He was just trying a little cowboy charm on her.

"I felt like an idiot last night, Amanda," Sean said. "But . . . I thought you were about the prettiest thing I'd seen in—"

"Ah, here it comes—country charm."

"And I didn't want a pretty woman like you going off thinking of me as an idiot," he finished with a smile.

"What makes you think I'd give you a second thought?"

"Because when I looked at you last night, thinking, 'God, she's gorgeous,' you looked right back at me the same way."

Dear Reader,

It's almost Thanksgiving time, but before you get too involved in the holiday rush, why not take a little time for yourself, sit back and enjoy this month's Silhouette Classics?

Joan Hohl appears most often in Silhouette Desire, where she frequently lands on the romance bestseller list. *Moments Harsh, Moments Gentle* was her first—and so far only—book for Silhouette Intimate Moments, but it has what I can only describe as that special Joan Hohl magic. Sensuous, intense, compelling—these are the words that describe any book by this talented author, so don't miss this opportunity to enter her world and experience the love shared by two very special people, Nacia Barns and Jared Ranklin, as they find each other amidst the glamour and flash of Atlantic City.

The professional rodeo circuit has a glamour all its own, a glamour you can sample for yourself in Kathleen Eagle's *Someday Soon*. This Silhouette Special Edition was Kathleen's very first book, and it won her the Romance Writers of America Golden Heart Award. You'll know why as soon as you join blue-blooded Amanda Caron and cowboy Sean Brannigan for their very unorthodox first meeting. Can a high-bred Eastern lady and a rough, tough Westerner find lasting happiness together? You bet they can—especially when their future is in the hands of Kathleen Eagle!

At Silhouette Classics, the hits just keep on coming, so join us in future months for books from more of your favorite authors: Ginna Gray, Carole Halston and Catherine Coulter—to name just a few!

Leslie J. Wainger
Senior Editor

Kathleen Eagle

Someday Soon

Silhouette Classics

Published by Silhouette Books New York

America's Publisher of Contemporary Romance

SILHOUETTE BOOKS
300 East 42nd St., New York, N.Y. 10017

Silhouette Classics edition published November 1988

Silhouette Special Edition edition published November 1984

ISBN 0-373-04626-X

America's Publisher of Contemporary Romance

Printed in the U.S.A.

Books by Kathleen Eagle

Silhouette Special Edition

Someday Soon #204
A Class Act #274
Georgia Nights #304
Something Worth Keeping #359
Carved in Stone #396
Candles in the Night #437

Silhouette Intimate Moments

For Old Times' Sake #148
More Than a Miracle #242
But That Was Yesterday #257

KATHLEEN EAGLE

is a transplant from Massachusetts to her favorite regional setting, the Dakota prairie. As educator, wife, mother and writer, she believes that a woman's place is wherever she's needed—and anywhere she needs to be.

For Clyde,
who loves the rodeo,
but loves me more

Chapter One

"Who is it? Who's . . . ?" Amanda slammed her hairbrush down on the counter top and secured the sash over her white peignoir. No one had knocked, but she was certain she had heard a key being fitted into the lock on the door to her hotel room. And the feminine giggle outside didn't sound as though it belonged to a maid.

"Just a minute, please, I'm . . . ," Amanda sputtered as the door swung open, but the rather tipsy blonde who was doing the giggling was already in the room. Good Lord, it was past one in the morning, and Amanda hardly knew a soul in Reno!

"There you go, Lacy," a man's voice crooned. "And here's your key."

The giddy blonde didn't take notice of the fact that the room was already occupied. She turned on her heel, bracing herself on the door, and reached out into the hallway. "Now, you weren't going to leave me to spend the night all alone, were you?"

"Wait just a minute," Amanda interrupted sharply. "There must be some . . ." As Amanda spoke the blonde gave a mighty tug and, like a deep-sea fisherman, hauled her catch over the threshold. ". . . mistake. I believe this is *my* room." Amanda lowered her voice, staring unabashedly at the tall man, who looked quite as surprised as she was. "That is, you must have been given the wrong key."

The man straightened, pulling his arm from the blonde's clutches as he inclined his head in Amanda's direction, boldly surveying her from head to toe. Left off-balance, the blonde, whom he'd called Lacy, fell a few awkward steps backward and found herself tumbling over the arm of a padded chair, into which her blue-jeaned bottom summarily settled. This struck her as even funnier than whatever their previous joke had been, and she launched into a new peal of giggling.

"Lacy! Keep your voice down. We're in the wrong room. Uh, pardon me, ma'am. The key says two-fourteen. The door says . . ."

"Yes, this is room two-fourteen. That's also what *my* key says." Amanda edged her way closer to the pair, keeping her voice calm. He was—at least he *appeared* to be—a cowboy. He had all the trappings: silverbelly-gray Stetson hat, cream-colored Western shirt, blue jeans and a wide belt with a big, flashy silver buckle. A deeply tanned complexion and black hair were visible beneath the brim of the hat, and his mouth was now curved in a somewhat sheepish grin.

"I'm sorry. We'll go back down and get this straightened out. Come on, Lacy, I'll . . ." He turned to the chair. "Damn it, Lacy, wake up. They gave you a room that was already . . ." He leaned down and draped the woman's arm behind his neck, her head lolling to the side as he curved one arm around her back. "Geez, I'm sorry about this, ma'am."

"Wait a minute," Amanda said. "Why don't you just leave her there and go down to the desk and get another room? You can't very well drag her through the lobby like that."

After settling the woman back in the chair, the man straightened again, looking relieved, albeit disconcerted. "You sure you don't mind?" His dark eyes searched hers for assurance. In contrast to the woman's drunken condition, he seemed quite in control of himself. Amanda nodded and told him with a wave of her hand that he should take care of things. "Be right back," he said with a quick, grateful smile.

Lacy's shiny red satin blouse seemed less than custom fitted to her ample bust, which was now threatening to pop the button holding the blouse together well below her cleavage. Her mass of blond curls was apparently caught up on the back of her head somehow, and a deep wave swooped down over her forehead. Her makeup was overdone, her false eyelashes too obvious, but underneath it all she looked like an attractive woman. Her age was hard to guess.

Amanda stood in the middle of the room staring down at her unexpected guest. If she were to write the rodeo story . . . if these were "rodeo people" . . . Interesting.

A tap at the door interrupted Amanda's perusal of the sleeping woman. She peered through the peephole and saw a brown neck and an ivory shirt. Stepping back, she admitted the cowboy, who grinned down at her as he pushed his hat back a little from his forehead.

"The clerk is most apologetic, ma'am. I'm sure you'll get your share of kowtows when you confront the desk in the morning."

"It was rather an absurd mistake."

"Yeah, well . . ." They stood looking at each other

for a moment, neither seeming to need an excuse for the action. "Well, I'm sorry for the disturbance."

"No problem, really."

As though he were just remembering why he was there, the cowboy turned quickly to the chair and leaned down to gather up his charge. "Okay, Lacy, let's go. Your room's just down the hall." The woman was like a rag doll, suspended from his neck by one arm, muttering incoherently, head jerking up and then flopping chin to chest. "G'night, ma'am," the cowboy said quietly as he stepped back into the hallway.

"Good night," Amanda answered, as the thought crossed her mind that his night was obviously not going to be as good as he'd planned.

"There was no harm done, really. The people who came in were embarrassed, and so was I, but no harm done," Amanda assured the clerk after his profuse apology. "The night clerk called and offered his apologies, so I've already been told that this virtually *never* happens, and no one knows how it *could* have happened, and really all is forgiven."

"You will consent to be our guest for dinner tonight?" the man behind the desk suggested obsequiously.

"And mine for breakfast," came a drawl from behind.

Amanda turned to find last night's midnight cowboy smiling quite confidently down at her. "Oh! It's you! Well, you're up bright and early."

"Sir," the clerk interrupted, "were you the other party involved in last night's embarrassing mix-up? If you and your wife would also—"

The cowboy laughed. "The lady in question is not my wife, and I'm not a guest here. Offer your complimentary dinner or whatever to Miss Lacy

Cook, room two-twenty-five. All I did was help her get there."

"Certainly, sir."

"Now, Miss . . ."

"Caron. Amanda Caron."

"Miss Caron, please let me try to make amends for barging in on you last night. Have breakfast with me."

"That really isn't necessary. Consider the whole matter forgotten," Amanda suggested. He looked somewhat different this morning, considerably more on top of the situation, exuding confidence. He was strikingly handsome, with a chiseled face, straight nose, full, sensual mouth, and a boyish sweep of black hair across his forehead.

"My name is Sean Brannigan. I'm here for the rodeo. And I've been waiting for you to come out of that room for an hour and a half now. So don't turn me down and leave me standing here feeling stupid. How about breakfast?"

Smiling, Amanda replied, "Okay, cowboy, you're on. Truthfully, I'm getting tired of my own company at the table."

The hostess marched past several empty tables en route to one near a huge window, shaded from the morning sun by a lush array of green plants. The hostess's bracelets jangled with her every step, a sound that was echoed by the clinking of silverware throughout the room. The sounds filtered past Sean Brannigan's senses as he hung back in the procession just enough so he could watch Amanda Caron move ahead of him.

Nothing about her jangled. On the contrary, Amanda Caron glided with stately bearing. Sean smiled, imagining a very steady book on top of her head and wondered, admiring the way she looked from this angle in her trim summer sheath and white pumps, if she'd changed any plans just for him.

After they had ordered Amanda asked, "Won't your *friend* be expecting to have breakfast with you, too? You may have to eat twice."

"Lacy probably won't remember how she got here last night. And, yes, we're *friends*. It isn't the first time I've gotten her a room after she's . . . Well, that's what friends are for, right?"

"Right. You must be a nice guy. I mean, I really wondered what you were up to when you said you'd been waiting for me for an hour and a half. Maybe it's just because you're a nice guy, hmm?" The waitress brought coffee.

"Yeah. Well, I felt like an idiot last night."

"Oh, please, let's forget it. It certainly wasn't your fault."

"And . . . I thought you were about the prettiest thing I'd seen in—"

"Ah, here it comes—country charm."

"And I didn't want a pretty woman like you going off thinking of me as an idiot," he said with a smile.

"What makes you think I'd give you a second thought, as an idiot or otherwise?"

"Straightforward, aren't you?"

"Always."

"Then let me be, too. When I looked at you last night thinking, 'God, she's gorgeous,' you looked right back at me the same way."

"Thinking, 'God, he's gorgeous'?"

He cocked her a wry grin, looking straight into her eyes. "At the very least thinking, 'God, he's not half bad.' And now, come to find out, I'm a nice guy to boot."

"Are all cowboys as self-assured as you are?"

"That's only a superficial trait. Underneath there's a shy little boy."

"Touching. Why do I get the feeling you've used that line before?"

His quiet laugh was easy and relaxed. He stirred entirely too much sugar into his coffee, the smile still crinkling the corners of his almond-shaped eyes. "I've never tried it on such a sophisticated lady before. It's obviously not the right one. Are you in Reno on vacation?"

"I'm here on business."

"Which is?"

"I'm a writer. I've been working on a series of articles about the Bureau of Land Management's wild-horse management program."

"Oh? Do you write for a magazine?" There was the sound of genuine interest in his voice now, perhaps even respect.

"My horse material goes to a lot of different magazines. I free-lance."

"Where are you from?"

"Massachusetts. Boston."

He raised an eyebrow in acknowledgment of the distance. She looked like Boston, he thought. Chic, but not that real high-fashion stuff. The luster of inbred polish. Her brown, shoulder-length hair was softly styled, and her blue eyes were cool, holding something in reserve. "You travel a lot to get your stories?"

"Not usually this far. I did do a feature story on the Denver Stock Show last year."

"Did you go to the rodeo?"

"No, just the horse shows."

"I was there. How did I miss seeing you?"

"Did you go to the horse shows?" She expected to make her point with a simple question.

"Yes, as a matter of fact, I did. I had a horse in the cutting class."

"Did you show him yourself?" Amanda inquired, her voice reflecting a spark of genuine interest as she leaned back slightly from the table to allow the waitress more room to serve her breakfast.

"No, the trainer showed him. Took fourth." He grinned slowly. "Not bad for the first time out."

"No, that's very good."

"I did better, though. Took first and third."

"What sort of rodeo riding do you do?"

"Calf roping and steer wrestling—dogging, we call it. Sometimes I ride bulls just for the hell of it, but that's not really my event."

"Riding a bull does seem like something one might do for a little taste of hell."

"It's not as bad as it looks. It's like any other sport—football, skiing—it's dangerous if you're careless or out of condition."

"Unlike football or skiing, you involve animals that have no choice in the matter, and there's danger for them. The bucking horses often snap their spines, from what I've read."

He cast her a curious glance from behind the rim of his coffee cup. "I've only heard of it happening once." He paused, then said, "If you write about horses, you must have done some riding yourself."

"My father has a couple of Morgans. I've done some showing."

"Are they volunteers?"

"What do you mean?"

"The horses you ride. Do they *choose* to be ridden in your shows? I know I said you were just about the prettiest thing *I'd* seen in a long time, but I don't imagine any horse, even a Morgan, would be impressed enough to offer you a ride."

"It isn't the same. Those animals buck wildly, out of control, just to throw you off their backs."

"Those animals are performing a stunt, just like the cowboys. Don't kid yourself. A good bucking horse is worth as much as a good show horse, and nobody wants to lose one. I watched the hunt seat equitation at the Denver show. That big black that fell taking a jump had to be put down, you know. Foreleg was broken all to hell. Shattered."

Now it was her turn to study him curiously. "How do you know that?"

"I saw it happen. I also knew the vet who took the

X rays." He shrugged. "It was a freak accident. But it happens, even to the classiest horsemen."

There's more to this cowboy than meets the eye, Amanda mused. "I saw it happen, too. I wonder how I missed seeing you." She smiled, and for the first time since he'd met her, her smile reached her eyes. "You have an interest in hunt seat?"

"I have an interest in horses."

"More than just for rodeo?"

He nodded, his eyes twinkling. "Yes, more than *just* for rodeo. I raise Quarter Horses."

"Oh? Do you live around here?"

"I have a place in South Dakota, not too far from Rapid City," he explained, polishing off his eggs.

"That's nice country, from what I've heard. I guess I thought rodeo people were sort of gypsies." She lifted the coffee server. "More coffee?" He nodded, and she poured him some before refilling her own cup.

"I guess that's a fair description."

"How do you manage to raise horses *and* follow the rodeo circuit?"

"I rent the place out. I tried hiring someone to run it for me, kind of like a foreman, but it didn't work out. So I sold the cattle, just kept the horses, and I leased the place to a young couple I knew pretty well. They take care of the horses, and I go home pretty often, help out with the haying, work my horses. I'll probably settle down and go back to ranching one of these days."

"How long have you been doing all this?"

"We started raising quarter horses when I was a kid. The roping was just another ranch chore then, at least up until a few years ago. I started out with the bulls about five years ago. Did it mostly for myself. After a couple of seasons of hitting local rodeos, I went PRCA—Professional Rodeo Cowboys' Association."

"How good are you?" There was a hint of surprise

in his smiling brown eyes, hinting that her question showed her ignorance of the rodeo world. "I'm sorry, but I don't have any idea who the champions are or how you get to be one."

"You get to be a world champion by winning the most money for the year in your event. In order to do that you have to hit a lot of rodeos. Right now I'm sitting first in calf roping, but I want the all-around championship this year too."

"Which means?"

"Which involves competing in more than one event *and* winning the most money. It's like the grand championship." He sat back in his chair, enjoying his second cup of coffee and the lady's company, even if sometimes she did think she knew it all. "Have you ever been to a rodeo, Amanda?"

"Only once. I guess I didn't find it a very entertaining sport. I hated seeing those animals kicked and strangled and raked along the shoulders with those huge spurs."

"Come on, it's not that bad. Do you think the ASPCA would let us get away with anything that gruesome? Why don't you come tonight? Judge for yourself whether I'm any good."

"Well, frankly, I . . ."

"You have a date?"

"No. I had intended . . ."

"Then come. I'll leave a ticket for you at the box office. I want you to sit right over the roping boxes where you can see how a good roping horse works."

"Actually, I did intend to go to the rodeo tonight. I'm interested in two of the bucking horses, Mean Machine and Mustang Sally. Maybe you know them."

"I'm not a bronc rider, so I can't say I've had the pleasure, but I've watched them. Mustang Sally will probably go to the national finals."

"Really? That's interesting. Did you know that they're both mustangs adopted through the BLM's adoption program?"

"And now they're worth eight, ten grand apiece, easy." Sean shook his head. "No, I didn't know they were mustangs."

Amanda sat forward in her chair. Physically the man was attractive, and he had an appealing way about him—intelligent, though that came as something of a surprise, yet unaffected. More to the point, they touched on common ground now and then. Amanda was a horse lover.

"The Society for the Protection of Mustangs and Burros is headquartered here in Reno," Amanda explained. "As part of this series of articles I'm doing, I'm following up on several horses that were adopted in the last few years. I want to show that they've become useful members of society, so to speak. Did you know that there's a bill coming up in Congress that would allow them to be rounded up and sold for slaughter again?"

"Yes, I knew that. I've sent my donation in to the society, and I've written to my congressman. You really don't look like a crusader."

"I have an interest in horses." Echoing him, she favored him with another genuine smile. "Wouldn't it be nice if the mustangs could be left alone, free to roam as they pleased?"

"Not in my pasture. They break down fences, steal mares, mess up your breeding program. The society's doing the best thing for the extra population—trying to place them."

"Well, I'm not sure about including the bucking horses in my article. I want to stir up public support for the adoption program."

"Rodeo's a popular sport in this part of the world. You let people know those horses might be headed for the finals, and the BLM will have a new pile of adoption applications."

"I'll have a look at them tonight. You can get me a seat over the roping boxes you say?"

"Best seat in the house. Then we'll do the cowboy

side of this neon town. That'll give you something to write the folks in Massachusetts about." Sean grinned.

"Yes, that would be different. I'll be there, Mr. Brannigan."

"Great! But the only person who ever calls me Mr. Brannigan is my banker. It's Sean."

As if to dispute that appellation as well, a voice startled them both with, "There you are, Johnny!"

"Some people can't get that through their heads, though," he muttered as Amanda's eyes darted from his to the blonde who approached the table, her breasts jiggling with each purposeful step. "Sit down and have some coffee, Lacy," Sean invited, turning a friendly smile in her direction. "How does breakfast strike you?"

"Like a ten-pound mallet, honey. No thanks. I will have some coffee, though." She sighed, seating herself in an empty chair.

"Amanda, this is Lacy Cook, one of rodeo's most devoted fans. Lacy . . . Amanda Caron, from Massachusetts." After the women had nodded at each other somewhat stiffly Sean continued. "We stumbled into Amanda's room last night by accident, Lacy, and she was good enough to let you sack out in her chair while I got a different key."

"Really? I don't remember. I really must have been out of it. Thanks, Amanda, I hope I didn't put you out too much."

"Not at all."

"I don't know what happened to Bud last night. I was with Bud, but all of a sudden he was gone, and then . . ." Her voice was twangy, oozing like frosting from a pastry bag.

"And then some trucker tried to pick you up. You've gotta be more careful, Lacy. You're gonna end up—"

She cut him off with, "Oh, Johnny, you're such a knight in shining armor, you know that? The gentleman cowboy—a dying breed." Lacy gave Sean a calf-eyed smile, which made Amanda feel very much in the way.

"I think I should get back to my typewriter so that I can go to that rodeo tonight," Amanda said as she reached for her purse. "I've enjoyed breakfast, Sean." He stood, assuring her, as though he had originated the phrase, that the pleasure was all his and that he would look for her at the rodeo.

When the hostess smiled back at her, Amanda realized that she was leaving the dining room with a big, silly grin on her face. Nobody had said anything especially funny, for Pete's sake. That country boy had her smiling for no particular reason but that she had enjoyed having breakfast with him. And she was actually looking forward to seeing him again.

Well, that was only because the rodeo invitation fit so neatly into her plans. She wanted to see those two horses, see what they had to do to earn their oats. Perhaps this Sean Brannigan would introduce her to the stock contractor. During her interviews for the wild-horse series, the topic of rodeo stock and Western performance horses had sparked her interest. It was a facet of the horse world that she'd largely ignored, having been involved only with English-style riding all her life.

These rodeo people might be interesting; they might be story material. Amanda felt a strange, encouraging curiosity about this man. He was so different from the men she was used to. In the hour they'd spent together, he hadn't asked her father's opinion of the commodity futures market, nor had he expounded in excruciating detail on the deal he was about to close with some computer outfit. But this wasn't Boston, and Sean Brannigan didn't know who her father was, and even if he did, she didn't believe he'd bat an eye. Ironically, she knew that before she decided how to proceed with her story, she'd give her father a call to see what he thought.

It was an unspoken pact. When Amanda had a new project under consideration, her father expected to be consulted. She, in turn, expected to consider his advice because it was generally sound, because they shared a love of horses and because he was her father.

These rodeo horses, though, they were horses of a different color. Amanda smiled again, slipping her key into the slot and clicking the lock on her door. Sean Brannigan. It had a nice literary ring to it. Behind an interesting man must lie an interesting story. Lately she'd been feeling as though she were stalled at an intersection. Maybe he could get her moving again. With her bottom lip tucked thoughtfully between her teeth, Amanda pushed the door open.

Chapter Two

$\mathcal{A}$manda's ticket was indeed waiting for her at the box office. The air was warm with the smell of hot dogs and popcorn, and it vibrated with the buzz of spectators wending their way through crowded aisles and up and down steps. Section C . . . row 10 . . . row 10 . . .

"Amanda! Over here!" Amanda searched the crowd for the owner of the voice, and her eyes finally fell upon Lacy, the only familiar person in the sea of faces.

"Hello, Lacy," Amanda said in greeting as she settled herself on the seat next to Sean's friend. "Thanks for saving my seat for me."

"I'm glad you came. Johnny would've been real disappointed if you hadn't shown up. I kinda didn't think you would."

"Actually, I'd been planning to see a rodeo before I left. I'm sure it'll be more exciting now that I know someone in it."

"Yeah, it will, and Johnny's the best. He'll get the all-around championship if he just keeps after it this year. And he's entered in bull riding tonight, too. Wait 'til you see him—he's beautiful."

"I'm looking forward to it. I know very little about any of this, so you'll have to explain the rules to me."

"Sure thing. I guess I know about as much about it as anybody. I love rodeo. Mostly, I love rodeo cowboys." Lacy's eyes brightened considerably, and she smiled at Amanda as though she thought they might have this in common. "Johnny's real special."

Amanda pasted a smile on her face and told herself not to roll her eyes. "Are you from South Dakota too?"

"Yeah. I've known Johnny a long time—since high school." Lacy suddenly looked at Amanda as though a thought had popped into her head, and Amanda wondered if it was lonely up there. "Oh, hey, Johnny and me are *friends,* that's all," Lacy explained. "He's like a brother . . . you know what I mean."

"And he and I are just acquaintances."

"He told me he's taking you out tonight after the rodeo. He's really looking forward to that. I don't wanna mess anything up for him by letting you get the wrong idea, especially after last night. See, I was with somebody else, and Johnny—"

"I know. I heard the story this morning. Really, there's no need to explain any of this to me. Sean strikes me as a very nice man, but, as I said—"

"Look, there he is! See, down there behind the chute, talking to Bud. That's Bud, the guy I was with last night. We kinda made up today."

Amanda's eyes picked through the assortment of cowboy hats until she recognized the silverbelly color atop the lean, tan face. Sean wore a friendly smile as he talked with the sandy-haired cowboy who stood near him. A big bay horse stood quietly at Sean's shoulder, and he reached up almost unconsciously as he talked, rubbing the animal's neck and raking his fingers through the well-groomed mane. As if he felt her eyes on him, he suddenly looked up into the stands, grinned at her and nodded slightly. She greeted him with a smile and a little wave.

The grand entry was announced, and a line of Western horsemen galloped in a serpentine trail of dust around the arena, flags fluttering on long staffs held by several of the horsemen. The national anthem brought the crowd to its feet, and Amanda chuckled inwardly at the Cowboy's Prayer that followed, in which the announcer assured the Lord that cowboys never asked for any special favors, only that He give them a kindly nod and admittance to that last great roundup in the sky.

The bareback event was first. The rider seemed to be attached to his horse only by one hand, which held fast to a handle on the leather rigging strapped behind the animal's withers, and by the seat of his pants. His free arm waved high in the air. The rider's legs stretched over the shoulders of the horse, the spinning rowels of his spurs catching with the horse's every jolting jump.

When Amanda caught the announcement ". . . on a horse called Mustang Sally," she leaned forward, studying the wild little mount that burst from the chute. The horse moved with the controlled contortions of a modern dancer—a leap, a kick, a turn, and the rider was down before the ten-second buzzer. Head held high in the air, Sally pranced once around the arena, letting the crowd know just who had won this round.

"Watch the calf roping close, now, Amanda," Lacy instructed later. "This is Johnny's best event."

Several ropers preceded Sean, but Amanda wasn't interested in their names or their scores. As always she watched the horse work, and in this event he was the man's full partner.

When his turn came, Sean and his horse stood quietly in the box, the length of narrow rope called a "piggin' string" held between Sean's teeth, a look of studied concentration on his face. At the black calf's release, the stout bay jumped from the box, and the loop of Sean's rope whirled briefly over his head before he threw it over the calf's neck and flicked back as the horse's sudden stop jerked the calf's legs out from under it. Quickly the little animal scrambled back to its feet.

Sean had performed his moves almost simultaneously—throwing the loop, jerking the slack and dismounting with such fluidness that he seemed only to be stepping down from a stool. The bay started backing as soon as he felt the jerk of the calf's weight, and the rope became a taut line from the saddle horn to the calf's neck. There was no wasted motion, no hesitation. The calf was thrown on its side, three of its legs gathered in a tripod, and the string from Sean's mouth came into play as he wrapped it twice around the bunch of legs, securing it with a half hitch.

"Why doesn't he tie up all four legs?" Amanda asked as she watched.

"Because . . . just because that's the way you do it. Three legs. Calf's not goin' anywhere with three legs tied up," Lacy explained with an open-handed gesture.

"No, I guess not."

A red flag in the hand of an official signaled the completion of the feat. Sean mounted the bay, nudged him two steps forward to release the tension on the rope and watched the calf as it struggled uselessly. Sean's time was announced as nine and two-tenths seconds, which was received by the crowd with hearty applause.

"See? What did I tell you?" Lacy beamed, her bust bouncing as she slapped her hands together. "Have you *ever* seen *any*thing like it?"

"No, I really haven't." Amanda smiled as she took

note of her own feelings. She was proud of him. Ridiculous. She hardly knew the man. But what he had just done was exciting.

"Bud ropes, too, and rides broncs, and usually hazes for Johnny. He's good, but not near as good as Johnny. Even when he beats Johnny, he's not as good, just lucky. Watch, now, and see the difference."

Amanda complied, studying the efforts of the sandy-haired cowboy and noting the obvious contrast. There was not quite the same continuity from one move to the next. The calf was caught and tied in under eleven seconds, but the pure liquid motion was not there. "That's real good for Bud. Looks like he'll place!" Lacy clapped for him, too, her eyes dancing.

The steer wrestling was an even quicker-paced event, and when Sean's name was announced Lacy warned, "Watch close, now, Amanda. You blink your eyes, you'll miss the whole thing."

Amanda nodded, training her eyes on the box where Sean sat his horse, a blaze-faced sorrel this time. The steer was suddenly free, lunging from the chute, and two horses lunged forward almost at the same instant. Lacy's friend, Bud, was on the steer's right, keeping the animal from veering away as Sean leaned down off the horse's right side and dropped his body over the steer's shoulders, a pointed horn tucked under his right arm and another gripped in his left hand. With a twist of its head, he forced the steer onto its side, leaving it flopping on the ground like a tackled quarterback. The red flag came down at five and three-tenths seconds.

Suddenly realizing that she wasn't breathing, Amanda sighed with something that sounded to her strangely like relief, whispering, "Good Lord, I thought he was going to come down on those horns."

"Johnny? No way," Lacy laughingly assured her.

Soon barrels were being set up for the ladies' barrel-racing event. Amanda glanced toward the aisle and smiled at seeing Sean. She moved toward Lacy, and Sean sat down. "Glad you could make it, Amanda. Has your opinion of rodeo been influenced for the better yet?" he asked.

"The first note I made was that you *are* good at this," she said evasively.

"I'm having a pretty good night, thanks. Did you see your mustangs? Ol' Sally's hard to beat, and Mean Machine gave Travis Steele quite a ride. Better score than I'd like to see him get. He's leading in the all-around—for the moment."

"It's hard to believe that a person can stay on a horse in such a ridiculous position. It looks pretty funny to see a grown man . . ." She allowed herself a half-chuckle. "But you—*you* could get hurt if you came down on the horns of one of those steers."

He looked at her meaningfully, his dark eyes twinkling with amusement. "Would that bother you, Amanda? Were you worried about me?"

She would not be flustered. "Of course it would bother me. Bloodletting spoils my day every time."

Chuckling, his gaze still fixed on Amanda, he asked, "What do you think, Lacy? Was she worried about me?"

"She looked pretty tense to me, Johnny. Scooted right to the edge of the seat, those pretty little knuckles turning just as white—"

"Don't be silly," Amanda countered. "It was all over before I knew it."

"It takes eight seconds to ride a bull. Maybe you can work up a little concern for me over that . . . unless, of course, you're pulling for the bull," he teased.

"I haven't chosen sides yet."

"While you deliberate, I could use something to drink. How about you ladies?"

Lacy declined. "I wanna watch the barrel racing. You two go on ahead."

As they made their way down to the concession stand, Sean's hand resting lightly on her back guiding her through the crowd, Amanda felt the stares they were getting. It was like being in the company of a celebrity. Several people greeted him, commenting on his good performances.

"What can I get you?" Sean asked, nodding toward the counter.

"Just a soda."

"I don't know if they can manage that here . . . Oh, you mean pop. I forgot, that's Massachusetts talk." He laughed, and then he put in his order.

They retreated a short distance from the concession stand crowd before she observed, "You sound like you've been to Massachusetts."

"A few times. I went to school in New York."

"Where?"

"Cornell. Good ag department there. I gave them geographical distribution and they gave me almost four years of animal science."

"You didn't finish?"

"No. My plans were changed. So tell me—what do you do about your mustang story now? Sally gets closer to the finals every time they buck her out."

"I'll need to talk to the stock contractor. Do you know him?"

"Gerry Strickland? Yeah, I know him. He's a good contractor. Runs good animals."

"Do you think I might be able to meet him?"

He turned his engaging smile on her, obviously pleased to be able to help. "Sure, I'll introduce you to him. I'll see what he's doing tomorrow. Should we buy him lunch?"

She smiled back. "Yes. In fact, I'll take you both to lunch."

"Uh-uh, Miss Caron. I've never let a lady pick up a check at my table, women's lib be damned."

"But I insist."

"Insist all you want, but since it's my football, you'll have to play the game my way, won't you?"

Traditionally the bull-riding event was the finale on the rodeo program, saving the most dangerous moments for last. After watching several bulls ridden by several cowboys, some successfully, some not, Amanda couldn't deny feeling a twinge of apprehension when Sean Brannigan's name was announced. The name itself was greeted with a round of applause.

A white gate swung open, and a buttermilk-colored Brahman plunged from the confines of the chute, kicking its hindquarters in the air. Reversing the direction of its motion, the animal tucked its head to the right, ducking into a spin, hindquarters following with a roll to the right from the midsection. Each jarring buck of its body seemed to drive the bull tighter into its spin, like a corkscrew. But Sean's lithe body seemed to move with the impossible motion, his free arm cutting rhythmic arcs in the air above his head. His black and white batwing chaps flapped with each rocking plunge of the animal's two-thousand-pound body.

At the sound of the buzzer Sean extricated his hand from the bull rope and swung himself off, hitting the ground and rolling clear of the deadly flying hooves all in one move. The crowd was delighted.

"Wow! I've never seen Johnny ride better!" Lacy sparkled as she bounced in her seat and clapped her hands. "He must be trying to impress somebody. And you can't say you weren't scared for him this time." She nodded toward Amanda's hands, clenched tightly in her lap, nails red and knuckles white from the pressure.

Amanda glanced down. "Well . . . yes! I guess it's like watching someone walking on a high wire. You feel like you're going to fall yourself."

"He's beautiful, isn't he? God, he can ride!"

"It's amazing he's able to stay on with the bull spinning like that. It looks pretty dangerous to me."

"Well, it *is* dangerous. I guess that's what makes it exciting for them." Lacy grinned, a decidedly lascivious look in her eyes. "And it's what makes *them* so exciting."

"Whom?"

"Cowboys! God, once you've known a cowboy, any other man is a joke."

"Really? That should give most women a laugh at least."

"Most women don't know any better."

"I see. Well, if it means watching your man try to kill himself every week, we're probably better off with the bliss of ignorance."

"Did you hear that?" Lacy chirped, paying no attention to Amanda's remarks. "He's gonna take first with that score."

Amanda marveled silently at Lacy's enthusiasm for Sean's success. Bud, her boyfriend, got much less praise, making it hard to believe the "just good friends" bit, although it certainly made no difference to Amanda.

"The guys'll be waiting for us back by the chutes," Lacy said as they edged forward with the departing crowd. But the men weren't waiting behind the chutes, and Amanda felt the tug of impatience at being expected to hang around, especially when a burly-looking fellow in a flowered Western shirt draped an arm over Lacy's shoulder and greeted her with, "Hey, Lacy, what brings you to Reno?"

"Hey, Jimmy, nice ride tonight," Lacy sparkled. "I rode out with Bud. Been on the road for five weeks."

"And who's your pretty friend?" Jimmy gave Amanda a one-sided grin. His reddish, round face was ruggedly good-looking under the thatch of straw-colored hair escaping from the hat that was tilted back on his head.

"Jimmy Stephens, Amanda Caron," Lacy offered in introduction.

"Howdy, ma'am," Jimmy drawled with a boyish grin.

"Put away the charm, Jimmy. She's *Johnny's* friend."

"Oh." The grin faded. "Nice meetin' you anyway, Amanda."

What did "friend" mean to these people, anyway? Amanda wondered. She felt as though an Off Limits sign had just been hung around her neck. "I just met Sean this morning, and we found that we had a mutual interest in horses. He invited me to the rodeo tonight to show me his style of horsemanship, which, I must say, he seems to be very adept at."

"Yeah, you gotta go some to beat ol' Sean Brannigan. One of these days I'm gonna buy a roping horse off him, and then we'll see."

"Is it the horse that makes the roper?" Amanda asked.

"Sean's got real fine horses," Jimmy replied.

"So why don't you buy one, Jim, and see if it helps?" Amanda hadn't noticed Sean's approach, and now he stood behind her shoulder.

"I might just do that. Wouldn't mind having a night like you just had. Don't know anybody else who can place in three events in one night. Pretty lady up in the stands sure can make a man try a little extra, too."

"Gotta admit, she did cross my mind once or twice," Sean agreed.

"You can always tell when Johnny's showing off for a girl," Lacy quipped.

"Sorry to keep you ladies waiting. Horses wanted supper."

Sean led the way to an area behind the stock pens, where an armada of campers, pickups and stock trailers stood waiting. Horses were getting walked, rubbed down and loaded up. Here and there people were sorting out their gear, stowing it away in pickup boxes and trailer compartments, hailing friends who passed by.

"What's your pleasure tonight, Amanda? Do you go in for casinos, or supper clubs, or . . ."

"I believe you said you'd show me the cowboy side of town, wherever that is," Amanda said lightly. "But what I'd really like," she suggested almost shyly, "is a pizza."

"Pizza! Sweetheart, you and I were made for each other," Sean declared with a grin.

Because Sean's vehicle was a big motor home, they decided to take Bud Eliot's, but not before Sean and Bud had showered and changed. It was a tight squeeze to fit four in the cab of the pickup, although Lacy made a genuine effort to share Bud's seat behind the wheel. She declared that his winning second place for the night in saddle bronc and fourth in calf roping were utterly commendable. Funny, Amanda thought, Lacy had been much less impressed with Bud's performance when they had been in the stands.

Amanda found herself tucked beneath Sean's arm. Realizing that this was her first date in a pickup, she allowed that; for the sake of her story she would have to be tolerant of the . . . inconvenience. While she concentrated on tolerance, her body willingly relaxed against Sean's long torso. He wore a light gray western shirt with black piping, and dark gray pants. All the good smells of a freshly showered man lulled Amanda's senses. Surprisingly there was a faint hint of masculine cologne.

Sean smiled to himself when he felt Amanda's body finally relax against him. He had met a lot of women on the road, women he knew he'd never see again, and it hadn't mattered. From the moment he'd seen this woman, though, he'd known it was different with her, that he wanted to see her again, that he would *always* want to see her again. She had the soft beauty

of a lady, the round-eyed innocence of a child that her
sophisticated posture didn't quite cover up, and the
statuesque, gently curved body of a woman. He had a
weakness for Eastern ladies, with their aloofness and
the contradictory hint of warmth somewhere underneath. That weakness had once nearly proved fatal,
but that had been in his young and foolish days. He'd
learned to take things easy.

After eating more than her share of a huge pizza,
Amanda alluded to the late hour and suggested that
they drop her by the hotel. Hearing that, Sean caught
the attention of several strangers in the parking lot
with, "Hey, I just placed in three events, girl! We've
got some celebrating to do. Besides, by now everybody's probably heard about my beautiful lady friend,
so I wouldn't want to disappoint them by showing up
alone."

"Showing up where?" Amanda asked.

"Where? is a good question. Where are we going,
Bud?"

"Everybody probably went to the Bootheel. I think
Janie and Buck's band's playing there," Bud offered.

"Well, Amanda, are you game for some country
music and a little pump-handle dancing?" Sean chal-
lenged.

"Why not?"

Why not, indeed. She soon learned the answer to
that. The Bootheel was basically a bar, and Amanda
did not frequent bars. The place was crowded with
cowboys, none of whom removed their hats in deference to being indoors. The laughter and the talk
seemed unduly loud, and the air was oppressive with
smoke. Amanda was out of her element, but she hid
her anxiety with a practiced dignity that always carried her through.

As they threaded their way past the bar Sean was
gracious, shaking hands, exchanging boisterous com-

pliments, all the while steering Amanda through the crowd. The way was suddenly blocked by a cowboy who swung down from his barstool and planted a lusty kiss on an apparently unsuspecting girl nearby. Amanda cowered back against Sean, and for the first time since they'd been in the pickup he put his arm around her shoulders, giving the top of her arm a reassuring squeeze as she looked up at him. He smiled. There was the wide-eyed innocence.

"Is this a free-for-all?" she asked, her apprehension unmasked.

"Not when you're with me. We'll find a table over by the dance floor, away from the bar."

Sean seemed to know everyone in the place, but each time someone called him, motioning him over, he would only grin and wave. He didn't leave Amanda's side, and for that she was grateful. She continued to feel out of place when Sean had to order three beers and a daiquiri, repeating the latter when the waitress asked, "A what?"

Amanda removed her white jacket, wishing her blouse were sleeveless. Despite the air conditioning the place was stuffy. She felt the need to say something to ease her own awkwardness. "Did you win, then? How is that determined?" she asked as the band picked up their instruments to get ready for the next set.

"First in calf roping and bulls, third in steer wrestling. My hazer wasn't where I wanted him." Sean clipped Bud lightly on the arm in a teasing gesture.

"I'm sorry, Sean. I should have—"

"Hey, I'm kidding, Bud. I was a little off-balance. But I had a real good night. That ol' Brahman was just the way you want 'em," he explained to Amanda. "You get a better score when they spin like that . . . if you can stay with 'em."

"But you prefer the roping and steer wrestling."

"I do better in those events overall, and that's what I train my horses for. The bulls are just for a little variety."

"Pretty dangerous variety. I hope you've got good insurance."

"Full coverage. Now, the question is, are you strictly a rock 'n' roller, or can you manage a two-step?"

"On the dance floor, Mr. Brannigan, I can do anything you can do."

Sean instructed Amanda in the cotton-eyed Joe, a lively Western jig that, as promised, she quickly mastered. The small dance floor was crowded, but Amanda began to enjoy this boisterous crowd's brand of entertainment. The drinks flowed freely, but though Bud and Lacy seemed to have bottles of beer in their hands at all times, Sean apparently preferred dancing to drinking, and Amanda certainly did. There was a lot of "Hey, Sean, who's the pretty lady?" and Amanda felt his hand at her waist or on her shoulder frequently. To her surprise, it felt fine.

When he retreated from the dance floor, Amanda close behind, her hand in his, Sean was met by a voluptuous young woman, who flung her arms around his neck and pasted the front of her body firmly against the front of his. "Sean Brannigan, you haven't asked me to dance once tonight, and that's not like you, sugar. How 'bout this next one, hmm?" she cooed softly.

Amanda tried to pull her hand from Sean's, but he held on tightly. "Thanks, Mona, but I'm—"

"Go ahead, Sean," Amanda put in over his shoulder. "I'm going to find the ladies' room." Pulling free, she gave him a quick smile and left him to the arms that were still fastened around his neck. He watched her even as, wordlessly, he picked up the rhythm of the music.

As she made her way back through the crowd in the direction of their table Amanda found her progress blocked by a big cowboy, who leered at her, beer and cigarette in one hand, his other hand on her upper arm, feeling clammy even through the material of her blouse. She couldn't back away as he leaned close to her face. "Would you like to dance?"

"No, thank you. Excuse me," she muttered, trying to push past him. He held her arm.

"Hey, lady, all I'm askin' for is a dance. Come on, your friends'll still be there."

"I'd rather not. Now, please, let go of my arm."

"The lady is with me." A hand gripped the cowboy's shoulder, and Amanda was released as he turned to face Sean.

"No offense, cowboy." The man grinned apologetically. "I was only askin' her to dance."

Sean reached for Amanda's hand and pulled her to his side. "The lady came with me, she's dancing with me, and she'll be leaving with me. Got that?" Sean's jaw was set, and his eyes, in which Amanda had thus far seen only pleasant expressions, were smoldering.

"Sure, cowboy. No harm done," the man said as Sean shouldered past him, his hand at Amanda's waist.

"I'm sorry about that. I should've sent Lacy with you."

She gave him an indulgent smile. "I've been going to the ladies' room by myself for years now."

"Do you have any idea what a temptation you are to a lonesome cowboy? We can't have anyone thinking you wandered in here by yourself."

"By the looks of it, cowboy, I'd say you haven't suffered too much from the lonesome-cowboy syndrome."

"Looks can be deceiving, as they say." Sean held Amanda's chair as she sat. "What do you think of this country music? Hardly Boston's style, is it?"

"Some of the lyrics wax a bit maudlin, but I love to dance, and this is fun, Sean. I'm glad I came."

"How much longer will you be here?"

"I should be getting back in a day or two."

"What about your story?"

"After I talk to the stock contractor I'll make a decision about including Mustang Sally's life story in my series. And I might be interested in finding out a bit more about Western performance horses. Like yours."

"Stock horses, you mean? Plain old *cow* horses?" He grinned.

"They're hardly plain. You've got some of the finest horses I've seen anywhere. I'd like to know more about them."

"I'd rather hear you say you'd like to know more about me. Is there someone waiting for you at home?"

Amanda fingered the little plastic straw that stood in the empty glass in front of her. "Just my parents. My father reminded me on the phone last night that I'm missing a lot of shows."

"There's always another show, just like there's always another rodeo. Keep that in mind, Amanda."

"And where are you going from here?" she asked as she traced the little boot on the cocktail napkin with the end of the straw.

"I want to be back in South Dakota by the Fourth, but I'll hit a couple of rodeos on my way home."

"Wouldn't it make sense to travel with someone and share expenses?"

"I had a guy with me as far as Gallup, but then I got involved in some side trips, so we parted company. Most guys do a lot of flying in this business, but I don't like flying."

"But you can't get to as many rodeos that way."

"Right." He grinned, then drained his beer. "But I see more country." Unexpectedly, his hand closed over hers on the table, and he leaned close to her ear. "Dance with me, Amanda."

She wasn't sure whether it was the daiquiris or his

charm, but she was letting go of her usual defenses, and she felt green-girl giddy. When he pulled her against him in an easy, swaying rhythm, she settled the length of her arm over his shoulder and rested her chin against his collarbone. His hand pressed warmly against the middle of her back, his fingers gently teasing her spine as he rocked her from side to side.

"You smell good," he whispered, nuzzling her hair.

"So do you." It was out before she caught herself.

"This is the kind of dancing I like. It gives a man an excuse to hold a lady in his arms—a lady who isn't quite sure what to make of him yet."

"As you pointed out this morning, I've decided that you're not half bad looking and a nice guy to boot."

"Not a bad start. Will you spend the day with me tomorrow?"

"I think tomorrow is today already."

"Today, then."

"I also think the music's stopped. There goes your excuse."

"The excuse was to get you in my arms. The pleasure I'm feeling is all the excuse I need to keep on holding you." The band obliged his mood by playing another romantic song. "There." Sean smiled. "Feel better?"

"You're a good dancer, Sean, and I enjoy dancing with you."

"And you're very good at evading the issue. What are you doing tomorrow—today—after lunch?"

"I haven't made any plans other than . . . spending the day with you."

"Sean Brannigan is here tonight, ladies and gentlemen," the lead singer announced when the song was over. Amanda thought that surely everyone knew that by now, but she applauded along with everyone else. "He gave quite a performance in the arena tonight. With a little encouragement, he might be persuaded to give us a song, too."

"A song?" Amanda smiled, incredulous.

"I haven't had nearly enough to drink to get me up there," he said, winking at her.

"Go on, Johnny. Sing pretty for us," Lacy drawled.

"How 'bout it, Sean?" came the voice over the microphone, followed by more applause.

"I'd love to hear you sing, Sean," Amanda encouraged.

"Then how can I refuse?" He squeezed her hand, then ambled up to the bandstand amid cheers and whistles. They hung a six-string folk guitar around his neck and pulled a high stool up to the microphone for him as he talked with the band.

"One of these days I'm gonna get Buck for this," Sean's deep, soft voice said over the mike. "I'm gonna call him out of the stands to ride my bull." After the appreciative cheers Sean continued, looking over in Amanda's direction. "This is a song about a lady, and I'd like to sing it for the lovely lady who's with me tonight." Amanda felt herself flush like a schoolgirl as his voice, a rich baritone, caressed her with romantic words sung to a lulling tune.

Afterward he was cajoled into singing an upbeat duet with the female vocalist, and he obviously enjoyed himself. The audience loved him, and they called out other requests. His soft laughter rumbled over the mike. "I know what you guys are up to. You're trying to keep me busy while some saddle tramp steals my date. Besides, somebody's paying Buck for this gig, so let's make him earn his keep."

A few minutes later, pulling his chair over close to Amanda, Sean looked pleased with himself. "You're a man of many talents," she said.

"Have I won a place in your heart?"

"You sure have. Right between Gene Autry and Roy Rogers." He caressed her wrist with his thumb, and she offered a smile.

"That sounds like worthy company." Sean swung his attention in Bud's direction and found him whispering to Lacy between nibbles on her neck, while she giggled and nodded. "Ready to go, Bud?"

Bud fumbled for the most recently acquired bottle among the assortment that he had lined up on the table. It was empty. "One for the road," Bud suggested, nodding to the waitress.

"Give me the keys, Bud," Sean ordered, and Bud complied meekly. "We'll have one more dance while you drink that." Amanda slid her chair back as Sean stood and leaned over in Bud's direction, laying a hand on his friend's shoulder and offering some words meant only for Bud's ear. Bud nodded, again meekly.

On the dance floor Sean held Amanda and moved her slowly in their small space. Being that close to him gave her a heady sensation. She enjoyed every minute of being snowed by his charm, the close contact with his body, the strength of the arms that held her, the unabashed pride in being Sean Brannigan's date in a room full of his admirers. She snuggled her face under his chin, and he answered by rubbing her back. When the music stopped he held her several seconds longer than was necessary, and Amanda waited until he was ready to let her go.

When they got back to the pickup Sean elected to take Bud and Lacy back to the fairgrounds, where Bud's gooseneck trailer was parked. The trailer was built to house both horses and riders, with a small camper in its front half. Amanda sensed some hesitation on Sean's part about leaving Lacy with Bud.

"He'll be all right, Johnny. He's gonna pass out pretty soon." Sean handed her a key. "I won't need this, Johnny. He'll be all right." Sean nodded as he gave Lacy's shoulder an affectionate squeeze, then slid behind the wheel of the pickup, realizing that what he had done had not escaped Amanda's notice.

"I don't sleep with Lacy, if that's what you're thinking," he said, starting the pickup.

"I'm not thinking anything."

"No? Then why did your eyes just bore two holes in

my back? Bud turns on her sometimes, and she's got no place else to go."

"Why did she come out here with him?"

"I don't know why." He put the truck in gear and followed the road that skirted the grandstands. "It's none of my business," he said finally. "Lacy just likes cowboys."

"You're the one she likes. Maybe she came with him to be around you," Amanda said quietly.

"I'm her friend when she needs one, but that's all. Lacy knows that."

"That's a lot, Sean, coming from someone like you. You obviously take that role more seriously than most people do. You don't interfere, but you're there when you're needed. Lacy's very lucky to have you for a friend." Amanda couldn't remember the last time she had felt inclined to make such an honest and complimentary speech to a man. She must have been affected by the drinks more than she had thought.

"Can I take that to mean you believe me about Lacy now?"

"Does it matter so much what I believe?"

"Yes. Yes, I guess it does. Have you watched a desert sunrise lately, Amanda?"

"We're a little old for parking, don't you think?"

Sean laughed. "I've been giving you answers, but all you give me is more questions. You must have led your share of merry chases."

Amanda didn't respond right away. She wasn't sure how she should handle this one. His honesty was disarming, and his insight enabled him to see through her cover. "No," she said finally, "I guess I haven't really watched a desert sunrise."

"Then you've missed one of the most spectacular scenes this country has to offer. Let's drive east of town a ways. Trust me?"

"Should I?"

"Well, there's no back seat in this thing."

"That doesn't answer my question."

"You haven't answered mine. But since we're not headed for the hotel, and you're not objecting, I'll assume that you're not afraid to be alone with me, which means you must have some faith in your own judgment. And that, you remember, has already told you that I'm a nice guy."

Amanda hadn't a clue as to how Sean chose the spot from which to watch the sunrise. They left the city behind and sought the empty desert, eventually leaving the paved highway for a gravel road. When they could see no signs of civilization Sean seemed satisfied to stop the pickup and shut the engine off. The sky was beginning to lighten, and the most distant stars had faded.

"Let's walk," he suggested, and he was out of the cab quickly, reaching for her hand. They walked in silence, hand in hand, away from the pickup. Amanda marveled at the tingling sensation that his hand awoke in hers. How long had it been since she had just held hands and walked with a man? And how long since she'd felt this good about such a simple pleasure?

There was nothing but sagebrush and sky. Feeling very small and detached from the world, Amanda brushed close to Sean's side as they walked. "There's a lot of . . . of space here, isn't there?" she said in a small voice. The stillness didn't seem to want to be disturbed.

"Space, yes, and peace, and simple beauty. There's no place to hide out here. You can't lose yourself in people and noise and commotion. Out here you're alone with yourself and God."

The observation surprised Amanda. "I didn't expect you to get me out here and start talking about God."

"I didn't get you out here, Amanda, you came with me. And you're still trying to hide behind that clever wit of yours. Unless I'm sadly mistaken, there's more to Amanda Caron than that."

She felt as though her father had just told her that

he was ashamed of her. Her face was hot with embarrassment, and her tongue, mercifully, tied.

"You don't have to figure me out, Amanda. I'm just as you see me. I say what's on my mind. I think you're a beautiful woman, and I'm enjoying your company." He stopped walking, moving behind her, and rested his hands on her shoulders. "And this is what I wanted you to see. Just be quiet, don't think about anything, and let it fill your whole body." The straight line of the horizon glowed with a hint of pink, a promise.

"Feel that color and warmth start to creep into your toes. Feel it as it moves gradually . . . inch by inch . . . ," he whispered beside her ear. She stood quietly and watched as the glow brightened and the pink grew, and the power of his suggestion led her to internalize the spreading dawnlight until the fiery ball hoisted itself over the edge of the world and spread white light through Amanda's eyes.

"My God!" she uttered.

"Exactly." Sean turned her to him and smiled at the rosy glow in her face. "Exactly, Amanda." Drawing her closer, he lowered his head, and she lifted her mouth to meet his lips, sliding her arms around his back. He intensified the quiet glow that he had planted within her, making her stomach shudder with the sensual caress of his mouth against hers. Teasing her lips apart, his tongue found a cache of sweet honey, which he tasted tentatively and lingered to taste again. Then slowly, reluctantly, his mouth released its claim, but his arms kept her close.

"That was everything I thought it would be," he whispered, brushing his lips across her temple, relishing the silkiness of her hair.

"I know what you mean," she replied, her eyes still closed, her breathing unsteady. She'd been kissed before, she told herself, so why did she feel so utterly helpless now?

With a gentle hand Sean brushed the hair back

from Amanda's face, smoothing it behind her ear, exposing her slender white neck to the butterfly touchings of his lips. "There's a woman inside you, Amanda, and she's as beautiful as the lady you work so hard at being." He lifted his head again and looked down into her eyes as they opened slowly, blue and wide. "But the woman wants to respond more honestly than the lady dares allow."

"Now I *don't* know what you mean, Sean."

"You know exactly what I mean."

"Obviously I find you attractive. I didn't mind your kissing me."

" 'Didn't mind' isn't an accurate description of what you felt just now. I caught you at a moment when you were feeling something honestly, from the depth of your soul. But now you've had time to regroup, and you're waiting for me to make a move so you can deftly parry. Relax, Amanda. I'm not driven by lust, and I'm not going to force anything on you."

She smiled up at him. "If I thought you were dangerous I wouldn't be out here with you."

"I didn't say I wasn't dangerous. Dangerous for you is whatever you can't handle." He bent his head and kissed her again, taking leisurely possession of her mouth and working his lips to awaken her response. Moving his mouth away, he breathed, "A kiss is not something to be handled, Amanda. A kiss is something you just let yourself enjoy."

Chapter Three

Sean dropped Amanda off at the hotel with a promise to be back with rodeo contractor Gerry Strickland by noon. Strickland would be catching a three-thirty flight to Vegas, Sean had told her. She would need to plan a brief interview, but, for some reason, she had difficulty keeping her mind on the upcoming interview and away from Sean Brannigan. Thinking of him, she felt the warm glow of the desert sunrise diffuse through her body. Finally Amanda decided that a few hours of sleep would clear her brain.

Later, wearing a gauzy summer dress and sandals with comfortably high heels, Amanda smiled at herself in the mirror, realizing that she had taken as much care with her makeup as she had for her first prom. For such a brief encounter—for Sean would surely be out of her life soon—she was allowing an inordinate amount of adrenaline to flow. And her ill-fated engagement and subsequent, equally lackluster relationships had demonstrated to her that adrenaline was highly overrated.

Amanda adjusted the straps on the pale aqua dress and thoughtfully fingered the opal teardrop pendant that had been a recent gift from her father, noting that her tan—what there was of it—would fade if she didn't start getting more sun. The phone rang, sending her bounding across the room, as though she had been afraid he might not show up. She caught herself and quelled her excitement before affecting a casual, "Hello?"

"Didn't wake you, did I?" Sean asked.

"Of course not. I've been waiting for you. I'll meet you in the dining room."

Gerry Strickland was glad to answer Amanda's questions about the care and feeding of rodeo stock. She asked about time spent on the road, vet care, death loss, rotation of animals. She explained her interest in the mustangs, and he proceeded to tell her about adopting several of them. Mustang Sally had taken to the life of a bucking horse with apparent relish, and he spoke of her personality as though she were a temperamental stage star. When Strickland began checking his watch Amanda expressed her appreciation for his time and assured him that she didn't want to keep him any longer. He was soon on his way to the airport in a cab.

"How was that, Amanda? Did you get what you wanted?" Sean asked, willing to linger over a lukewarm cup of coffee with the company he had so quickly come to savor.

"He's pretty excited about that mustang, which is the kind of endorsement I need for my defense of the adoption program."

Enthusiasm simmered in Amanda's voice as she talked about the mustang owners she'd interviewed. The sparkle in her eyes grew steadily as she told her story, leaping a bit higher when she laughed. When she told the tale of a tricky little mustang who'd become a handicapped child's pet her whole face shone.

"We had a colt like that once," Sean contributed, and a wistful smile settled in his eyes before he explained. "My little sister brought him in the house once for a drink of water. Never found out how she got him up the steps." Sean watched as Amanda braced her hands on the seat of the chair by her knees and rocked forward on her arms, shrugging her bare shoulders in childlike delight. He was enchanted. "He learned to open the yard gate by himself. Of course Mom put her foot down about letting him in the house, but when he came to the back door Shelley knew he wanted water."

"Now, you see—if that colt had been a mustang, what sympathy we could get with a story like that! I'll bet your sister would never part with that horse. I'll bet you still have him around."

The smile on his face faded quickly, and Sean lowered his eyes, tilting the coffee cup, examining its contents. "No . . . I sold him." Banishing the whole topic, Sean tossed his linen napkin on the table. "Is there a pool in this place? Let's go for a swim."

"But, Sean, I . . ."

"I know, you're all dressed up, but I may never see you again after today, and I can't help wondering what you look like in a swimsuit. Mine is out in the camper."

She looked the way his hours of fantasizing about her had told him she would. She was long limbed and long waisted, and she had the well-toned muscles of a horsewoman. Her one-piece black swimsuit was tastefully provocative, and he sat with his legs dangling lazily in the water as he watched her stride gracefully toward him.

"I'm not getting my hair wet, cowboy, so don't try

anything funny," she warned, seating herself beside him on the edge of the pool.

"You don't have to get anything wet, pretty lady. I'd be happy just to sit here and watch you walk around the pool. Besides, you probably can't swim."

"I'll bet you dinner I can swim more laps than you can."

"What about your hair?"

"It'll be dry in time for dinner."

"You're on," he laughed, pulling her to her feet.

The pool area was almost deserted in the late afternoon, and they were free to swim laps until they dropped, which was about what they did. Sean had intended to show off a bit, so he was surprised when Amanda kept pace with him. In the end he was satisfied to best her by two laps. She was sitting back up on the edge of the pool, winded, when he stood in the water, pushing the wet hair back from his face and inhaling deeply. Then he grinned at her, resting his tanned hands just above her knees.

"Lady, you are one hell of a swimmer!"

"But you beat me," she admitted.

"You're messing with a professional athlete, sweetheart. Gentleman that I am, my professional pride won't allow me to throw a sporting contest, not even to a lady." He levered himself up on the pool's edge and wiped his face on the towel that she draped around his broad shoulders.

"Ah, but in the end your pride isn't served by winning."

"How's that?"

"Because, Mr. Brannigan, you will have to allow a woman to pick up the check at your table tonight." The grin on Amanda's face lit up her eyes, and Sean enjoyed the sense that she was having honest fun with him. "Hang around here and watch the girls while I shower and change. Then you can use my shower."

Sean leaned back on his elbows and watched her

walk away. The back view was as pleasant as the front.

Amanda left Sean alone to take his shower, and when she returned found the door to her room open and Sean lounging in a chair. "That was quick," she said as she swept into the room, the mellow scent of her perfume wafting past his nose.

"It's nice to use a shower that I don't have to accordion myself into. You look great, Amanda. No one would guess that you'd just lost an important race."

"As the victor, the choice of restaurants is yours. What do you like besides pizza?" She was putting a pair of pearl earrings into her ears as he stalked her from behind, settling his hands at either side of her small waist. The black dress was soft and clingy.

"I like uncrowded, intimate places."

"Oh? Like the Bootheel?"

"You had a good time last night, didn't you?"

"Yes, I really did."

"Then trust me. You might not want to wear that dress, even though . . . I like it very much."

She turned to him, smiling. "Then I'll wear it. Now, where are we going?"

"Someplace where we can have wine and candlelight, a simple supper and a nice, long, uninterrupted talk."

"That sounds lovely. Where is it?"

"My place."

"Your . . . you mean your motor home, or whatever it's called?"

"It's called transportation with portable conveniences."

"The agreement was that I take you out to dinner."

"The bet was dinner, and I want you to cook it."

"What makes you think I can cook?"

"I underestimated you once, and you swam your

little heart out. Consider this another challenge. A picnic supper."

"You're a victor seeking pretty slim spoils," she concluded.

"Yeah," he chuckled. "Pretty and slim, but not spoiled. I can't stand spoiled."

The camper boasted all the conveniences Sean had promised. It was custom fitted for pulling a horse trailer, had a forty-gallon gas tank, and afforded freedom and comfort on the road. Amanda noted that the interior was immaculately clean; either his belongings were carefully put away or he didn't have any. Behind the plush, padded swivel seats in the cab there was a small couch on the driver's side and a booth with a table on the passenger's side. The galley had a stove, a refrigerator, a sink and cabinets. Amanda glimpsed doors on either side near the rest; she assumed that one must lead to a bathroom. Another couch traversed the back of the camper beneath a full back window. The berth over the cab was curtained.

Evening drew down slowly as they headed for isolation in the vast Nevada desert. Purple shadows softened the stark angles of the surrealistic landscape.

"You didn't ask Lacy and Bud to join us?" Amanda asked.

"They left this morning."

"Oh. Had you planned to leave today too?"

"Originally, yes."

"And I delayed you for that luncheon date. I'm sorry. You should have said something."

Chuckling, Sean assured her that it wasn't unusual for him to change his plans on the spur of the moment.

"You won't be late for your next rodeo, will you?"

"There's always another rodeo. I like to stay around and collect my winnings, whether it's money or dinner."

If you think you'll be collecting any more than that, Amanda mused, think again. Aloud she asked, "And what sort of dinner have you planned for me to make? I've no doubt you've got it all figured out, from soup to nuts."

"'A loaf of bread, a jug of wine, and thou.' How does that sound?"

"Familiar."

"Then you've been courted before."

"I've had communion."

"And you have a heartier appetite than that."

"Definitely."

"Good. I'll have prime rib, baked potato, bleu cheese dressing on the salad, a decent rosé and . . ."

"Will midnight be soon enough?"

". . . pecan pie."

"I haven't mastered piecrust yet."

"I'll wait." He flashed a grin at her. "Sunset with you is going to be as great as sunrise."

When he found an isolated expanse of placid desert Sean parked the camper.

"How do you choose these spots, Sean? We've driven past miles of country just like this."

"Listen," he said, signaling for quiet.

After a moment she said, "I don't hear anything."

"That's why I chose this spot. I had it reserved. How about a glass of wine?"

Cooking was unnecessary. Sean had indeed thought of wine and a plump loaf of French bread, as well as cheese, fresh fruit and cold ham. Amanda had only to do some slicing, which she bungled by slicing into her middle finger. She let Sean bandage it for her. He didn't fuss, and when he was done, though she half expected him to kiss it for her as country charm would dictate, he winked at her and predicted her survival.

Dinner was served on a blanket spread a short distance from the camper. True to his word, he had provided candles, wine glasses and a simple supper.

Also true to his word, the rosy-golden glow in the sky warmed her and the orangy orb that had thrilled her with its appearance that morning gave her a deep sense of serenity as it slipped below the horizon.

Amanda sat with her legs tucked to one side, the soft black fabric of her dress fanning over them as she sipped her wine. She caught an appreciative look from Sean, who lay on his side, propped up on one elbow.

"You are an enigma, Sean Brannigan. I can't imagine you packing candle holders and stemmed wine glasses along with your ropes and spurs."

"I didn't. I just bought them today."

"I must say, there's method in your madness. This was a lovely idea."

"Watch the eastern sky, Amanda. The best is yet to come."

The full moon was a huge orange balloon, rising as quickly as if it were filled with helium. Amanda leaned in its direction slightly, as though magnetized, her eyes round with awe. "Oh, wow! I've never seen it like that, so big and orange. Oh, my . . . Sean, you're not watching. Look! It's beautiful." She glanced at him, but her eyes were quickly drawn back to the spectacle in the sky.

"I am watching it. I can see it in your eyes. Tell me, Amanda, how long has it been since you've said 'Oh, wow'?"

Amanda giggled, realizing how ingenuous she must have sounded. "It's been . . . a long time."

"I think I've discovered a weakness in your designer facade."

"Do I seem haughty to you?"

"If I thought there was nothing behind that beautiful facade I'd be in Salt Lake City right now."

"And what do you think is behind my facade?"

"Someone I'm going to like very much when I get to know her. Someone who'd rather see the desert sky at night than a star-studded floor show in town.

Someone who doesn't mind getting her hair wet or her white pants dirty." He reached across the candleglow to refill her glass and then refilled his own.

"I think you know me about as well as you're going to. You'll be leaving tomorrow, won't you?"

Sean was quiet for a moment, swirling the wine in his glass. "I'm leaving soon." He looked up, catching her eyes, holding them with his will. "I want you to come with me."

It took a moment for her brain to process the statement. "Come . . . where?"

"Through the desert to Salt Lake City, over the mountains to Greeley, and on to South Dakota by the Fourth."

"That's a lot of driving by the Fourth."

"Plenty of time before then, lots of beautiful countryside along the way."

"I . . . no, really, it's not possible for me."

"That isn't true, Amanda. Not only is it possible for you to come with me, but there are other possibilities for us. You sense that, just as I do. Are you afraid to see what they might be?"

"No, it isn't that. I'd like to go on seeing you, Sean, if we were going to be here for a while. But traveling with you in that . . . And, really, I wasn't planning to . . ."

"The camper bothers you?"

"It would be like moving in with you. I'm not like Lacy, Sean. I don't attach myself to a man and follow him around."

"You're a writer, and you're interested in writing about Western performance horses—rodeo horses. I'm just offering you some transportation, a little insight into the business and good company. You don't have to share my bed. When we get to a town you can stay in a motel if you want to."

Amanda sipped her wine, avoiding his eyes now. It was ridiculous to even consider this . . . this proposition, innocent as he made it sound. "I know so little about you, Sean," she said quietly.

"A thousand miles down the road you'll have heard more about me than you ever wanted to know. And vice versa. More wine?" She shook her head. He leaned forward to blow out the candles, which he moved off to the edge of the blanket. He took the glass from her hand, setting that aside, too, but keeping her hand in his. Her palm tingled when he brought it to his lips. A subtle change of position and she was in his arms, her lips parting as his closed over them, his tongue dipping between them.

Sliding her arms around his tapering back, Amanda sought only to steady herself against the surge of quivering that beset her insides. She welcomed him with the warm pressure of her own lips, a shy, tentative flickering of her own tongue against his. It was a contact that incited them both to deepen the kiss, and he pressed her back to the blanket, interrupting himself only to reposition his mouth and kiss her again.

Sean felt his need for her quicken, and he tempered it, holding his body away from hers, slowing his kisses to soft caresses of her mouth, her chin and jawline. "Come with me, Mandy," he whispered.

A ragged sigh eased its way from her chest. "I don't know, Sean. I just . . . don't know."

Sliding his arm beneath her shoulders, he settled on his back beside her, pillowing her head in the pocket of his shoulder. "You haven't said 'I don't want to.' Do you know why?" She didn't answer, so he answered for her. "Because you like being with me, and you're not anxious to see me go out of your life."

"But I haven't said that I want to, either."

"If I stayed all week and asked you out every night, would you go out with me?"

"Yes."

"Would it matter where we went or what we did?"

"No . . . well, not as long as—"

"As long as I behaved like a gentleman and didn't take you to an orgy somewhere."

She laughed a little. "Right."

"Look up there, Mandy," he commanded, his voice a husky whisper. The black canopy of deep space ran riot with white jewels. "If you just lie here and watch them long enough you get to thinking that if you lift your arm you can touch them, that they're hanging just above you. Then you can reach up, and you watch your hand reaching up, and it looks like you just plunged your hand into the sky, like you're just about to touch those little white lights. Then you remember that the light we see is millions of years old, and the light they're making now is so far away that it'll be seen by some being far down the evolutionary road from us. And some of the light we see is from stars that aren't even there anymore."

"Now I'm waiting for you to quote Andrew Marvell to me. 'Had we but world enough, and time, this coyness, lady, were no crime.'"

He chuckled deeply. "I'm not one for quoting poetry, Mandy. I like it, though, so if you want to quote it to me, I'll enjoy that. No, I'm not accusing you of being coy with me. What you're doing is being coy with yourself. You want to come with me, you want to see what a different kind of life might be like, and you might even want to do your story. But you're shying away because Amanda Caron doesn't do that kind of thing. You're making assumptions about all of it; your mind projects the possibilities for you, and what you see doesn't jibe with who you think you are, so you back off from something that deep down you're at least curious about." Suddenly his long arm pushed into the sky above them. "From this angle I can almost believe I'm there, but it's an illusion. I'd have to venture away from everything I know if I were really trying to touch the stars."

"I don't dream that big, Sean."

"I'm not talking about dreaming. A dream is an illusion of life. If you want life, Mandy, you have to listen to what's inside you, that woman inside you who wants to *do* more."

"What do you think she wants to do?" Persuade me, she thought; make it seem sensible. . . .

"She wants to respond to life honestly. She wants to see what it would be like not to have to worry about what everyone else thinks, or about how to outmaneuver other people. I think you've maneuvered yourself into a box."

"They called Will Rogers the cowboy philosopher. Who are you? The cowboy psychoanalyst? You make me sound very shallow."

"No, you're not shallow. If you were I'd be bored with you already. You work hard at your . . . your image, but when you forget about that for a while you enjoy yourself, and you're fun to be with."

"I can't see myself as being that complicated. I'm certainly not interested in putting on an act. What I might be interested in is doing a story, and you could give me an 'in,' which is what I really need. Just what would you expect of me on this trip?"

"Intelligent conversation, keep me awake while I'm driving, help me with the horses, maybe fix a meal once in a while."

"I'm not much of a cook. I'll share expenses fifty-fifty."

"You'll screw up my tax return, lady. My expenses are deductible."

"So are mine. Fifty-fifty."

"I'm pulling two horses, which takes a hell of a lot of gas, and I eat twice as much as you do."

"Sixty-forty, then."

"Eighty-twenty if you'll drive once in a while."

"Deal," she murmured. "But don't try anything funny, cowboy."

"How about a kiss to seal the bargain?" he whispered, then caught her lips with his before she could answer. His free hand held the back of her head for a moment; then his fingers found the silkiness of her hair irresistible, and they tangled themselves in it. Amanda curved her hand under his arm and spread her fingers across his broad back, excited by the strength she sensed there. Reluctantly Sean lifted his mouth, his tongue hovering a second longer on the soft pillow of her lower lip before he whispered, "That ain't funny, lady."

Chapter Four

$\mathcal{A}$manda called the wisdom of her decision into question over and over again as she packed. She hadn't told her father the whole truth over the phone. She'd said that she was doing some follow-up, which would involve looking into the rodeo business, and that she wouldn't be returning home for a week or two. He had argued, but she'd reminded him of his promise to let her make her own decisions, a promise he'd made when she'd agreed to take an apartment in Brookline rather than move to Hartford with a girl-friend. Her father had taken it hard when her engagement to Paul was broken, and he had become all the more protective of her in the three years since then.

Sean announced his arrival with a knock at her door. She was dressed, packed and ready when she admitted him. He took her luggage out to the camper while she checked out. It was a delaying tactic on her part when she asked if he wanted coffee before they left.

"It'll be ready and waiting by the time we get out

there. Let's go, lady; it's at least four hundred miles to the state line."

While Sean stowed her belongings Amanda poured the coffee he'd made. From the back of the camper he was telling her that it would be a long haul. "We'll eat on the road, stopping just for gas and to take care of the horses. It should be evening when we hit the desert—Great Salt Lake. It can be a killer in the middle of the day. You don't mind, do you? It'll be pretty late when we get to Salt Lake City."

"No, I don't mind. I don't want you to do anything differently from the way you normally would. I'm just along for the ride. When we get there I'll get a room." She lifted the cup to her lips as she turned from the counter. He was there, smiling.

"I'm glad you're coming with me."

She returned the smile, but she wasn't ready to echo his enthusiasm for this venture. She handed him a cup with, "Here's your coffee."

After stopping to pick up the trailer and horses, which he had left with a friend, Sean pointed the camper's nose in a northeasterly direction. Amanda watched the sage and greasewood roll by, quiet in her contemplation of what she was doing in this camper with this man. Her mind admonished her, then rationalized, then admonished her again, moving in a circle as tedious as the Nevada vegetation that she watched. He probably knew what she was thinking, and she wondered if he was thinking along the same lines.

"On the right is the Humbolt Sink," Sean announced after a long silence. "Corresponds with your mood, doesn't it?"

"What?" She was startled out of her reverie, jumping a little at the sound of his voice.

"You have a sinking feeling that you're stranded in the middle of the desert with a total stranger."

"Oh, no, I was just thinking that I should be able to get some typing done along the way. I have quite a bit of—"

"Come on, Mandy. If there's one thing I'm not a stranger to it's feeling uncomfortable in foreign territory."

"You strike me as the sort of person who makes himself comfortable wherever he goes."

"You should've seen me when I first went east. I was shier than hell, stayed in my room at night for the whole first semester."

"What made you decide to go to Cornell? I'd have thought you to be a Texas A&M prospect."

"Cornell offered me a better scholarship. I was two things that looked good on their records—a South Dakotan and an Indian."

She looked at him as though for the first time. "I didn't realize you were Indian."

"On my mother's side. She was Sioux, at least mostly. You mean you just thought I had a great tan?"

"I didn't really think about . . . well, now that you mention it, I do see a resemblance between you and Jay Silverheels, who's the only Indian I know."

Sean chuckled. "Back east, people would look at me sometimes and finally ask me if I was from Italy or Brazil or someplace. From you I get Jay Silverheels."

"What a matinee idol you'd have been a few years back. So tell me more about this interesting family of yours. Your father is obviously Irish."

"Kevin Brannigan, Irish as they come. His parents came over from the old country. They left him the ranch. Oddly enough, my mother was part Irish as well."

"Your mother's dead?" she asked, gentling her voice.

He nodded. "She and my little sister were killed in a car accident. Drunk driver."

"How long ago did it happen?"

"Six years. That's when I left school."

"And your father?"

"Dad died two years later. He . . . didn't want to live anymore. So I'm the last of the Brannigans."

"Have you thought of going back to school?"

"Crossed my mind once or twice. Dad wanted me to be a veterinarian. Correction, he wanted me to be *educated,* and I went along with the animal science idea. And it was interesting."

"Did you want to be a veterinarian?"

"I'd been accepted for the program at South Dakota, but after the accident I needed to be home. And then I started to rodeo, and right now that's what I want to do."

"What do you like about being in rodeo?"

"Well, I like the action, the physical challenge and the risk, I guess. And I like winning. I enjoy training my own horses and showing 'em off, and I like to travel."

"Do you like the bright lights and applause and being *the* Sean Brannigan?"

"Yeah," he laughed. "Yeah, I like that part, too."

"I can see why. It's kind of fun just being *the* Sean Brannigan's date. You're a talented man. You sing really well, too."

"Must be the Irish in me. I'm really at my best when I'm driving down the road, radio backing me up."

"I'll enjoy that," Amanda said honestly. It occurred to her that her father never sang, even when he thought he was alone. Neither did Paul. They were two of a kind—too serious for singing.

Sean grinned broadly. "How about a chorus of 'Happy Trails'?" A strange shiver tantalized her when he winked at her. "You know what I'd like? A ham sandwich. Think you can brace yourself against the curves and fix us some?"

Amanda rummaged through cupboards and drawers, boldly familiarizing herself with the whereabouts of supplies. Sandwiches were easy enough, and she found soda and chips as well. Continuing her search, ostensibly for napkins, she found a drawer full of boxes labeled with the names of towns or sites. Some had lids on them, but some didn't, their contents open to view. There were old pieces of bone, bits of rock and pottery, and arrowheads.

"Sean, what's all this?"

"All what?"

"These artifacts. Are they yours?"

"No, I stole them."

"*Stole* them! From whom?"

"From some long-since-departed cliff dwellers, some prehistoric farmers, and some from my own more recent ancestors, the buffalo hunters."

"Do you dig for artifacts?"

"That's one of my stranger interests, and it's why a lot of guys get tired of traveling with me."

"May I look at some?"

"Sure, help yourself. Are you interested?"

"Oh, yes, very," she answered, taking a box and closing the drawer carefully. After handing him lunch on a paper plate, she settled back in the passenger seat with her own lunch and the small box. "I used to think I wanted to be an archaeologist, but I know I haven't the patience. You really do this yourself?"

"I really do. It's good to get off by myself once in a while and just dig around and think. It's like treasure hunting, or looking for petrified rock, like I did when I was a kid. You find an arrowhead that some guy made hundreds of years ago, and you think, 'I'm probably the first person to touch this since that poor, dumb bastard who spent all his waking hours making stuff like this and using it to try to get enough food to stay alive.' Then you think that maybe he wasn't poor, because everything he made seems like a work of art now, and maybe he wasn't so dumb, either, because surely he breathed clean air and drank clean water, and he usually didn't kill any more than he could eat."

"And maybe he wasn't a bastard, either. They probably got married and stayed married. They were probably truer to their value system than we are to ours."

"Is Amanda Caron questioning our venerable social values?"

"I question our inability to live by them. How is your sandwich?"

"Ah, now there's a good question," he said, taking a first bite. "Excellent. So you don't think you have the patience for archaeology, huh? Ever tried digging?"

"Only for night crawlers."

The mental picture which that conjured up in his mind made him chuckle. "I'll take you out digging sometime, then. I have a sifter along—stopped in a few places in New Mexico and Arizona this trip. You'll love it, I guarantee."

"Has anyone ever done a story on you?" she asked.

"On me? You mean for some magazine?" Amanda nodded. "Sure, my name pops up now and then. Sometimes they'll ask me a few questions."

"I mean an article just on you. You lead a very interesting life, and your interests and talents are so diversified. I don't imagine there are many cowboys who sing, collect artifacts—"

Laughing, he interrupted with, "Every cowboy thinks he can sing."

"But I doubt they all think the way you do."

"Of course they don't all think the way I do. Cowboys are just like any other group of people, Mandy. There are some who think about beer, broads and broncs, and there are others who have a string of college degrees."

She was more than skeptical, but she wasn't going to argue the point. "Be that as it may, you would be an interesting subject for an article."

"Tell you what, I'll give you an exclusive."

"I might take you up on that."

It was early afternoon when they pulled off the road to look after the horses. Sean carried a large water tank, fastened over the fender of the horse trailer.

After dishing out water and alfalfa pellets Sean and Amanda gave the animals a five-minute walk to stretch their legs. The heat was oppressive, bearing down on them from the sun overhead and rising from the largely barren earth. Amanda was grateful for the lack of humidity and for the air conditioning once they were again under way.

At the state line they stopped for gas and, once again, to feed and water the horses. This time Amanda took time out to attempt to cook hamburgers. She found herself not wanting to appear totally undomestic. In fact she wanted to give the impression that it was unnecessary that she put any effort into such tasks, since they really took no thought and anyone could handle them. Unfortunately the meat stuck to the pan, and when she tried to turn the patties they fell apart. Worse, she was angrily shoving the spatula under the pieces when Sean came in.

"Oh, Sean, this is embarrassing!" she wailed. "I'm not always so bad at this."

"This little stove takes some getting used to. Start with low heat and work up to what you need."

"I made a mess," she complained.

"No problem, Mandy. Look . . ." He opened a can of sandwich sauce, chopped up the hamburger and said, "Easy barbeque. That's what you had in mind anyway, isn't it?" he teased. With that he left her to put the rest of the meal together while he busied himself in the back of the camper.

"I made up the bed in the back," he told her in answer to her call to come and eat. He joined her at the small table. "It'll be late when we get to Salt Lake, so you grab some sleep when you get tired."

"You're the one who needs rest."

"No, I'll let you know when I do. But you go ahead and sleep when you feel like it."

"I'll be fine. Part of the deal is for me to keep you awake while you drive, and that's what I plan to do."

Amanda had no idea what time it was when she

couldn't keep her eyes open any longer. They had had coffee and long conversation, but two nights with little sleep and the monotony of the highway forced her to succumb.

"Hey," Sean said quietly, reaching to pat her knee, "go on back and lie down."

"I'm all right," Amanda yawned. "I don't know how you're staying awake, though. You haven't slept much the past two nights, either."

"And if I have to sit here and watch you nod off I'm gonna start thinking I'm tired, too."

"Okay, I'm going. Can I get you anything first?"

When he shook his head Amanda lifted her weary body from the seat, but he caught her hand before she moved toward the back of the camper. "You're a good copilot, lady. I like having you along." Her hand responded with a squeeze, and something inside her responded with a burst of good feeling.

Neither the daylight nor the wailing country music on the radio some distance away nudged Amanda from sleep. She was aware of those things only after she smelled coffee and bacon in her dreams. The realization that she had slept through the night, that they were parked and that it was morning brought her fully awake. At some point Sean had been back there. The windows were open at the head and foot of the bed, and they had been closed before. The folding curtain had also been drawn. She avoided glancing in the kitchen when she took herself and her makeup case into the little bathroom.

"Have you given up on my cooking?" she asked when she emerged, feeling fresh.

"No way! I'll cook when I feel like it; you cook when you feel like it. And if neither of us feels like it, we'll go out."

"I hadn't intended to spend the night back there, Sean. I want to stay in a motel. Why didn't you—"

"Wake you up so you could move to another bed?

What kind of sense would that make? Come on, have some coffee."

"Sean, it isn't that I don't trust you."

"No?"

"Of course not. But I don't want you to feel you have to provide for me. You're free to go where you please, eat where you please and with whom you please. I'm just going to ride along with you for a little while."

"How do you like your eggs?"

"Benedict."

"How else do you like your eggs?"

"I'm not fussy, and you're not listening."

"You're getting over-easy."

"Fine. Sean, you're not responsible for me. You can just let me off at a motel when we get to where we're going," Amanda insisted.

"Will you relax, Mandy? I'll take you to a motel after the roping tonight. You don't want to spend the day in a motel, do you?"

"No, but I don't want you to feel like you have to—"

"I don't feel like I have to do anything. I asked you to come along with me because I like being with you. And you like being with me, don't you?" It was more a statement than a question.

"It isn't that I—"

"*Don't* you, Mandy?"

"Yes, I do."

"You don't have to tell me what it is or isn't, Mandy; I know what's bothering you. You're afraid of what people might think, even people you don't know from Adam. When you step out of this camper you're gonna think everybody out there figures you spent the night with me. And you know what?" He paused as he set two plates on the table, then retrieved utensils and the coffee pot.

"What?" she asked quietly.

"Most of them won't think about it at all, but a few will probably figure that you did. You know what else?"

"What?"

"You did spend the night with me. Do you feel like a fallen woman?"

"No, but . . ."

"But nothing. Mandy, look at me." She felt like a child as she raised her eyes to meet his. "What happens between us—or doesn't happen—is nobody's business but ours. If you like, I'll have a bumper sticker made: We Are Not Sleeping Together."

"They'll say that 'the lady doth protest too much,' " she countered, unable to hold back a smile.

"Whoever *they* are, they'll be right. She doth. And you know what else?"

"What else?"

"When I cook, you clean up."

If Lacy was surprised when Amanda arrived with Sean, she didn't show it. Amanda was uncomfortable with any assumption that they had become a couple, like Lacy and Bud, but Sean was right: Explaining or denying their relationship wouldn't make any difference to anyone. At any rate Lacy was friendly.

They were in Salt Lake City for a roping. Sean explained that the local roping club sponsored the event, and that it was a good stopover between the Reno and Greeley rodeos. Only roping events would be held, and as she fell in beside him, helping him feed the horses, he warned her that there would be countless ropers. Amanda insisted on helping him with the washing and grooming as well. The bay, he told her, was called Medicine Man, and the sorrel was Deke. They were prime animals, well-fleshed and well-kept, and she told Sean that.

"I think they like you, too. They're not used to all this fussing." He rubbed the sorrel's neck. "What do you think, boy? Do you want to offer this lady a ride after she's done all this to pretty you up?" He tickled the horse under the jaw, causing the animal to bounce his head in something like a positive gesture.

"Good Lord, cowboy, you've even got your horses trained to be charming!" Amanda laughed.

"Don't knock it—he'll be the first horse to give you a ride voluntarily."

Bud and Lacy joined them for supper in the camper. It was hot, but there was some relief in the cross breeze that came in through the windows. Bud had come in with a can of beer, and when that was gone he asked Sean if he had another one.

"No, Bud, I don't. And I don't know about you, but I'm roping tonight. You look like hell. How'd you do last night?"

Bud shook his head. "Not too good."

"Tell the truth, Bud, the *whole* truth," Lacy put in. Bud cast a sharp glance in her direction.

"Yeah, well, I threw my loop away. Then I bought a team in the Calcutta, and I lost."

"Sounds like a tough night, Bud," Sean commented, then turned his attention to Amanda's attempt at frying steak, which she had always thought should be broiled. Once he had adjusted the heat for her, he offered Lacy and Bud a "pop" and Amanda a "soda." To Amanda he whispered, "I speak several languages."

"I'm not surprised," was her retort. "What's a Calcutta?"

"They auction off the teams for some pretty high stakes before they rope. You can make a bundle if your team wins—even if it places. Some of these local clubs get into that kind of thing. Only 'stakes' I'm gambling on are the ones in this pan," he assured her, cocking a thumb in the direction of the stove. She waved him away with her meat fork, determined to prove herself with this meal.

Sean slid into the booth across from Bud, who

continued to recount the mishaps of the previous night. Finally he sighed. "Sean, the team roping's still open, and I mean it's wide open. How 'bout gettin' in with me?"

"Team roping! I'm not here for team roping."

"Lot of money in it, Sean, lot of local boys."

"I don't care about that; I'm not here for that. I don't use my calf horse on steers; you know that."

"Sean, you could use that horse on elephants."

"But I don't, and that's what makes him a good calf horse."

"I won't ask you again, Sean. I wouldn't now, except—"

"Don't make me any promises, Bud. You'll forget them tomorrow. I'm just not a team roper. What do you want to do, ruin my image?"

"Image!" came the feminine bellow. Amanda stepped slowly around the counter, her eyes dancing. "Did I hear you say that you were worried about your *image,* Sean Brannigan?" She stood beside him, arms akimbo. "My, my, a hang-up like that could take all the enjoyment out of your life," she warned, laying a hand on his shoulder and grinning down at his handsome face. "This kind of an attitude could bring on acute horse-opera neurosis."

Sean laughed, enjoying the familiarity in her gesture. "Unfortunate choice of words, I guess. Touché, sweetheart. You got me where it hurts—right in the old philosophy."

"Would you care for steak sauce with your crow?" she taunted, returning to the stove. "I'll have it ready in just a minute."

"Looks like you met your match, Sean," Bud laughed, but his laughter was guarded.

"So you think we could win it, huh, Bud?" Sean asked.

"Piece of cake, Sean."

"You drink any more between now and then, and

I'll give you a piece of this, Bud," Sean threatened quietly, his fist under Bud's nose. "And I'll tell you something else. You walk out on Lacy again before you get her home, and I won't ever bail you out again." Bud nodded like a child who'd learned his lesson. "I mean that, Bud. You won't even get me to rope fence posts with you in the backyard."

Amanda didn't want to put the food on the table until she was sure that this conversation was finished. Sean's tone wasn't unfriendly, but he was serious about what he said. She glanced at Lacy, who sat quietly on the couch staring at her fingernails. Lacy felt Amanda's eyes on her, and she came to her feet suddenly, offering to help serve dinner.

Before the subject was dropped Sean grumbled, "I suppose I have to pay your entry fee, too, huh?"

"Well, yeah, but you'll get it back."

"I damn well better."

The roping did seem to drag on and on, and Amanda lost interest in the endless lineup of ropers. She was more interested in the activity behind the roping boxes. She listened to the boasts and the compliments, the complaints and the jokes, and the inevitably colorful language. Lacy was a popular lady, and Amanda noticed a number of different arms draped over the other woman's shoulders.

"I told you, Travis, I'm with Bud," Lacy protested to a particularly lanky-looking, dark-haired cowboy. "I wouldn't want him to mess up that pretty face of yours." Amanda pretended not to notice that the cowboy had patted Lacy's bottom when she leaned forward on the railing to peek into the arena.

"You gotta be kidding. Bud Eliot? Thought you only went in for real cowboys, Lacy. Eliot's just a party boy. Last night he didn't even know his calf was out."

"Bud was just having a good time. Now that

Johnny's here he'll get serious. Johnny's gonna enjoy beatin' the pants off you, Travis, and the rest of us are gonna enjoy watching him do it."

"Still Brannigan's cheerleader? When're you plannin' on growin' up? If Eliot passes out early on ya', honey, you know where to find me. I'll give you somethin' to shake your pom-poms about." A wink and a click of the tongue punctuated his promise.

Watching the man's departing back, Lacy grumbled, "Travis isn't the kind of guy you want to be introduced to, Amanda. He's the one Johnny's gotta go after in the all-around. He'll come on to you, too, when he finds out about you and Johnny, just to make him mad. Johnny can't stand him."

"Johnny can't stand who?" Sean stepped over to join the ladies.

"Oh, that Travis Steele; he was bothering me again."

"And?" His eyes grew hard.

"And nothing. I told him to get lost."

"I have to know," Amanda interrupted, suddenly feeling she was finding herself privy to more than she wanted to know about the intricacies of these relationships, "why Lacy is the only person I've heard call you Johnny."

"I used to tease him in school about the way he spelled his name. I told him it should be S-H-A-W-N," Lacy explained gleefully.

"Can you imagine my Irish daddy spelling Sean like that?" Sean laughed.

"He told me that Sean was Irish for John, and he's been Johnny to me ever since."

"I guess that makes sense." It occurred to Amanda that she resented even that bit of intimacy between Sean and Lacy.

"As much sense as Lacy ever makes." He grinned and threw a playful wink at Lacy. Amanda felt her jaw tighten.

"Sean Brannigan, you're in the hole," someone shouted from behind the boxes. Sean started to turn back to the bay, but, impulsively, Amanda caught his arm.

"How about a kiss for luck?" she offered quietly. His expression was momentarily surprised, then pleased, and he lowered his head to plant a firm kiss on her waiting mouth.

Sean licked his lips. "Yeah, that tastes like luck, all right." He grinned as he stepped into the stirrup and swung his weight into the saddle. "Sweet."

It was. Sean won the calf roping, and he and Bud placed third in team roping. Lacy bubbled over Bud's performance in calf roping as well, even though he placed fifth and out of the prize money. After returning to the camper Sean showered while Amanda made some notes on her observations. Then came the pounding on the door.

"Come on out, you guys! We've got a campfire going out here, and what we need is a singing cowboy." Bud stuck his head in the door. "Where is he?" he asked Amanda.

"I'm here, Bud, and you just overstepped your bounds. If I want to let you in I'll open the door."

"Sorry, Sean, just wanted you to come on out and—"

"Play? I heard, Bud, no thanks. Amanda's tired."

"No, Sean, a campfire and cowboy talk sounds like fun."

"I thought you wanted to get a—"

"There's plenty of time. It's still early," Amanda said.

A few minutes later Sean sat on the ground, his back against a pickup tire, and Amanda, situated in front of him, lay back against his chest. He had sung several ballads, he and another man strumming guitars that someone had produced. Now he sipped a beer and watched the fire, stroking Amanda's arm, relishing the fresh smell of her hair. The talk was quiet now, the jokes and laughter no longer outrageous, the mood serene, one of comfortable, easy comradery. He hated to do it, but he said, "We'd better go, Mandy. We're gonna have to drag some poor inn-keeper out of bed to get you a room tonight."

Sitting nearby, Lacy overheard the suggestion, and she turned a questioning ear on the conversation.

"It would be kind of silly this late at night, wouldn't it?" Amanda allowed.

"Yeah, it would be, but it's up to you."

"I want to stay and listen to you sing some more, cowboy," she murmured. "How about 'Happy Trails'?"

"Jimmy, hand me that guitar back. The lady wants more music," Sean announced amiably.

They all sang together this time, remembering the words to songs like "Happy Trails" and "Montana Cowboy." Finally Sean's quiet voice brought compa-rable quiet to the group when he said, "This is for my lady," and he sang the song that he had done at the Bootheel, a song about a lady, a love song. His use of the possessive wasn't lost on Amanda, and she real-ized that she wouldn't have accepted it from any other man. He looked at her when he sang, and she basked in his sincerity.

When they went back to the camper he showed her how the couch in the back turned into a bed. She started to contrive an explanation for not being con-cerned about getting a room, but she stopped herself. Instead she thanked him.

"For what?" he asked.

"For telling Lacy and Bud that I planned to stay in a motel."

"I didn't tell—"

"You made sure they could hear. Trying to make me look good."

"But you tried to cut me off. Did you think it would hurt my ego to let people know that you weren't?"

"No, but you were right. I don't need to let

everybody know what I'm doing with my personal life."

"My ego takes pretty good care of itself," he assured her, tossing her a pillow from an overhead compartment.

"No doubt. And maybe I do worry too much about what people think. I feel comfortable with you, Sean."

"Are you comfortable with what you're doing yet?"

"I'm getting there."

"And with what you're feeling?" he asked as he gathered her slight shoulders in his big hands, drawing her to his chest. Amanda lifted a willing mouth to his, her breathing checked in anticipation. His kiss stirred a warm feeling in the pit of her stomach, and her arms stretched eagerly around his back. Sensitive to the turbulence he was causing, and feeling some of his own, Sean stroked her back, pulling her body tight against his, reasserting his claim on her mouth.

"This is a scary feeling, Sean," she breathed when he drew his lips away.

"Why?" he asked between light kisses.

"Because I'm losing my perspective."

"Your control, you mean. Don't be afraid of it, Mandy. I won't push you. I want you, but I won't push you."

"What do you want from me?" she asked, a catch in her voice.

"Whatever you have to give me." He looked earnestly into her eyes. "You want something from me, too; you're just not ready to ask for it."

"I don't go in for recreational sex."

"I know that, Mandy. That isn't what I want from you. I want much more," he assured her before closing his mouth over hers again, rolling his tongue over the soft inner surface of her lips. Her hesitation was brief. That fluttering feeling inside prodded her tongue to seek his and her fingers to knead the hard musculature of his back.

"Mmmm," he groaned, wresting his lips from hers. "That's what I want, Mandy," he whispered. "When I kiss you, I want you to kiss me back. There was feeling for *me* in that kiss."

There was, she thought, and tears welled in her eyes, unbidden, unexpected. *Oh, God, what's going on with me?* Attempting to hide her confusion, she buried her head in his shoulder, her face under his chin, and she took a slow, deep breath to try to ward off the tears. Feeling something was possible for her, then. "Yes, Sean," she whispered at last, "I felt something real for you." Unable to hold them back, she let the tears roll.

"Hey," Sean exclaimed softly, "it's nothing to cry about, honey. It's a nice thing. In case you didn't recognize it, there was feeling for you in my kiss, too."

"I know. I'm not crying," she sniffed.

"This is the best imitation I've seen, lady. I've never made a woman cry with just a kiss before."

She felt comforted by his gentle rubbing of her back. "I'm not unhappy. It's been a long time since I really felt anything when a man kissed me. I've . . . managed to keep men at a distance. But you've been so different from anyone else . . . any man . . ."

"Do you want to tell me about anyone else?"

"No. Not now."

He brushed a kiss against her temple and started to pull back, but she resisted. "I'm not going anywhere," he assured her, keeping an arm around her as he reached to prop two pillows at the head of the bed. He turned out the light, and he felt her tremble. Finding her hand, he drew her to him as he lay down, moving toward the wall to make room for her. "Come here, Mandy."

"No," she sobbed, almost inaudibly. "I can't . . ."

"It's okay, honey, I'm just going to hold you for a while. Do you think I'd try to make love to you with my boots on? Come here and just let me hold you."

She went to him gratefully, and he held her, brushing the tears away, smoothing the hair back from her temple and rubbing her back in that comforting way he had. "Sean," she whispered finally, "you'd never guess this by the way I'm acting, but I'm glad I came."

"So am I, hon."

"I dreaded it, you know. I've avoided it for so long. But it's good to feel this . . . this fluttery feeling again, and I don't want to run away."

"I know what you mean."

She fell asleep that way, lying in his arms, and then he slept, too.

Chapter Five

$\mathscr{B}$efore leaving Salt Lake City Amanda shopped for a small wardrobe of jeans, boots and Western shirts. She was "going native," she decided. Sean suggested a fleece-lined denim jacket for cold nights in the mountains. He chose her boots himself and wanted to buy them for her, but she refused to hear of that. "These people will think I'm your mistress," she whispered.

"Here we go again," he sighed. "Mistresses aren't part of the rodeo circuit—at least I've never seen one. What do they look like?"

"They look . . . kept."

He eyed her up and down, then shook his head. "Nobody'd mistake you for *kept*, lady. You're too mouthy. If you don't stop arguing with me all the time they'll think you're my wife."

They crossed the state line into Wyoming and, after stopping briefly at the site of Old Fort Bridger, drove through the low green hills and tawny meadows of

Green River country. Sean pointed out the striated buttes and rock formations along the way.

There was a quiet between them that afternoon, the motor droning in the background and the radio largely ignored. Amanda watched the hills roll past the window. Sean looked toward the water mirage on the road ahead. But it was the kiss from the night before that lingered in both their minds like the refrain of a song.

Amanda offered to help drive when she noticed that Sean had rubbed the back of his neck more than once. "The good thing about a camper is that you can stop for the night when you get tired—if nobody gets huffy on you and starts agitating for a motel."

"Nobody will," Amanda said.

Amid the quiet pines of Medicine Bow National Forest they stopped for the night. They saw to the horses and had supper, and then Amanda suggested a walk. She wanted to talk, and he let her know that he was there for her in the way he held her hand, in the quiet conversation and the comfortable silences between them.

During one of those silences Amanda reached back for the story that she had tried to relegate to her mind's remotest files. "I was engaged to a man when I was in college. He was handsome, had all the right family credentials, a med student—perfect. We were the perfect couple. What's more, I loved him. It didn't work out. We broke it off shortly before I graduated."

"He broke it off, or you did?"

"I did. He turned out to be an illusion . . . or maybe *I* was the illusion. . . . The relationship certainly was. He wasn't the man I'd thought he was."

"He was cheating on you."

"Yes."

His knowing chuckle gave Amanda an icy second's dismay. But he wasn't laughing at her, and the arm he slipped about her shoulders reassured her. "Ah, the sorrows of the sincere lover," he said. "The girl I loved when I was in school was all those good things, too. There was just one problem. She didn't know what love was, and I was too stupid to see that. We had a great time in bed together. We even talked about marriage.

"Then I came home when my mother and sister were killed. I called Alisha and told her that I wasn't going back to school. I even went to see her—went all the way back there for a weekend—and it was great, just like it had always been. We got her sheets all sweaty, and then in that quiet afterglow I told her I'd missed her, and that I wanted to marry her right then, the next day."

He paused, as though marveling that he had ever been that naive. "She laughed. She said, 'Sean, you're a fantastic stud, but I have no intention of being a farmer's wife or living in some godforsaken desert.' She had already made plans to marry some damn preppie, even had the date set, and there she was in bed with me."

"How long did it take for you to stop hurting?"

"As long as it took for me to stop feeling sorry for myself, which was a while. I felt stupid, and that bothered me long after I stopped caring about her."

"I know what you mean. After I discovered Paul's other . . . his girlfriend . . . I felt like an utter fool. So gullible!"

"So what does that leave us? A couple of emotional cripples?" he said, his voice mocking them both.

"I'm sure you've known lots of women since."

"I haven't loved anyone since."

"But you don't seem bitter."

"I was. At that time I was bitter about a lot of things, but I've worked it out. I enjoy my life, and there's no place in it for someone like her, whoever she was. I was in love with some fantasy I cooked up."

"How is it possible to be so wrong about people? I was going to be the model wife: supportive, loyal—

and blind." Amanda bent to pick up a pine cone. "At least, that was the role I was assigned. But we really choose our own roles, don't we?"

"Play yourself—Amanda Caron. You put up a front, and you're gonna get the same thing back. You'll be surrounded by fakes, and you'll lose yourself, 'long about act three."

"I was ridiculous last night, wasn't I?"

"No. You felt something, and you enjoyed it. Were you afraid of it or relieved to find out it's there? You're not a model of anything, Mandy; you're a woman."

For a long time she said nothing, as though she were digesting all of this. They had walked aimlessly and had come full circle. "How far is it to Greeley?" she asked.

"About a hundred and forty miles."

"When is the rodeo?"

"The day after tomorrow."

"I'm going to be honest with you, Sean." She held up an open palm, as though swearing the truth. "I didn't think much of Western horsemen until I met you. But I'm interested now—in your 'plain old cow horses,' in your methods of training and in your sport. I think I could write about rodeo people . . . once I get to know them a little better."

"I don't have any etchings to show you, but I've got a hell of an arrowhead collection," he chuckled, opening the camper door.

"That sounds like an interesting gambit."

"Gambit, hell. For the next two hours I'm gonna show you arrowheads, lady, not to mention pottery shards, bones and one corroded cavalry insignia off some dead trooper's hat. I like to think he was scalped."

They were in no hurry the following day, but Sean wasn't interested in Laramie or Cheyenne except for gas and groceries. They crossed the state line into

Colorado on a two-lane mountain road. In a grassy meadow they parked the camper and took the horses for a ride. The mountains loomed purple in the distance, and the air was clear. Dipping their noses into the water of a little stream, the horses relished a long cool drink.

"What are you doing?" Sean asked. Amanda had looped her reins over a bush, sat on the ground, and was pulling off boots and socks.

"Going wading. Come on."

"Hell, no, that's cold water. You'll slip on those rocks and—"

"Chicken."

"If I found some deeper water, would you take off the rest of your clothes and go skinny-dipping?"

"Maybe," she replied with a teasing smile.

"I'll keep that in mind." She had rolled her jeans up to her knees, and he sat on the ground, forearms draped over his knees, admiring her shapely calves.

"Oh, this is cold! The stream bed is gravelly. I won't slip."

"Let's have a picnic," he suggested.

"Good idea." She made her way to a rock big enough to sit on, which she did. The warm sun felt good. She left her feet dangling in the cold water.

"Warm body, cold feet," Sean observed. "I'm getting hungry."

Hopping too quickly off the rock, Amanda lost her footing and settled with a splash on her bottom. Sean's laughter rankled at first, but as she looked down at herself, waist deep in water, Amanda couldn't ignore the humor of the situation. With her head tilted back, eyes closed to the sun, she shook with laughter of her own.

"How many laps you gonna do, Mandy?" Sean chortled.

Her jeans were heavy with water. Dragging herself up was tricky, especially in her fit of giggles, and she slipped twice before stumbling back to the bank. She reached for the hand Sean offered her, then gave him a mischievous smile as she tugged on him.

"Don't try it, lady," he warned with a grin, pulling her to dry ground. He watched her hold her arms out from her sides, dripping, and he howled. "You looked almost as surprised as you did the first time I saw you." He put a hand on her wet shoulder. "Now this is where I say, 'We've got to get these wet clothes off you before you catch cold.'"

"And I say, 'Don't try it, cowboy.'" Then she gave him another saucy smile. "Or better yet, I say, 'I was terrified that I would drown! Hold me in your arms!'" Arms quickly fastened around his waist, she plastered her wet body against his.

"Oh, God!" he groaned. "Forget what I said about warm body."

"You wouldn't cast me from your arms, would you?" she giggled.

"I might even cast you back in the water," he said, but his arms belied that empty threat, settling around her body. The brim of his hat shaded both their faces as their lips met. Amanda felt the surging heat inside her begin to pulsate, and she pressed closer to him as his mouth grew hungrier, more demanding. She felt a need to be even closer. Abandoning her inhibitions, she arched her hips against him. His hands clasped her wet buttocks, and he pulled her against himself.

Her gasp of pleasure startled him, and he eased her away, dragging his mouth from hers. Making every effort to control his ragged breathing, Sean slid his hands to her back, whispering, "You're very sexy in these wet clothes."

"Sean," was all that escaped her sighing chest. She trembled with the force of her longing.

"You're damn sexy in dry clothes, too. I'm going crazy with wanting you, Mandy."

"Sean, I want . . ." She couldn't finish.

"Say it, honey," he whispered next to her ear.

"Oh, Sean . . . Sean . . ." She had given herself the moment she needed to calm herself. "I want to . . . go back and . . . change clothes."

He was disappointed, but he did his best not to let it show.

A straw cowboy hat perched over his forehead, his nose and chin just visible, Sean rested on the blanket, one arm tucked behind his head. He resembled a well-fed cat stretched out in the sun. They had elected to bask in the early-afternoon sunshine as they picnicked, Amanda barefoot in shorts and a halter top, and Sean wearing jeans and boots. She had seen nothing more beautiful than his long, bronze torso, totally hairless, gleaming in the sunlight. His broad chest tapered to a flat, hard belly, underscored by a big, flashy silver buckle on a tooled leather belt.

Leaning closer, Amanda read aloud, "Range Days Rodeo, Rapid City, South Dakota, All-Around Cowboy, Sean Brannigan. How many of these do you have?"

"I don't know," he mumbled beneath the hat. "Quite a few. Got a nice one in Reno the other night."

"Do you ever let anyone else win?" she asked, plucking a long stem of grass, which she used to trace tickling lines on his belly. She watched the muscles contract along the path she was making, but that was the only response she got.

"Not intentionally. And that won't work," he told her.

"What?"

"I'm not ticklish."

"Would you like me to give you a massage?"

His wide smile revealed a flash of white teeth under the brim of his hat. "That's an interesting suggestion."

"All the driving you've been doing must be building up a lot of tension in your back."

"Massaging my *back* isn't going to relieve my tension, sweetheart." He tilted the hat back and lifted his head enough so that he could see her face. "Come here, Mandy," he said with a smile, gently pulling her arm. She went to him, stretching herself along his side and resting her hand on his chest. "You don't have to come up with an excuse to put your hands on me," he teased. "I'm warning you, though, I've just about reached the limit of my resistance."

"I know. I think I have, too," she said seriously.

He rolled over easily and looked straight into her wide blue gaze. His eyes searched for the truth in her declaration, and when he thought he'd found it, he lowered his head to her mouth. This time he let the fire build in him. He made no attempt to beat down the flames. His hungry mouth delighted in the slightly salty taste of her skin. She gave him greater access to her neck when she twisted her head to nibble the hard satin of his shoulder.

The halter top fell away under his hands, and she knew vaguely that one breast brushed against his chest while he fondled the other nipple with the tender torture of his fingertips. He lifted himself above her, his eyes feasting first on her firm, creamy breasts before his mouth would taste. Amanda admired the thick blackness of his hair, and she laced her fingers in it at the nape of his neck. Then she felt the feathery flickering of his tongue, and she gasped with pleasure.

Sean's body responded to the sound. One long leg hooked over hers as he raised himself slightly, reached down to flick open the snap of her jeans and mumbled, "I want you, Mandy."

She heard the words, saw the need in his eyes, felt his hand on her belly and his weight insinuating itself against her in a gradual advance. Her own body trembled with weakness, and his huge chest heaved above her. His invasion would overwhelm her. She saw herself lost in the onslaught, being consumed by him, and fear unseated all her needs.

"No! No, you can't, Sean!" Amanda twisted away from him, clutching the halter top to her breasts. She sprang to her feet and ran to the camper.

It was dark when Sean finally came back to the camper himself. She had angered him, frustrated him, confused him, and he'd needed to keep his distance from her for a while. He had needed to ride. If there had been a bull or a bronc handy, that would have suited his mood even better, as it had years ago when he had first started riding, when he could ride out all the hatred he felt.

The darkness wasn't what brought him back. It was the rain, a gentle, cleansing evening rain. It cooled him, then it chilled him, and he was damned if he was going to stay out in the rain just because she was in the camper. Now he knew why he'd bought a pack of cigarettes the other day. He seldom smoked; he had been able to take it or leave it even when he was a kid, when everybody who thought he was a cowboy smoked. Tossing his wet shirt over the back of the driver's seat, he lit a cigarette and sat down on the couch to take off his boots, the cigarette dangling from his mouth. He didn't travel with liquor, but if he had, he would have had a drink about then.

He didn't hear her. She moved quietly into the kitchen on bare feet, and he didn't know she was there until he leaned back on the couch, drawing deeply on the cigarette before plucking it from his mouth. She was wearing the same outfit he'd first seen her in, that satiny-looking white robe or whatever. She crept toward him as he let the smoke drift from his mouth.

"I didn't know you smoked," she said hesitantly.

"I don't . . . much."

"I was afraid you weren't coming back."

"You forgot that this is my camper?"

"No, but it started raining, and I . . ."

"I came back because I was getting wet. Sometimes I can read signs pretty well."

"I'm sorry about . . . the way I acted before."

"Forget it," he said, dragging on the cigarette again. The smoke was acrid. He didn't even want it now. "Let's just chalk it up to male intuition. I guess there's no such thing."

"That isn't true," she said, closing in on him like a beautiful white bird. "You've been so intuitive about me that it's uncanny. You've been right at every turn."

"Look, Mandy, I'm going to bed. I've got a job to do tomorrow that requires a positive mental attitude and a little rest, so I'm gonna work on both of those right now. And I don't sleep in my jeans, so I suggest you glide right back in there and close the curtain."

She stood there, her back to the light, not moving. Her voice trembled. "Be patient with me, Sean. I hardly know you, really, but I feel—"

"Now *that* isn't true. I told you before, I'm exactly who I seem to be, and you like me, and you want to be with me. I'm not forcing you into anything, sweetheart." His voice was quiet and even.

"But I feel," she repeated slowly, "a strong . . . attraction for you. I've always *dealt* with my feelings rather than—"

"I know all that, Mandy. I made a mistake. Now go on back to bed." He moved toward the dash, pulling out the ashtray so he could get rid of the cigarette. When he turned back, she hadn't moved.

"Don't send me back there, Sean. I'm trying to tell you that I want to stay up here . . . with you."

His hands rested on her shoulders; he was wondering whether she was an inveterate tease. "I'm not playing any more of your games, lady. If you had kept your distance, I would have kept mine. I've never forced myself on a woman, and I'm not going to start now."

"I want to be close to you," she whispered, and she felt his hands and arms stiffen as though in defense.

"If you come to my bed, Mandy, I'm going to make love to you."

"I know."

"Then tell me that's what you want."

"Sean . . . I want you to make love to me."

There was a quiet moment before he folded her in his arms, rubbing the satin that covered her back. "Are you sure?"

"Yes." Her arms went around him.

"Mandy, I wanted you so damn bad today. It hurt when you ran away from me."

"I know. I was afraid. I don't know what I was afraid of. I won't run away this time. I've wanted . . . felt . . ."

He pulled back from her and untied the peignoir. "If you don't want me now, honey, I'm going to make you want me. Will you let me do that?"

"Yes," she whispered.

"I want your naked body next to mine," he said, sliding the garment off her shoulders. "And I want to touch you and kiss you and make you want me as bad as I want you."

"Yes, Sean . . ."

"And then I'll need to be inside you," he whispered hotly, slipping the thin straps of her nightgown off her shoulders as he bent to nibble at her earlobe. "And I'll become part of you, Mandy. Do you want that? Do you want me that way?"

"Yes, Sean, yes . . ."

His mouth came down hard over hers, his tongue taking the first risk of venturing inside her. She received him as a hungry new bird receives sustenance from its mother. When he withdrew his mouth he rasped, "I have to believe you."

Catching her at the waist, he lifted her easily into his bed. When he followed, she was aware that he had divested himself of his remaining clothes.

He sought to arouse her, to make her want him desperately, as he had promised. Her passion mounted on the stairway of his. His kisses were warm and wet, his tongue probing and tantalizing. His mouth found her breasts again, and he loved them until she moaned softly with pleasure. Pushing her nightgown past her hips, he whispered to her between kisses, telling her what she was doing to him, promising what he would do for her.

Amanda was consumed by sensation. Fear or shyness or whatever she had felt initially had flown, and she returned his kisses, stroked his back, sought ways to be closer to the magnificent man who brought her this pleasure. The hand on her belly slid between her thighs, and she writhed with need.

"Oh, God, Sean, I need you . . . ," she gasped. "Please, Sean . . ."

"Tell me what you want, honey. How can I make you happy?"

"Love me, Sean . . . Sean . . . Sean, love me . . ."

He was not prepared for what he found when he entered her. She gasped with pain. "Oh, Mandy," he whispered, then covered her outcry with a kiss and rocked himself within her gently until he felt her relax. Then he increased the pace in response to her need until she gasped and groaned and shuddered in a moment of total ecstasy, a sensation in which, seconds later, he joined her.

In the languid silence that followed, Amanda was awash in the wonder of fulfillment. His hand rested possessively on her stomach, moving just slightly now and then to caress her.

"Why didn't you tell me?" he asked finally.

"Tell you what?"

"That you were a virgin."

"Why did you assume otherwise?"

"You know why. You told me all about him."

She didn't answer right away. She had expected some feeling of guilt, but there was none. Instead there was the innocence of pure joy. "This may sound silly to you, Sean, but I never wanted to give myself to a man before. I guess it didn't occur to me to tell you."

"I wish I'd known why you were so scared. Did I hurt you?"

"It hurt a little at first, but then . . . I feel beautiful even now. Does giving myself to you sound old-fashioned?"

"From the receiving end, I'd say that old-fashioned is pretty nice." Then, almost shyly, he asked, "Does it still hurt?"

She turned to him and stroked his thick hair. "No." She paused. "I'm glad you were the first. Do you know why?"

"No, why?" He stroked her back.

"Because for such a tough cowboy, you're the gentlest, kindest man I've ever met. I thought about it while you were gone, and I knew what I was doing. You said you wanted whatever I had to give."

"What you gave came as a surprise."

"It shouldn't have. I haven't been what one might call a very giving person, not in any real sense. But I truly felt a need to give you pleasure. I . . . I did give you pleasure, didn't I, Sean?"

"Yes, Mandy. More than you'll ever know."

"I believe that I gave myself to you . . . because I care for you, Sean."

"I believe you did, too," he whispered.

They held each other quietly for long moments, touching lazily with gentle fingers and slow-moving lips. Raindrops pattered on the roof, the sound enhancing the warm feeling of security they shared. Amanda suddenly broke the mood with a throaty giggle.

"What's so funny?"

"We seem to be sleeping together. So much for the bumper sticker," she laughed.

Inexplicably Amanda felt a moment of fear when she awoke to find Sean gone. Sounds outside the camper reassured her that he was nearby. He was giving her some privacy, and she closeted herself in the little bathroom to take advantage of it.

The shower and shampoo felt good. Once they dried, her soft brown curls would wave in casual disarray. Looking at herself in the mirror, Amanda sought signs of the change that had undoubtedly taken place in her in the last few hours. There had to be a look in the eyes, a new worldliness, the knowledge of good and evil, *something*. What she saw in her own eyes was a soft glow. She smiled at her reflection, and the girl in the mirror smiled back, a conspiratorial smile. They shared a secret, she and this girl, a remarkable discovery. Amanda Caron was not a cold fish.

"Good morning," Amanda offered tentatively, even shyly, when she went outside. Sean had the right hind hoof of Medicine Man, the big bay, wedged between his knees, and Amanda greeted the top of Sean's head as he nipped off the end of a horseshoe nail he'd just driven.

He glanced at her quickly, smiling briefly as though she were a casual acquaintance who had just happened by. "Morning, Mandy. Horse was trying to throw this shoe. Never trust a farrier you don't know. This ought to take care of it."

Amanda felt as though she were looking through the wrong end of a telescope. She didn't know what she had expected from the man who had just taken her virginity, but it certainly wasn't a discussion of the condition of his horse's shoes. Until that moment she had not felt ashamed. Now it occurred to her that her place in his hierarchy of needs came somewhere below his farrier and above . . . above what? Perhaps above a partner for team roping. The heat of a blush suffused her face.

Sean released the horse's leg and straightened his own back, ironing out the kinks with his hand. "A good horseshoeing is more important than the fit of my own boots," he mumbled. Finally he looked at Amanda and read the hurt in her face for the first time. You idiot, he told himself. He dusted his hands on his pants.

"I . . . made coffee," Amanda said quietly. "I just wondered if you were ready for breakfast."

He put his hands on her shoulders, sending a shock wave of awareness through her nervous system. "You look like an angel when you sleep, Mandy," he told her. "I hated to get out of bed this morning, but I thought you might want some time to yourself."

"Yes . . . thank you," she murmured.

"Are you . . . sorry?"

"No," she said in a tiny voice, but without hesitation. His arms went around her, and she sighed heavily.

"I was scared to death you'd wake up and find me next to you and say, 'My God, what have I done?'" he whispered, holding her close in the morning sunlight.

"I didn't think that way at all until you started the morning off with a dissertation on horseshoes."

He chuckled. "That wasn't what was on my mind, believe me."

"Look at me, Sean," she said, pulling back so that he could see her face. "Do I look any different to you?"

He studied her for a moment. "You know, I think you do look different."

"How?"

"Well, this morning you remind me of the Mona Lisa. Before you were the perfect image of the Statue of Liberty. Nice change," he said with a wink.

Her face brightened. "I feel good! I feel especially

good because I don't feel the way I was afraid I'd feel. I'm not a promiscuous person, you know."

"No kidding," he said with a grin.

"Well, I guess you of all people can believe that," she said, chattering in a flustered manner that he had not seen her demonstrate before. "But I thought I would feel guilty, and I don't, and it's silly, I know, but such a relief. I've been accused of being . . . well . . . cold."

"By your fiancé?"

"Yes, by him . . . and others I've dated since . . . I couldn't stand the way . . ." She realized how childish she must sound. Looking up at him, she vowed, "It's different with you, Sean. It has been since you first touched me. I'm not cold, am I?"

"Not by a long shot, honey," he said, and his lips touched hers.

"Breakfast?" she whispered.

"Mmmm." He touched the corner of her mouth with his lips. "Let's forget food and horseshoes and rodeos . . ."

"If you start missing rodeos, I won't have a story."

"Breakfast, then. Let's see if becoming a woman has improved your coffee any."

Chapter Six

$\mathcal{S}$ean wrestled a steer that afternoon in the "slack," the name given to the time when some of the cowboys performed before or after the actual rodeo since there were always too many entrants for the three-hour show. Walking the sorrel back toward the camper and trailer, he laughed when Amanda commented that it was a shame to deny the audience his performance. "As long as one pretty girl is watching, I have an audience. That wasn't a winning time, but I might place. A friend of mine plans to use Deke tonight, so it's just as well I used him early."

"What if he beats you on your own horse?"

"Since he's leading the standings in dogging, he probably will. Then I get a percentage of his winnings, and he realizes what a good horse I've got. I've sold a lot of horses that way."

"Very sporting of you," Amanda allowed, putting one booted foot up on the running board of the trailer and considering for a moment that it looked as if it belonged to someone else, clad as it was in brown alligator wing tips. "These are comfortable," she admitted aloud, turning her ankle to give herself a side view.

"But?" Leather creaked as he lifted the saddle from Deke's back.

"But they still look funny on my Yankee feet. Aren't Lacy and Bud going to be here? You had a different hazer."

"Yeah, I can't always depend on Bud, but there's always someone I can work with. Bud's entered, so I imagine he'll get here sooner or later. You in the mood for a laundromat?"

"Bubbling with enthusiasm."

Amanda clicked her tongue in reproof when she caught herself fingering the pearl snaps on one of Sean's shirts as she carefully arranged it on a hanger. It's just a shirt, she told herself. She had offered to do this chore while he ran an undefined errand, leaving Amanda and the camper at Dee Dee's Wash and Dry with a promise to return in less than an hour. Pulling his shirts and her blouses from the dryer together somehow seemed as intimate a statement as sharing a bed. A statement of what? She smiled, straightening the collar.

As she carried their clean clothes back to the camper, Amanda imagined what her father would say if he came walking down the street at that moment and saw his darling daughter with an armload of Western shirts and some strange man's shorts and socks. "You've known this man less than a week, and you're doing his laundry!" her mind's ear heard him gasp. Sleeping with him would be bad enough, but doing his laundry would be deplored as totally unworthy of Amanda Caron.

Sean had been gone well over an hour, and she had found places to put all the clothes and had made sandwiches. He surprised her when he came in the back door, dropping several packages on the couch in

the back before he brought one into the kitchen. He
grinned when he saw the bright look of welcome on
Amanda's face. "Hi, lady. Miss me?"

"Only when I had to fold your clothes," she answered, but the smile was there when she handed him
a sandwich.

"Mmm, thanks. I wonder what all those housewives
with the fat pink curlers in their hair thought when
they saw you—Amanda Caron—folding a man's shirts
and pants."

"I hung your shirts up—not a wrinkle in them. It
wasn't the shirts that got them thinking, as a matter of
fact; it was the underwear. I overheard one lady
whisper to another, 'I'll bet she's living in sin with
some cowboy.' Then they both stared at me while I
matched up your socks."

He had stopped chewing to stare at her himself.
"You're kidding," he croaked.

"Of course I'm kidding," she said, chuckling.

"I meant to be back in time to fold my own clothes.
I don't mean to take advantage of you."

Amanda was quiet for a moment, sizing up the
response she was about to offer, avoiding his eyes. "I
was glad to do it for you, Sean. I'm not too stuck-up to
do a friend a favor."

"I want to be more than a friend."

"I know that, and I want that, too. But some people
become lovers without even liking each other. I want
you for a friend, too. I like you, Sean, as a person. It's
just occurred to me recently that I really have very
few friends, and your friendship means a lot to me."

"You've let yourself accept me as a person, sweetheart, and I have the feeling you don't do that with
too many people. All I ask of a friend is honesty. Stay
honest with me and I'll be your friend for life."

"Okay, honestly now, I still want to get a room
when we stay in town."

"All right," he said quietly.

"I'm not moving in here with you, Sean. Our relationship is new and fragile, and we shouldn't presume . . . I mean, we have to give each other room to . . . to find out . . ."

"Mandy, I said all right."

"It would just be better if we didn't expect too much too soon."

"I thought we'd go on to Cheyenne tonight. I've already made you a reservation at a motel."

"You have?"

"I'd better get back over to the fairgrounds. I'm not in the bull riding tonight, so I thought we'd leave early, have dinner."

"I'd like that."

He started to get up from the table, then turned to her. "You're still afraid of your feelings, Mandy. You're afraid to let yourself get too close to me."

"I may be unsure of *myself* at this point, Sean, but I do trust *you,* and I want to be . . . I'm enjoying your company."

"I know that, honey. That's why you came to me last night. So now the lady is trying to make it a little harder for the woman to have her way."

"It's not that at all, Sean; it's just—"

"Hey, you're one hell of a sophisticated lady, and I like that. But I'm betting on the woman." He smiled and bent to kiss her briefly, his hand lifting her chin. "The one who made love with me last night," he whispered, and then moved to the driver's seat.

Lacy and Bud had arrived at the fairgrounds, Bud offering profuse apologies for missing Sean's steer wrestling. "No problem," Sean told him. "Gary Reed hazed for me."

"Reed? He can't ride worth a damn," Bud spat.

"He was here, and he did all right."

"I'll buy you a drink to make up for it, Sean. Let's do the town tonight, the four of us," Bud suggested.

"I don't know what town you've got in mind, but
we're leaving for Cheyenne as soon as I'm through
here."

"You did real good in Reno, Sean. You oughta ride
bulls all the time. It's really boosting your standings in
the all-around."

"Too much strain on the arm. What I ought to do is
quit it altogether, but I still get a kick out of it once in
a while."

"Where's Lacy?" Amanda asked, although she
could see someone moving around in Bud's gooseneck.

"She's in the trailer, probably sleeping again.
Maybe we'll go to Cheyenne tonight too. Can you
wait around 'til after the saddle broncs? You'll stay
and watch me ride, won't you?"

"I don't know, Bud," Sean said. "I'm taking
Amanda out to dinner in Cheyenne tonight, just the
two of us. Maybe we'll run into you after that."

Amanda decided to look in on Lacy. It was a
wonder that she hadn't appeared immediately with
her everlasting "Johnny" this and "Johnny" that.

"Lacy, it's just me. Those two men are talking bulls
and broncs . . . Lacy! What happened to your face?"
Amanda was stunned by the blackened bruise that
covered Lacy's cheekbone. The other woman's hair
was disheveled, and her eyes looked hollow and
sunken.

"I ran into a door," Lacy replied sullenly. The
gooseneck had a small kitchen area, a booth with a
table, and a bed in the gooseneck area, the part that
jutted over the box of the pickup. Lacy plopped
herself into the booth and rested her chin in her
hands. "Have a seat, Amanda."

"Some door, Lacy. Who hit you?"

"I already told you," Lacy said sullenly. "Actually,
the door ran into me. It was an accident, but don't tell
Johnny. He'll start hollering around about how dumb

I am." A second thought quirked the corner of Lacy's mouth. "No, he won't either. Johnny doesn't holler around. *Bud* hollers around."

"What happened, Lacy? Did Bud do that?"

"Not exactly. I was sort of playing up to another guy, just to get Bud jealous, and when we got back to the trailer he kinda got mad. He went in, slammed the door, left me standing out there. I was yellin' at him, and he opened the door up kinda fast. Smack! I was standing right there. But really—don't tell Johnny."

"You know I won't have to tell him, Lacy; he'll see it."

"You'd be amazed at what I can do with makeup."

"If it was an accident, why not tell him? What would he do?"

"Nothing. Johnny just keeps telling me what a fool I am. He doesn't understand. Bud's having a hard time, and he needs me."

"He doesn't treat you like someone he needs."

There wasn't a tear in Lacy's eye, but there was quiet outrage in her voice. "You and your high-and-mighty kind, you don't understand what a man needs. You're just another Alisha. I don't know why Johnny goes looking for trouble."

"You're out of line, Lacy, but then, so am I. In his own way Bud must care for you, and I had no right to imply that he doesn't. It's none of my business."

Lacy's anger suddenly dissipated. "No, it's none of your business. But he doesn't care for me, not like Johnny does. Johnny cares for me, but he doesn't want me. And Bud . . . well, Bud at least *wants* me. So I teased him a little bit, just to remind him that he's got no hold over me, and I guess I wanted him to get mad. *I* care for *Bud*—in my own way." Lacy ended the explanation with a wry smile. "Kinda mixed up, isn't it?"

"You care for Sean more than you care for Bud."

Lacy's expression hardened again. "Damn right I

care for Johnny. I'd do anything in the world for him, but he doesn't want me to. He says I'm his best friend."

"Sean's a good man. He's a good friend." Amanda made an effort to sound casual in the face of her strong feelings about her own friendship with Sean.

"Yeah, I know. Don't tell him what I said, Amanda —about you being like Alisha. He'd hate me for that. And I hope to God you aren't, because he deserves better than that. Johnny deserves the best, and if you can't stand by him like . . . like a woman should, then leave him alone. Don't hurt him."

"Sean seems to be able to handle all our shortcomings. He's a big man, Lacy."

Currying horses was Amanda's favorite therapy. Sean was visiting with several cowboys behind the pens, and the animated gestures and deep laughter among the group told her that it was man-talk. As she fished tools out of the saddle compartment of the trailer, the truth of what she had told Sean earlier rang in her head. Sean had many friends, people who admired him, enjoyed being with him. But she was different. There was really no one she missed at home, except her parents, of course. As for the rest, there was a distance. *But,* she smiled to herself, Amanda Caron was not a cold fish.

Deke's blood-sorrel coat shone, and he seemed to know what a flashy beast he was. As she combed Medicine Man's tail she admired Deke's proud head and alert ears.

"You can always count on Sean Brannigan to come up with choice stock." The voice startled Amanda, but she caught herself before she allowed her surprise to show. She cast a glance over her shoulder at the tall, dark-haired cowboy who stood behind her. She'd seen him before, and she knew she wasn't going to like him.

"I don't believe I know you," she said crisply.

"Travis Steele, ma'am. Friend of Brannigan's. And you're Amanda. Everybody's talking about Brannigan's new lady friend."

Dropping the bay's tail, she moved to the other side of the animal and began pulling his mane, feeling some satisfaction that she had put the horse between herself and this man, whom she remembered even Lacy didn't like.

He continued, unprodded. "Everybody's talking about what a classy lady you are, Amanda." Eyeing her over the horse's back, he patted the bay's stout rump. "Yes, ma'am, Brannigan has an eye for good stock." Amanda said nothing. "You don't strike me as a buckle bunny, Amanda. Are you one of Brannigan's friends from back east?"

"I met Sean just recently, but I am from back east."

"Looks like you know horses," he observed.

"I do some showing." Amanda's voice was tight.

"Ol' Brannigan hit the jackpot this time—a real lady who doesn't mind getting a little manure on her pretty hands." Travis chuckled as he moved to Amanda's side of the horse. "He's quite a collector, Sean is," Travis continued, his lanky frame closing in on her. "Always got room in his stable for one more filly. Looks like he picked up a thoroughbred this time."

Amanda ducked under the bay's neck and came up facing Sean on the other side.

"Oh, Sean, I was just going to look for you," Amanda said quickly. Sean stood with both hands resting easily on his hips, and she looped her arm through one of his.

"Is he bothering you?" Sean growled.

"No, he was just admiring your horses."

"What's the matter, Brannigan? The lady had her heart set on meeting the top contender for the all-around buckle. She wasn't aware that you've slipped a lot lately," Travis drawled.

"I don't know too many ladies who enjoy knowing

you, Steele. Understand this: If I catch you annoying *this* lady in any way, you'll find out how hard it is to babble your garbage with your jaw wired shut."

"Anytime, cowboy," Travis invited as he moved around the bay's rump.

"How about right now?" Sean asked, stepping around Amanda.

"No, Sean, he didn't bother me, really." Amanda made the mistake of grabbing Sean's arm just as Travis moved within reach. Travis had a clear shot at Sean's mouth. Amanda heard herself gasp.

Travis was a gloater. He hesitated long enough to enjoy the fact that he had landed the first blow. It was also long enough for Sean to recover and land the second and third. A quick pop to Steele's jaw was followed by a fist to his solar plexus. Amanda heard a grunt and a whoosh of breath, and then Travis's long body lay sprawled on the ground.

"Come after me again and you won't ride tonight, Steele," Sean warned, wiping the back of his hand across the corner of his mouth, which trickled blood. Travis couldn't answer. He was clutching his stomach, trying to recover his wind. "Better get away from my horses before you get kicked."

Travis got to his feet slowly and cast Sean a menacing glance before stumbling away.

Amanda stared at the man's retreating back, then at the face of the man who stood at her side. "Good Lord, Sean, you're bleeding. Your lip's cut." She dabbed at it with a tissue from her pocket.

"Mandy, I knew I could take him with one arm tied behind my back, but you didn't have to make me prove it."

"I'm sorry, Sean. I didn't think *that* was going to happen. You actually hit each other . . . just like a couple of . . . Let's go inside and take care of your mouth."

Sean sat on the couch in the back of the camper while Amanda wiped the blood away with a wet cloth, dabbing gently at each new trickle until the bleeding stopped. Then she held a piece of ice to his lip. "Your lip is swelling. Does it hurt?"

"Only when I laugh."

"Do you think it would hurt if I kissed you?"

"I don't know. Try it." She bent to plant a soft kiss on his bruised mouth. Pulling her down on his lap, Sean deepened their kiss. "I can handle that," he whispered.

Amanda slid the ice over his lip again. "Don't you think you should limit this contest between you and Travis Steele to the arena? This kind of activity could get you hurt."

"Travis Steele is a snake, Mandy. I meant what I said: I don't want him around you. You don't know what he's like. He doesn't care what he . . . you can't trust him. He *uses* women."

"Don't worry, Sean. I don't like the man, and I'm an expert at keeping men at a distance. In another thirty seconds he'd have found himself chatting with two horses. Speaking of which, you'd better get your act together." She dabbed once more at his mouth. "You sure you're okay?"

"I think I'll need more of this kind of attention later. Right now I want to make sure I beat Steele's time—in calf roping." Sean grinned, then put his hand to his mouth. "Ow! It does hurt to laugh."

From her vantage point near the box Amanda watched Sean rope. A band played fast-paced fiddle and banjo music as Medicine Man bounded from the box, staying with the calf and allowing Sean to drop his loop over the animal's head and neck within a few short strides. The calf stubbornly splayed all four legs, and the horse backed on the line to keep him still. Amanda admired the fluid grace, the economy of motion, in Sean's easy dismount and in his quick overturn of the calf, and the final gathering and tying of the three legs. His time was eleven seconds.

"Johnny's gonna be disgusted with himself over that time," Lacy observed over Amanda's shoulder. "That's not too good for him."

"What was Travis Steele's time?" Amanda said absently.

"Eleven-eight, I think. Why?"

"Sean beat him, then."

"Did they get into it again?"

"Again?" Amanda questioned. "Is this a feud?"

"Not exactly. Travis has a bad mouth and a mean streak in him, and he's always been jealous of Johnny. Then he and Johnny got into it over . . . something Travis did to me. When the two of them get near each other everybody just sort of backs off and watches. Of course Johnny's no brawler. In fact, I don't think I've ever seen him really have it in for anybody like he does Travis."

"They're rivals for the championship, I take it."

"That's got nothing to do with the way Johnny feels. Johnny's always a good sport, although there's nobody he'd sooner beat than Travis Steele. So what happened this time?"

"Travis hit Sean in the mouth, and then Sean hit Travis a couple of times. They were arguing one minute and fighting the next. I couldn't believe it was happening—grown men!" Amanda said.

"Did Travis come on to you?"

"Not really. I was currying the horses, and he came over. He made some stupid comments about Sean having room in his stable for another filly and having an eye for good stock. He was pretty insulting; I wouldn't call it 'coming on.'"

"Take my advice, Amanda," Lacy warned, "and don't trust Travis Steele alone with you for a minute. He's a pig, let me tell you."

When Sean appeared, leading Medicine Man, the smile on his face did not betray any disappointment he might have felt in his performance. Lacy, Amanda noticed, turned the bruised side of her face away from him when he asked where she'd been hiding all day. Her answer was obviously evasive, a ploy to get him to ask her what was wrong, Amanda thought, and she awaited the inevitable somewhat resentfully. With a frown and a gentle hand Sean tilted Lacy's chin in his direction. "Do you need a ride home, kid?" he asked quietly.

"No, Johnny, I'm okay."

"Suit yourself. I'm gonna load up and head for Cheyenne. You change your mind in the next fifteen minutes, let me know."

"It was my own fault, Johnny."

"Right. Staying with him is your own fault, Lacy, and it's none of my business, if that's what you want. We'll see you in Belle Fourche."

"Aren't you gonna stay and watch Bud ride? He'll be disappointed."

"I've had a bellyful of Bud lately, and I've got better things to do tonight. See you later, Lacy."

Amanda strode right along to keep up with Sean's angry pace. The steer wrestler who was borrowing Deke was getting ready for his run, and Sean asked him to return the horse as soon as he was through. Then he headed for the trailer. Amanda stood out of the way and watched him unsaddle the bay and stow his gear. Together they watched the horse grind alfalfa pellets between his teeth, Amanda wondering about the mental teeth gnashing that Sean seemed to be doing. Later, while Sean took care of Deke, Amanda wrapped Medicine Man's legs and blanketed him, both of them still silent.

Once they were on the road Amanda decided to broach the subject that had apparently caused this cloudy mood. She could no longer deny the jealousy she felt where Lacy was concerned, though she sought to erase it by telling herself that the relationship was, as she had been told so often, just friendship.

"Lacy asked me not to tell you about the bruise on her face when I saw her this afternoon. I think she really hopes you'll go after Bud the way you went after Travis Steele for whatever he did to her."

"Travis Steele?" The allusion surprised him. "Did she tell you about that?"

"Only that you fought with him before over something he did to her. What did he do?"

"He's done a lot of things I didn't like. Lacy got in a fight with him one night, and he left her stranded on the side of the road. She had no money and was too damned drunk to care. The police picked her up. They came and got me. When I saw how he'd left her, I was so mad that I . . . She's such a kid, such a crazy, mixed-up kid."

"Are you her caseworker?" Sean turned a hard look on her. "I'm sorry, Sean, but she does seem to rely on you to take care of her when she gets into trouble, and she seems to gravitate to men who inevitably cause trouble for her."

"Lacy has a big heart. She gives and gives, but nobody ever gives back." Sean sighed quietly. "First it was her father, who just sort of drifted in and out of her life—a cowboy, of course. Then there was a husband—she was married and divorced before she was nineteen. He used her for some con game, which he went to the pen for. And then there were more cowboys—Bud, Travis, some others, myself included. Back when I lost my mother and sister, and then went through that thing with the girl back east, Lacy was there. She helped me get through . . . all that." He flashed her a wry grin. "And I wasn't as easy to get along with then as I am now."

Jealousy squeezed icy fingers around Amanda's heart again, but she managed a quiet, "How did she help you?"

"She kept me from closing up, I guess. She was there when I needed a friend. When I rode, I rode angry, and I made a lot of mistakes, but she encouraged me. She was my biggest fan. Hell, she was my *only* fan for a long time. I used to run my dad's stock ragged, and Lacy would come out and keep time for me."

"She was your best friend," Amanda said, echoing Lacy's claim.

Sean thought about that for a moment. "I tried to give her more than that, but it just wasn't there."

"She's in love with you."

"I know," he said, "and I can't help her with that. I care about her too much to have what you call recreational sex with her anymore. All I can do for her is be her friend, bail her out when she gets in over her head."

"Maybe that's why she gets into trouble," Amanda offered carefully. "So you'll bail her out."

"Lacy's a born martyr. She's always trying to take care of some cowboy who needs her, even if he only needs her for one night. She takes care of them 'til they throw her out. Whatever happens to her while she chooses to be with them is her business. All I can do for her is take her home when it's all over."

"She said they argued and he slammed the door in her face. Bud doesn't seem to be—"

"I don't believe that." Sean shook his head. "Born martyr."

"She said you wouldn't believe it, and what's more, I don't think she wants you to believe it. She wants you to rescue her."

"I offered her a ride. Why didn't she take it?"

"Maybe she wants you to punish him for it, just like you punished Travis Steele."

"That was different. That was something she didn't bargain for. With Bud, it's her choice."

"She told me he got angry because she teased him, flirting with some other guy."

"So you think she started it all?"

"I think you feel guilty because you think you've used her, too. And I think she knows that, and she wants you to make her choice for her . . . because if you do that, then you'll be stuck with her."

"Oh, for God's sake, Mandy, will you stop trying to figure people out? You have no reason to be jealous of Lacy."

"Jealous! I'm not jealous of Lacy. Why should I be? I've only known you for a few days, and I certainly—"

"Calm down, lady. You're protesting too much again. Let's leave Lacy and her problems in Greeley and take ours to Cheyenne."

Sean had arranged to leave his horses with a friend just outside of town. At the motel Amanda graciously offered Sean the use of the shower. "You sure are generous, lady," he mumbled with a smile. Amanda was dressed and ready by the time he emerged.

Watching him from a safe distance across the room, Amanda detected an increase in her own pulse rate. She wondered if watching Sean dress could replace aerobic exercise. He stood in front of the mirror toweling his hair dry, wearing tan, Western-cut pants. Barefoot and bare-chested, he looked like something long and lean and carved out of smooth, polished wood.

"I'll be ready in five minutes. You can time me," he promised.

"Five minutes is pretty slow, cowboy. You can rope and tie a calf in less than ten seconds."

"Yeah, but that only has to be good enough to satisfy a judge. I'm dressing to please the critical eye of a lady from Boston."

The fan in the bathroom drowned her quiet, "She's pleased already."

"What?"

"I said, 'She'll be pleased when you're ready.' I'm starved!" Amanda said loudly.

Quickly Sean brushed his hair, splashed some after shave on his cheeks, and pulled on his socks and boots. A black shirt with tan piping was snatched off a hanger. Quick hands tucked the shirt inside the pants, zipped them, and laced a tooled belt through the belt loops. When the buckle was fastened Sean threw his

SOMEDAY SOON   107

hands up in the air in the calf roper's signal that he
was finished.

"Not bad." Amanda smiled, sauntering toward
him, the softly draped knit fabric of her ivory-colored
dress clinging to her curves. "Four minutes flat."

He reached for her waist. "With a little incentive, I
can always improve. You look good."

Amanda put her hand on his cheek. "How did you
get away with such a smooth face?"

"I take after my mother. She didn't have a beard
either." Amanda rolled her eyes. "No kidding," he
protested. "Have you ever seen a bearded Indian?"

"I told you, I've seen very few Indians."

"Well, we're not hairy." He nuzzled her jawline
with his soft cheek.

"Mmm, so I see. I like that." She slid her hands
around his shoulders and drew her head back. "How's
your fat lip? It looks a little purple."

"It needs a little sympathy from a soft, female lip,"
he suggested, and Amanda's lips, since they fit his
description, tenderly healed him.

Chapter Seven

*D*inner was quiet, intimate and candlelit in the inn's own dining room. They found enjoyment just in looking at each other, smiling with the pleasure of looking across the table to see the other one there. They were aware of no one else in the room.

"There's a band in the lounge," Amanda observed.

"If that's an invitation for me to hold you in my arms I'm all for it." He reached for her hand.

It was late, and the music was slow and easy, the dancers few. Amanda moved as one with Sean, her body pressing close to his, seeking complete contact with the source of the warm current that he was sending through her. He rubbed her back in slow, lazy circles as her hips swayed suggestively in time with the music. She could feel his desire for her. She listened to the pounding of his heart and exulted in its quickening. She did this to him, and she was pleased in the knowledge of the effect that she was having.

Sean felt her lips against his neck, and he knew he couldn't take much more. He slid his hand to the small of her back and held her tightly against him. "Mandy," he whispered, "do you hear the music?"

"Mmm-hmm."

"There isn't any, honey, and we're still dancing. You know what you're doing to me, don't you?"

"Yes. That's why I don't want to stop dancing. Everyone else will know, too."

Sean chuckled wickedly in her ear. "Honey, anyone who might be watching us is probably waiting for me to tear your clothes off right here and now."

"Is anyone watching?"

"Just everybody. Let's give them a little thrill, okay?" The swaying stopped when Sean lowered his head and found her lips. Where she was or who was watching suddenly became immaterial as Amanda's tongue reached to answer the probing of Sean's.

"Sean . . . let's go," Amanda whispered without opening her eyes. His arm was around her shoulders, and they were walking toward the door before she had a chance to qualify her suggestion.

Amanda watched her room door swing open as he turned the key in the lock. She glanced furtively at the bed and then watched him pull his hand back from the doorknob. He made no further move, and Amanda wished that the pounding of her heart would be quiet so that she could hear what she would say.

He was looking down at the top of her head, willing her to look at him, but she resisted. She was like a shy colt who wanted the feed that he held out in his hand, but who paced nervously on the brink of taking it. "Please come in," he heard her say finally in a soft, steady voice. He touched her back to move her in ahead of him, then closed the door behind him. The room was almost dark, illuminated only by the night light at the base of the wall. Sean reached for the switch on a table lamp, and a dim light came on. It was enough.

"Would you like a drink?" he asked.

"No, thank you."

His hands on her shoulders were warm, but she shivered at his touch. "I feel like I've cornered a wild doe, Mandy. You don't want me to leave, do you?"

"No, Sean. No," she groaned. She turned, and they were in each other's arms at once, raining kisses on each other while he unzipped her dress. Her clothing was allowed to fall to the floor, uncovering delicate shoulders and porcelain skin. For a moment his hands rested on her upper arms while he admired the stunning beauty of her breasts, where he longed to bury his face. Her trembling hands found his shirt-front, and the snaps popped open one by one at her insistence; then she pulled the shirt impatiently from his pants.

Looking for the reaction in his eyes, Amanda touched the hard muscles of Sean's chest with cool hands. "I want to be close to you, Sean," she whispered, sliding her arms around his back and pulling his chest against her breasts. Her smile shone in her eyes, and it was seductive. "A vision of holding you against me like this flashed through my mind when we were dancing," she confessed.

"No wonder you were searing me right through my clothes. You're a timid little girl one minute and a temptress the next. I'm trying not to expect too much all at once," he said, "but you're making it pretty difficult, lady." Her neck was irresistible, and he nibbled down to the ledge of her collarbone.

"I think I . . . ," she began in a breathy whisper.

"Don't think, Mandy. That's what makes you pull away from me. Don't think." His hands caressed her back gently, but when they moved to her buttocks the caresses became urgent, drawing her tight against him. Amanda moved instinctively against him, stretching her arms around his neck to plunge her fingers into the thick hair at the base of his skull and pull his head down to hers.

She *couldn't* think. Her mind spun in an eddy of sensation, and their mouths seized each other greedily. If he had disengaged himself suddenly she would have crumpled into a shapeless mass, for she was certain that his support was all that kept her on her feet. So she clung to him and drew this dizzying high from his kiss. It was as though she were swept along on a warm ocean current when she felt herself lifted in his arms and set down on the bed. Somewhere along the way she let her shoes fall to the floor.

Sean whispered to her while he peeled away the rest of their clothing. "I'm going to make you mine, Mandy. I'm going to brand you, honey—I can't help it—you've got this fire going inside me, and I can't control it anymore." He began plying his warm, wet kisses along the midline of her naked torso, his hands gripping her hips. "Do you feel it?" he breathed against her belly, teasing her sensitized skin with his tongue. "Am I scorching you where I touch you?"

"Yes," she groaned, "and it feels wonderful."

His hands crept steadily along her sides as his mouth traveled upward along her midriff. When they reached the swells of her breasts, his hands seemed hesitant to claim the tender prize, and so his fingertips skittered lightly over the silky white curves until they reached her nipples. There his fingers played her like a skilled harpist coaxing music from the most delicate of strings. Round and hard, like new spring peonies, each delicious nipple in turn was taken into his mouth, where he reacquainted it with his tongue.

Amanda groaned as the fluttering in her stomach became racing desire, alive throughout her body. She kneaded her fingers into his biceps and muttered, "Sean, I'm losing my . . ."

"Control?" he whispered, lifting his head, sliding his body up so that his mouth would reach her earlobe, which he caught briefly between his teeth. "I'm taking it from you for the time being. You can have it back later." He nipped at her again. "This pleasure is uncontrollable anyway, sweetheart." His hand had found its way to her thighs. She arched toward him, but she did not readily give him access until he assured her, "It's all right, Mandy. Let me touch you . . . there . . . that's right, honey . . . You're so beautiful . . . I want to make you feel beautiful . . . I want you to be mine."

"I am, Sean . . . I am . . ."

"Because when you take me inside you, I'm going to be all yours. . . ." He took a nipple in his mouth again, and she found that she hardly breathed, hardly needed to breathe. She was in a sense-heightened limbo, poised breathlessly beside a precipice.

"Oh, Sean! Please."

"Please—what?"

"I can't . . . I know you want me, too."

"Want you . . . *need* you, Mandy." His voice was almost strangled with passion.

"Please love me, Sean."

He reached for her hand and guided it to him. "Help me, honey. Show me. I want an invitation. I want to know I'm welcome."

"Sean!" she gasped. "Oh, Sean, I . . ."

"It's all right, sweetheart. Don't be afraid of me now. I'm going to give you nothing but pleasure; I won't hurt you this time . . . there, that's my girl . . . Mandy . . . Mandy."

"Show me how to please you. I don't know what . . . how to . . ."

He moved slowly within the cradle of her long legs, exhorting her to move with him, and then there were no more words as their lovemaking gathered momentum, pitching Amanda to the summit of passion, where Sean held her as she shuddered and gasped his name. When she began to drift back to him, he took her on another upward spiral, sharing with her in exquisite release.

He had been awake for some time, admiring the lovely sleeping face next to him. He'd thought about calling room service for coffee, so it would be there when she woke up, but she huddled so close to him as she slept that he couldn't move without disturbing her. Besides, he was comfortable.

Now he watched her awaken. His head was propped up on his elbow, and he had a good view of the momentary surprise on her face when she first saw him. Then she smiled. If she had been a cat, she would have purred. "Hi, cowboy."

"Hi, pretty lady."

"How soon do we have to be out of here?"

"It's early," he said. "There's no hurry."

"Good." She put her arm across him and snuggled up to his chest. "I must confess that waking up and seeing you first thing is pretty nice. I don't know why I made a big fuss over getting a room just for myself."

"I have a confession to make, too. When I made the reservation I didn't make it just for you."

"You assumed that we'd . . ."

"I knew that something happened between us the other night that I wanted to happen again. I thought you felt the same way. But if you were going to persist with that 'giving each other room' stuff, I wasn't going to push."

"I don't know, Sean; it's all happened so fast. We can't take it for granted."

"Mandy," he began with a sigh, lightly rubbing her shoulder, "I made that mistake once—took it for granted that someone else felt the same way I did. I've guarded against that for a long time now, and I'm not likely to take anything for granted again. But it gets pretty lonely when you don't even take the chance because you're afraid."

"I *am* afraid. I want to be sure I know who you are, Sean."

"Don't you think I'm scared, too?" he suggested.

"I can't imagine you being scared of anything."

"You're a heck of a lot scarier than a bull with

twenty-inch horns, honey," Sean replied with a chuckle. His hand slid down her arm and found her breast. "But you're worth the risk," he whispered.

Amanda's breath caught in her throat and she shivered as his careful fingers molded her nipple into a hard peak. "Sean, you must be . . . we should get dressed and have breakfast. . . . You must be hungry."

"I sure am," he said, leaning over her, smiling, his eyes bright. "You know what I want?" Sliding down a little, he answered himself. "I want a ripe strawberry floating in a bowl of cream," he whispered, tracing one areola with the tip of his tongue.

"Are you going to lap at your breakfast like a cat?" she asked, thoroughly enjoying the role of repast.

"Um-hmm," he affirmed lazily as he took the nipple gently in his teeth and tantalized it with his tongue until she moaned softly. "Delicious," he whispered. "I think I'll have seconds." And, with a slight shift of his weight, he did. She required no instructions this time. Willingly she opened herself and welcomed him inside.

Time became unimportant as they lay together in a haze of contentment, holding each other, giving soft kisses and warm touches.

"I take it we don't have to hurry to the next rodeo," Amanda observed quietly.

"I'm not in any hurry. Are you?"

"No, but then I don't have to worry about being on deck when my calf's in the chute."

"Do I look like a man who's worried about catching calves?" he asked, propping himself up and smiling down at her so that she could judge for herself.

"Hardly," she giggled. "You look like a tomcat who's just gorged himself on two bowls of cream."

"Gorged? You underestimate my appetite, little kitten. I think I'll keep you here until I've drunk my fill of you."

"Your rival calf ropers would be pleased to hear that, not to mention all those poor little calves."

"I know of one calf who's going to head for the chute again pretty soon unless I get him into the shower," Sean chuckled, rolling over and swinging his feet to the floor.

"Not unless you can outrun me," Amanda quipped, jumping out of bed unexpectedly and snatching the bedspread around herself at the same moment. "And I'm closer." She sailed into the bathroom, bedspread trailing behind her, leaving Sean sitting on the bed. He heard the water running in the tub, then the spray of the showerhead. Amanda's head popped around the corner once again, her chestnut waves tousled, a saucy smile in her eyes. "By the way, I liked the strawberries-and-cream metaphor, but that one about the calf heading for the chute was crude."

"Hell, lady, I'm a cowboy. Crude is part of the package." His back was to her, but he winked at her over his shoulder. She disappeared again, and he muttered to himself, "One out of two ain't bad."

He lay on his back and listened to the shower for a few moments before she called to him above the noise. "Sean, would you hand me my shampoo? It's right there on the counter."

Sean smiled and mumbled, "That sounds like an invitation," and then swung himself off the bed. "What'd you bring this bedspread in here for?" he demanded as he picked it up off the bathroom floor and tossed it back to the bed.

"Because I didn't want to parade around naked," Amanda answered.

He pushed the shower door open and grinned at the sight of her bare back, covered with rivulets of water that coursed from her wet hair down the slope of her spine and spilled over her round bottom. "What was it that you didn't want me to see?" he drawled.

"Good heavens, Sean, I'm in the shower! What are

you doing?" she demanded as he stepped in. "It's getting crowded in here, Mr. Brannigan," Amanda said with mock exasperation. "Just who do you think you are?"

"I'm the guy who had first claim to the shower," he explained patiently, pouring a dollop of shampoo on top of Amanda's head. She reached up to work it into her wet hair, but his hands were there first. Her back kept most of the spray from reaching him as he worked the lather through her silky hair. "In our house, before Dad put in a second bathroom, we had a rule, and the rule was that the first guy to say that he was going to take a shower had first claim to it. And anybody who weaseled in before the one who had first claim was a rotten claim jumper. And claim jumpers," he explained slowly as he took her by the shoulders and forced her to step back, her head directly under the showerhead and the water washing lather over her face, "could legitimately be drowned."

Amanda sputtered under the water, eyes tightly shut, pushing water and suds away from her face as he moved to change places with her. He rolled a bar of soap in his hands while she sputtered, "Sean Brannigan, you have no respect for other people's privacy." He began soaping her neck and shoulders, massaging her with strong, sensuous hands.

"You're sleek and beautiful, as if you just swam under a waterfall," he murmured appreciatively as his hands moved diligently along her arms to the hands that hung by her thighs.

"I didn't swim under. I was *pushed* under."

"Quiet. I'm trying to improve on my metaphors."

"I'll bet your English teachers loved you," she said, unable to deny the delicious, tingly feeling that he was generating inside her.

"They did, as a matter of fact. There was one who said I had a knack for inventing future clichés."

"Mmmm . . . Sean . . . you   definitely   have   a

knack with your . . . hands," Amanda breathed, quivering at the slow circles his soapy hands made over her breasts and belly. When he slid his hands around her back she stepped close to him, wrapping her arms around him while he treated the back of her to his stimulating ministrations. Their bodies were slippery against each other, and she tasted the hot water on his shoulder with the tip of her tongue.

"Don't get too carried away, lady. I expect you to return this favor in kind."

"Gladly," she offered, and they changed places so that the spray pelted her back again. She made her own hands soapy and used them to explore the muscles of his wide shoulders and deep chest, his tapering torso and flat belly. He smiled reassuringly when she gave him an awkward look. "I need more soap," she croaked, and vigorously rolled the bar in her hands again.

"I don't need to be scrubbed and disinfected, sweetheart," Sean chuckled.

"I know," she sighed, forcing herself to be relaxed. "You just need to be touched."

"I need to be touched by you. Touch me, Mandy," he whispered, and her slippery hand, untaught, brought him to a fever pitch of passion that had to be assuaged then and there, under the warm downpour.

After a late breakfast in their room Sean went down to the lobby to check out, and Amanda took the opportunity to call her father at his office.

"Amanda! When are you coming home, dear? Are you finished with that rodeo business, or just ready to give up?"

"Neither, Daddy. I'm just getting started."

"It's been almost a week, Amanda. Where are you?"

"I'm in Cheyenne."

"Cheyenne? Wyoming? What are you doing there?"

"I'm going to rodeos. It's more interesting than I had thought, Daddy, and I've met some fascinating people."

"I can't imagine whom you would meet out there except cowboys and saloon girls, for Pete's sake. You don't want to miss the Berkshire Open, Amanda." His tone was firm and decisive, as always.

"I'm afraid I will miss it this year, Daddy. I'm going to South Dakota for the Fourth."

"South Dakota! Where in South Dakota?"

"Oh . . . several places. There are quite a few rodeos over the Fourth, and I want to—"

"Amanda, where will you be staying? How can we reach you?"

"Actually, you probably can't. I'll be going to rodeos, you see, and . . . well, I'm not really sure . . ." She looked up to find that Sean was in the doorway, leaning against the doorjamb. He tossed a paper sack onto a nearby chair.

"Amanda, what is going on? If you're flying to South Dakota, surely you can give me the name of a city, if there is such a thing out there." She didn't answer. "Are you flying, Amanda?" her father asked sternly.

"Not exactly, Daddy. I'm sort of . . . hitchhiking."

There was a silence on the line, and then he said in a low, even voice, "I'm sure you're going to explain what you mean by that ridiculous remark."

"I'm riding to South Dakota with someone I've met out here. He's a very . . . interesting man who's . . . involved with the rodeo, and he's been a great help to me in getting started with this story."

"Just what kind of story is this, Amanda?"

"It's more complicated than I have time to explain right now, Daddy, but it'll make very interesting reading. I'll tell you all about it when I get home."

"And when will that be?"

"I don't know yet. I'll call you. Tell Mother that I called and said hello."

Amanda watched Sean as she hung up the phone. He pushed himself away from the doorjamb and took several slow steps toward her. "You're a master of evasion, Miss Caron."

"He wants me to go home."

"And how old did you say you were?"

"Did I say? I'm twenty-four."

"Old enough to make your own decisions, aren't you? So when does Daddy expect you back?"

Amanda bristled only slightly. "I told him that I didn't know when I'd be back. I told him that I'd be here for the Fourth."

"Your description of me was pretty sketchy. I have a name, an occupation, and more than a casual friendship with his daughter. Which part of the picture would he object to?" he asked, putting a firm hand on her shoulder.

"I don't know."

"The hell you don't," Sean grumbled.

"All right, he probably wouldn't like any of it, but, as you say, I'm old enough to make my own choices."

"And do you?"

"I choose to be here with you now, and I don't understand this third degree you're giving me. I couldn't tell him about us over the phone. The details of our relationship are private—just between us. And I couldn't tell him when I might be home because you and I haven't made any plans beyond the Fourth, right?"

A fierce, almost pained expression flashed through Sean's eyes as they shot an inscrutable message into hers. She was left to ponder the meaning of that look before he caught himself and turned away. "No, I guess we haven't. After the Fourth I'll probably head back to the ranch, go to Dupree, Mitchell, Aberdeen maybe . . . I was hoping you'd go with me."

"Without being asked? I told you that I wouldn't just attach myself to you and follow you around."

"I was going to talk to you about it. I'd kinda like for you to see the ranch," he said, turning toward her again.

"I think . . . ," she began quietly, "I think I'd kinda like to see the ranch."

His arms closed around her, and he drew her to him in a gesture of relief. "Don't talk about leaving, Mandy. Not yet."

"When you're this close I can't even *think* about leaving." He tightened his hold, and she continued with a small laugh. "Mainly because your arms are like steel stays, and I don't know how I'd get away while you've got this kind of hold on me."

"I wonder if I can drive with you on my lap."

"And I *am* working on a story."

"How long will that take you?"

"At the rate I'm going, quite a while."

"I'll introduce you to everybody who's anybody in rodeo."

"That sounds promising," she murmured, rubbing his back affectionately.

"Of course we'll have to do some traveling to run them all down, but it'll be a Pulitzer Prize winner by the time we're done. You can't turn down an opportunity like that, can you?" he asked, grinning down at her.

"I'd have to be crazy to deny the chance of a lifetime. I'm sure no one's ever won the Pulitzer Prize for a horse story before. How about a kiss to seal the bargain?"

His mouth closed over hers with a hard possession that surprised her after the light turn the conversation had taken, but Amanda responded to him with resolution of her own.

"I have something for you," he whispered when his mouth released hers.

"I liked what you just gave me," she said, grazing his angular jawline with slightly parted lips.

"There's lots more where that came from, sweetheart, but I've got something I want to see you wear with these new jeans—which look terrific on you, by the way."

"Really? Do you think I could be a cowgirl?"

"Right up there next to Dale Evans." He reached for the paper bag that he'd tossed on the chair and produced a tastefully tooled leather belt with a heart-shaped silver buckle. The word *Amanda* was engraved in script in the center of the buckle.

"Oh, Sean, it's just lovely. I really will feel properly dressed out here now."

"It's not too . . . you don't think it's too gaudy, do you?" he asked shyly.

"Of course not. It's perfect." She threaded the belt through the loops on her jeans and buckled the small, feminine buckle. "Is this the cowboy's version of giving a girl a locket?"

"Something like that."

"Well, do I look gaudy?"

"Hell, no, you're a cowboy's dream." He grinned, producing another box. "This is what I did yesterday while you were washing clothes."

Amanda opened the box to find a large trophy buckle, silver with turquoise and coral inlay. The engraving proclaimed that it was the all-around cowboy trophy buckle from the Reno rodeo, and that Sean Brannigan had earned the honors. "Turn it over," he suggested. On the back it said, "Mandy— This is for my lady" and the date of their first meeting. "I know this one's too big for you to wear," he explained quickly, as though he were suddenly embarrassed by his own gesture. "It would cover your whole stomach, and it's gaudy, and it was probably a dumb idea, but I wanted you to have it."

"This is the one you just won in Reno," Amanda said, stating the obvious as she fingered the engraving.

"Yeah, I . . . I just thought you might . . ."

"Oh, Sean!" Her arms were around his neck before he could finish. "I love it, and it wasn't a dumb idea. I feel like a schoolgirl, and the captain of the football team has just given me his class ring. My palms are even sweaty."

"I suddenly felt about as awkward as a kid asking for his first date," he laughed.

Pulling her head back to look at his face, Amanda smiled delightedly. "You're cute when you're nervous."

"It seemed like a good idea at the time, but I sure felt stupid watching you open that box!"

"Does this make me a buckle bunny?" Amanda asked, still smiling.

"Where did you hear that expression?" he asked, his smile fading a little.

"Oh . . . I guess . . . well, Travis Steele said that I didn't strike him as a buckle bunny."

"That son of a—" Her forefinger came up to his lips, and he kissed it, hugged her and said calmly, "No, you're not a buckle bunny. That's what they call women who hang around the circuit and pick up cowboys."

"Like Lacy?" she asked, and realized at once that it was an unfair barb.

"Yeah, like Lacy."

"That wasn't fair. I'm sorry."

"It's true, and she doesn't deny it. She is what she is. But she's a friend of mine, Mandy; try to remember that."

Amanda snuggled her face against Sean's neck and kissed him. "Thank you. I happen to be very sentimental, and I'll treasure this always."

"Touching," he chuckled as he shook off the temptation to say something more committal; he gave her bottom a playful smack instead. "We'd better hit the road, lady. We're headin' for the hills."

Chapter Eight

The little village of Belle Fourche, South Dakota, had the look of a settlement that wasn't on the interstate's handiest exit and didn't much care. It yawned and stretched before rolling itself into bed for the evening, winking a streetlight here and a porch light there, wishing a breeze would cool its bedrooms now that the sun had set. The cowboys were pulling into town, and tomorrow night the hometown boys would show them what the town had to offer. Tonight they'd turn on the window fans and lie on top of the bedcovers and dream of making the whistle.

No, it was not good sleeping weather. Amanda felt clammy and closed in and conscious of the fact that the space next to her in the bed was occupied. Though she was awake, she was startled by a rapping on the camper window just above her head. A reflex prompted her to sit up, but Sean's arms came around her and settled her back down beside him.

"Hey, Sean, you in there? You asleep already?"

"I was," Sean growled.

"Hey, good buddy, it's early yet! I just pulled in. Let's go over to the Elkhorn and have a few beers."

"Go to hell, Bud. I'm tired. If I come out it's gonna be to break your neck."

"No need to get so touchy. Just wanted you to know I'm here to haze for you."

"Not if I kill you first, Bud."

"Okay, okay, sorry I woke you up."

"See you in the morning. Lacy with you?"

"Yeah, over in the trailer. You still got that lady along?"

"That's none of your business, Bud. Catch you later."

"Testy, aren't we?" Amanda whispered.

"That idiot. It's the middle of the night."

"Sean," she began hesitantly, settling in his arms, "if I'm none of Bud's business, then why is Lacy your business?"

"Don't start that stuff again, Mandy. She just is, that's all." His lips found her temple and planted a soft kiss. "Go back to sleep, honey."

The sun turned the hot, still night into a morning of the same caliber. Amanda draped her arms over a whitewashed rail fence and watched the wild-eyed bucking horses trample down the trailer ramp, darting one by one through the crowding chute into a pen. Powdery corral dust billowed against her face, and she closed her eyes against the grit and tipped her head aside as the herd passed. Then she watched the horses crowd around the long stock tanks, jostling for position, stretching long sweat-slick necks toward the smell of water. Amanda's mouth was dry as she turned away.

Sean was well rested and ready to ride, anticipation evident in his demeanor. Amanda knew that love of competition, the thrill of putting oneself on the line for all the world to see. As she shared in the pre-event

excitement she was comfortable with Sean's close-
ness, his hand on her back or her shoulder when he
introduced her to someone, but she still chafed at the
thought that she might look like the many girls she
saw who walked around with their thumbs hooked in
the back belt loops of their cowboys' jeans. Despite
her disdain for such blatant behavior, Amanda
hooked her arm through Sean's when she caught sight
of Lacy a short distance away. Catching the connec-
tion, Sean chuckled inwardly.

Belle Fourche was a small rodeo, a small crowd, but
Sean was close to home, and his performance was
big-time. Afterward, much to Bud's delight, Sean
agreed to check out the local night life, promising
Amanda that the Elkhorn would be an experience.

"This must be a real honky-tonk," Amanda observed once they were inside the crowded, Western-
style tavern.

"This is it. Chance for you to practice your Western
dancing and maybe witness a real barroom brawl if
you're lucky," Sean said.

"From the looks of the band, the brawl might be
the best part of the entertainment." Amanda eyed the
three men settling on the small platform where drums
and two guitars were waiting for them. A slightly
overweight woman dressed in fringed satin took her
place at the microphone. Her voice was as twangy as
the electric guitars, and her first song bemoaned the
fact that she'd been lied to, cheated on and deserted
by her man.

"That's a real nice belt, Amanda," Lacy commented after the first round of drinks was served.
"Real pretty buckle. It'll be a nice keepsake to take
back east with you."

"Looks to me like Amanda ain't gonna get away
from this ol' cowboy that easy," Bud announced,
clapping a hand on Sean's shoulder. "You better
watch yourself, girl. He's tricky with that rope. Two
wraps and a hooey, and you ain't goin' nowhere."

Amanda laughed indulgently. "Heaven spare me from rodeo metaphors," she said, giving Sean a mischievous glance from under one raised eyebrow.

"I don't know what that means, but for the price of a dance, I'll keep my mouth shut."

"Who're you trying to kid, Bud?" Sean chided, raising his beer bottle to his lips. "You couldn't keep your mouth shut for the price of the Black Hills."

"Here it comes," Bud groaned, eyes rolled toward the ceiling. "Let's dance, Amanda, before this Indian gets started on his damned broken treaties again."

Dancing with Bud was like trying to dance with an oil rig. Amanda found herself seeking glimpses of Sean as Bud tipped her from side to side in triple time. She saw Sean pay for the round of drinks that Bud had ordered before he left the table, and then she watched Sean and Lacy share a laugh and caught herself wondering what it was about. When Bud kept her on the floor for another dance Amanda maintained a tight smile and watched Sean lead Lacy by the hand in their direction. She had a strange, constricted feeling in her chest as she watched Sean take Lacy in his arms and move smoothly with her in time to the music.

The band let the music die ignobly, as though they weren't sure of the final notes. "It's time for another beer for this cowboy," Bud announced, hooking an arm over Lacy's shoulders as Sean slipped his arm around Amanda's waist and pulled her into his embrace for the next dance.

"I have a confession to make," Sean whispered. "I don't enjoy watching you dance with another man."

The constriction in her chest miraculously went away, and Amanda expressed her relief with a small giggle. "That wasn't dancing. I felt like a human seesaw."

When the set was over Sean and Amanda returned to the table, which was surrounded by people for whom Sean had jovial greetings. "Amanda, here's somebody you ought to meet," Lacy insisted cheerfully. Amanda turned toward Lacy, who was pushing a rather embarrassed, nice-looking blond man. "This is Mark, Amanda. Mark . . . uh . . ."

"Mark Coleman," he supplied.

"Mark's a newspaperman from Rapid City," Lacy explained, "and Amanda's from Massachusetts. She writes for magazines. She's here writing about rodeo." Lacy stood aside as though she'd just introduced Grant to Lincoln and solved everybody's problems.

As the air thickened with smoke, laughter and the flow of reminiscences among old friends, Amanda found herself feeling left out. As more old friends dragged chairs into the circle and ordered more drinks and offered more stories, Amanda began to feel as if she weren't even there anymore. She was an attractive alien, detached, out of touch and looking on. She didn't even speak the same language, and the man she'd begun to feel close to belonged to them now, these people in funny hats.

Half a dozen drinks she hadn't asked for and didn't want accumulated in an absurd little collection on the table, and she left them there when Mark Coleman coaxed her onto the dance floor and away from the rest of the group. Mark seemed almost as much out of his element as Amanda was among these cowboys. He was an ordinary, pleasant man, and Amanda found herself slipping into the old routine of feigning interest in his career, smiling at his lukewarm witticisms and offering very little conversation of her own. She was on automatic pilot.

Sean was involved in his own discussion, and Lacy, standing behind him with a hand on his shoulder, was enjoying every minute of it. When Lacy leaned down to whisper in Sean's ear Amanda felt that tightening in her chest again. She wanted to sit the next one out, she told Mark.

"It's pretty crowded over there." Mark nodded toward the table. "Why don't we sit over here?" There was an empty table by the dance floor, but Amanda shook her head in reply.

"I'd really like a breath of fresh air," she said, and Mark agreed that the room was stuffy. She made a point of not glancing in Sean's direction as she walked to the side door, which opened to a parking lot.

"How long will you be staying in this part of the country?" Mark asked as he lit a cigarette.

"What? Oh . . . until I finish my story."

"I'm here with friends tonight," Mark was saying, "but I have my car if you'd like to go somewhere else. There's a nice—"

"The lady's with me, hotshot."

Amanda and Mark turned around simultaneously, and Amanda knew immediately that Sean had assumed the worst. He looked bigger than he ever had before, his eyes dark and smoldering, and his jaw set. She almost wilted when he turned his angry gaze on her and said, "Or have you had a sudden change of plans?"

"No, Sean, it was getting stuffy in there, and . . ."

Sean's eyes shifted back to Mark after dismissing Amanda with a scathing glance. "And you just thought you'd take her somewhere else?"

"I didn't realize you had a claim on her evening," Mark said evenly.

"I just wanted to . . . ," Amanda began, but she was ignored.

"When I take a lady out I see that she gets home," Sean explained carefully. "That gives me a claim on her evening." He stood within a foot of Mark's face, and Amanda wondered why Mark, by far the smaller man, didn't back away.

Mark turned to Amanda. "If you'd like a more attentive escort, Amanda, I'd be happy to take you to a quieter—" He stopped abruptly when Sean grabbed his shirtfront.

"I'll show you just how attentive I can be, you prissy-mouthed preppie."

"Sean!" Amanda gasped, clutching his arm. "Sean, there's no call for this. I had no intention of—"

"I'm not going to fight with you, cowboy," Mark said quietly. "I've never found it necessary to drag a woman around by the hair. I just asked if she was interested, that's all."

Sean's shove sent Mark reeling backward; the reporter was saved from landing on the ground only by a car parked a few feet behind him. Sean turned to Amanda. "There you go, Mandy, are you interested? Your preppie friend wants to rescue you from the clutches of a womanizing cowboy." Mark made an effort to peel himself away from the fender of the car, but Sean turned on him, his eyes glittering with anger beneath the brim of his Stetson. "Don't you move, hotshot. If you're not gonna fight me, then you're obliged to stay put while the lady makes her choice."

"Sean, you're acting like a maniac! Mark hasn't threatened you in any way."

"Damn it, Mandy, he wants to take you—"

"What's she supposed to do, cowboy? Sit there and listen to your rerides all night?"

It was probably Amanda's quick dive at Sean's lunging body that kept Mark from getting a broken nose. As it was, his face suffered only a glancing blow. As though he had come to his senses, Sean dropped his arms to his sides, and Amanda released her hold on him, standing between the two men. "You just made my choice, Sean. I'm going to find a motel, and I'll find a way to get to the fairgrounds in the morning to pick up my things. For your sake I hope Mark doesn't press charges."

"I won't let you get picked up by some—"

Amanda's eyes flared. "*I* will not allow *myself* to be picked up by *anyone*. I was merely talking with the man." Thoroughly disgusted, she turned away from them both.

"Don't walk away from me, Mandy. You made me look like a fool when you left with him. Now you're leaving with *me*."

"Not unless you drag me by the hair. You just made a fool of yourself, Sean."

"I'm not chasing after you, lady."

"I don't expect you to. Your pride precludes any chance of that," she said, turning on her heel and summoning her self-confidence.

"My car's over here, Amanda," Mark offered.

"I'm not going anywhere with you, either," she informed him without looking back.

In fact Amanda did expect Sean to follow her as she pranced down the main street of the little town in a determined huff, but he didn't. All she had when she checked into a motel, after walking she didn't know how many blocks, was her purse. She undressed and turned the shower on. That presumptuous, self-possessed . . . man! For several minutes she just watched the water beat down until steam began to roll toward the ceiling. She didn't feel like calling her father. That was unusual. She didn't want to make plane reservations. What she wanted to do was cry, and dignity be damned. Sobbing like a child, she stood under the pounding water until it turned icy and her tears had run their course.

He had let her go. She was alone in this strange town in the middle of nowhere, and he had stood there and watched her walk away. And now she cried out her frustration and her helplessness, angry with herself for wanting him back, angry with him for . . . for everything.

She had put her shirt on with her underclothes when she heard the gentle knock at her door. This was a motor court in which all doors opened onto the parking lot, making Amanda feel anxious about her security, but she managed to pump some strength into her voice as she stood behind the closed door and asked, "Who is it?"

"It's me, Mandy." The sound of his voice was so welcome that she was inclined to throw the door open, but her pride intervened and wouldn't let her answer. "I just want to talk to you," he said after a pause.

"About what?"

"About what happened tonight."

"Are you drunk, Sean?"

"After you left I had one more beer to wash my pride down. I swallowed it, Mandy, and I just want to talk. Please let me in."

She opened the door, peeking around it as though to confirm his identity. He leaned with one shoulder against the doorjamb, his fingers thrust in the pockets of his jeans, his hat pushed back on his head and a sheepish grin on his face.

"Are you sure you're not drunk?" she repeated.

"I'm sure I'm not sober, but I won't do anything stupid, I promise. May I come in?"

Amanda opened the door to admit him, then closed it behind her and leaned her back against it as though she might need an escape route. She could say nothing. Tears were burning in her throat. She was wary, but he seemed steady and calm, although unsure of himself.

"You were right," he said at last, not looking at her. "I acted like a maniac. I saw you leave with that guy, and I went crazy. I think I leaped over the table and pushed about ten people out of the way to get to the door."

"What did you think I was going to do?"

"I thought you were leaving with him."

"Did you actually think that after a couple of dances I would go sailing off with a perfect stranger?"

"I didn't think, Mandy. I just saw you go out that door with him, and I couldn't think."

"I tried to tell you, I just needed air. I'm not like . . . I don't make a habit of . . . Sean, you *do* know what a lady is?"

"Of course I do. And I know . . . I know I made a fool of myself, and I embarrassed you, and I'm truly sorry."

His face was the image of contrition. Amanda let the tears roll again. Holding them back was just giving her a headache. "Sean, I was afraid . . ."

He took a step closer, but he wasn't sure she'd let him touch her. "I know, honey. I'm really not a fighter, but you've seen me do it twice now, so I guess I can't expect you to believe that. I didn't mean to scare you."

Amanda shook her head, trying to gain control over her own voice. "I wasn't afraid of the fighting. I was afraid you weren't coming after me . . . that you were just going to let me go, and that would be the end of it."

He gathered her into his arms and let her spend her tears. "My insanity was only temporary. I started to track you down as soon as I came to my senses. I guess I was scared, too . . . scared you wouldn't want to see me after all the ruckus I caused."

"Oh, Sean . . . I've never been so glad to see anybody. I must be crazy, too," she sobbed.

"Don't cry now, honey," he crooned, rubbing her back. "Will you let me stay here with you?"

Amanda nodded, sniffling and wiping impatiently at her eyes. "I don't usually cry like this. I know that's hard to believe, since you've seen *me* do *this* twice now."

Sean set his hat on the desk and went to the sink to soak a washcloth in cool water. "I see you took a shower without me."

"I was trying to drown my sorrows," she admitted.

He lifted her chin in one hand and sponged her face with the other. His black hair fell across the corner of his forehead, and he smiled, a somewhat glazed-eyed, crooked smile. "I put these tears here, and I want to take them away."

"I'll overlook the corniness of that statement, since you've obviously had too much to drink," Amanda offered, trying to smile past the washcloth.

"Listen, lady, stop making fun of my clumsy attempts at sweet talk. If this doesn't work I'll have to resort to cowboy courtship."

"What's that, Tex?"

"I might find it necessary," he grinned, imitating Mark Coleman's superior tone of voice, "to drag you around by the hair."

"Ah, the womanizing cowboy. You find that to be an effective technique, do you?"

"Tones 'em down pretty fast, but then you end up with a hank of hair in your fist and a ragged woman at your feet."

"I prefer the sweet talk. In fact, I'm becoming an admirer of the endearing way you have with words." She cupped her hand around the underside of his jaw and waited for his kiss. It was in his eyes, and she felt drawn to his mouth, but he suddenly turned and tossed the washcloth back to the sink.

Taking a couple of steps away from her, Sean avoided her eyes, not wanting her to see his confusion, but wanting, at the same time, to get his feelings out in the open. "I haven't felt . . . jealous . . . in a long time. I didn't handle it very well," he said quietly.

"Were you jealous over me, Sean? Or was it someone else? I doubt that Mark Coleman is a preppie."

"Yeah, that part of it was a flashback. That smugness, that social superiority . . ."

"I'm not Alisha."

"It wasn't Alisha, Mandy. I was jealous over you. And jealousy is a stupid, selfish emotion I thought I'd outgrown. I saw him open that door and usher you out, and it was like a fire alarm went off in my head."

"As long as confessions are in order, I guess I

should admit that I didn't handle my own jealousy very well either." Amanda sighed.

"*Your* jealousy?"

"I suppose I wanted you to see me go outside with Mark. I was feeling a little sorry for myself because I was losing the game."

"What game?"

"Sort of a 'who-does-he-like-the-best?' game. There's definitely a home field advantage, you know."

"I can tell this is going to be some pretty sophisticated metaphor already. Remember, I'm just a country boy."

"I thought you'd abandoned the country boy routine."

"You can't take the country out of the boy, lady. Now, what's this game stuff?"

"I let Lacy get to me, that's all. She dragged Mark Coleman over, made a big deal about us both being writers, and then your old buddies joined her team. Before long I was pretty far out in left field. She pitched a very controlled game and had you hitting strictly to the infield, and planted old Mark out there in the outfield to keep me company—and the only way I could get your attention was by walking off the field."

"Now that's what I call a metaphor," Sean teased.

"It just sort of grew as I was talking. You don't believe me, do you?"

Sean put both hands on Amanda's shoulders. "It's hard to imagine Lacy coming up with all that strategy."

"Sean, I didn't imagine all those triumphant glances she shot across the floor at me. I didn't imagine seeing her hands all over you, and I didn't imagine seeing her whispering in your ear. That's about the time I needed some fresh air."

Sean raised his eyebrows, considering the evidence. "Lacy's been like part of the furniture to me for so long that I guess I just didn't notice."

"You weren't meant to. *I* was supposed to notice that I didn't fit in but Lacy did. She fit very nicely."

Sean shook his head. "You shouldn't feel jealous of Lacy."

"I know. You've told me that. You're just good friends, and she knows you have nothing more to offer her. Tell me something, Sean. What was Lacy's reaction when you decided to look for me?"

"Well, she just said you had no place to go, and I should wait for you to come back on your own." Amanda said nothing, and Sean acknowledged the implications of that with a slow inhalation of breath and a long sigh.

It was Amanda who closed the distance between them by sliding her arms around his back and stepping closer to hold herself against him. "You needn't have felt jealous of Mark Coleman, either, but you did."

"I stood there and watched you walk out of that parking lot and I felt sick, Mandy."

"I did, too. I made a dramatic exit, and then here I was, in this crummy room, with not even a toothbrush, wondering how everything had gotten so out of hand."

"Am I forgiven?" His hands played along her spine.

"You were forgiven when you knocked on the door," she answered, tilting her chin to offer him access to her mouth. His lips moved over hers slowly, and she returned their gentle caress with her own.

"Do I taste like beer?" he murmured, his mouth still brushing hers.

"Um-hmm."

"You don't like beer."

"I like it this way. Let me have another taste," she whispered, and she reached to capture those full lips, delicious on hers in spite of the bitter beer flavor. Her tongue asked to play with his, flickering delicately past his teeth. Sean groaned, tightening his arms around her and pulling the full length of her against him. His hand slid to her thinly clad bottom, and his caress made their chests heave against each other as the kiss ended.

"Does your male chauvinist code say anything about sleeping in a bed that a lady's paid for?" Amanda nuzzled the area under his collar.

"When the code poses a serious inconvenience, I'm willing to set it aside," was his answer.

She reached down to fflick open his belt buckle. "And you don't sleep in your jeans," she said with a coy smile.

"Boots first," he said, dropping a kiss on her forehead before he sat down in the straight-backed chair by the desk. He started to lift one booted foot, but Amanda took it in her hands, stretching his leg out and grasping his heel.

"I intend to undress you," she said. "Completely."

"If I thought I'd get this kind of treatment all the time, I'd see you got jealous more often."

"It has nothing to do with jealousy. You're a bit tipsy, so I thought I'd—" One last tug sent Amanda tumbling backward, boot in her hands, giggling as she landed on the carpet.

"Who's a little tipsy?" he chuckled, reaching to remove the other boot. She got there first. She caught her balance this time when the foot was free. Then she moved in front of him, kneeling in the vee that his legs formed. "You look pretty cute dressed like that, lady," he remarked as she unsnapped his shirt.

Pushing the shirt aside, she pressed her palms to his chest and smiled her delight. "This may sound shameless, but I think you have a gorgeous chest."

"Shameless. I wish you'd move right along so I could get my hands on yours."

"Maybe it would help if you stood up."

"Just waiting for instructions, ma'am." Supporting her by the elbows, he brought her to her feet with him. Then he switched off the lamp. The room was blue-white from the moonlit window. "Now what are you going to do?" he asked.

"Finish undressing you . . . after I turn the bed down, okay?"

"Tell you what, sweetheart, even half-shot, I think I could've handled this seduction with more finesse."

"It's my first time," she said lightly, following her own suggestion, "and you, I'm sure, have been practicing for years." She got a chuckle out of him, but no denial. Sliding up to him, she pushed his shirt over his shoulders, pulling it down along his arms until it became stuck at his wrists.

"Then take it from an old pro, honey," he said with a wink and a broad grin as he unfastened the snaps on his cuffs, "cuffs first. Then the shirt slips right off." The shirt was tossed on the chair. "Like this," he instructed, taking first one hand, then the other to undo the snaps at her wrists. She watched his face as he released the snaps on the front of her shirt, slipped it off and tossed it atop his own. He smiled. "See how that works?"

"Slick. Anything else?"

He glanced down at his pants. "Yeah, there's something else. I think you're back where you started." He draped his arms over her shoulders while she busied herself with his jeans. Brushing his lips along the side of her face, he muttered, "Be gentle with me, Mandy. I'm really very shy and sensitive."

"Your secret is safe with me, cowboy. Lie down."

"What?" His voice skittered around a laugh.

"Lie down. I don't know how else to get your pants off."

Sean let himself fall backward on the bed, laughing in the dark. "You'll have to work on your approach, honey. 'Lie down so I can take your pants off' is a little too direct."

After some wrestling Amanda dropped his jeans on the floor. Then she sat next to him, smiling. "I give up."

"What do you mean? You said you were going to undress me completely. No guts?"

"I guess I'm just . . . not in the mood anymore."

"I can fix that," he promised, and he drew her to him, lifting his head to meet hers. He didn't break the kiss as he rolled over her, settling her back on the bed, tasting her honeyed lips. "Do you think it would set the women's movement back any if I helped this seduction along a little?" Sean whispered against Amanda's mouth.

"I don't know, but I wish you would." He wanted her naked, and he soon had his way. In the end she had her way, too, because she did undress him completely. She explored his body with a relish equal to that with which his eager fingers and avid lips trekked across hers. The kisses he gave her breasts brought gasps of unmitigated pleasure from her lips. His stroking of her belly made her sigh as she nibbled at his neck. When his hand slid lower she moaned, and her hand sought to hold and touch him, too.

Feeling bolder now, Amanda tilted her head back to watch Sean's face, to see his reaction to her caress. His eyes were closed, but when her hand moved experimentally, they opened, heavy-lidded with his pleasure, and he smiled at her, encouraging her to continue the experiment. His broad chest expanded with a sharp intake of breath, and then he groaned her name before fastening his mouth greedily on hers. Sliding himself out of her grasp, Sean moved down to lave her tingling nipples. And when his fingers found her, she was aflame with desire. He touched her, teased her, tantalized her until she begged him to take her.

"I want to be with you, Sean. I want nothing, no one but Sean . . . Sean . . . Sean . . ." She gasped when he filled her with all that she wanted—the sound of his rapid breathing, the musk and leather and beer smell of him, the salty taste of him—and the undulating roll of his hips, which she met with the driving need to pull him deep within her forever and forever and forever.

"Sean, wake up," Amanda whispered frantically.

"Mmmm?"

"Somebody's at the door!"

"Well, answer it," he groaned, eyes still closed. "This is your room, as I recall."

"Who is it?" she called out.

"It's Bud Eliot. Is Sean still there?"

"Damn you, Bud," Sean roared, hooking his arm over his eyes. "You're worse than an ol' rooster."

"I just thought you might want a ride back to the fairgrounds."

"Geez, that's right," Sean whispered to Amanda. "He let me off here last night." Then in a friendlier tone he shouted, "Meet you at the café across the street in half an hour, Bud."

"Sure thing. Took care of the horses already, Sean."

"Hey, I appreciate that. I owe you one."

"Hell, I owe you more than one. Take your time."

Sean cast an apologetic glance at Amanda, lifting his arm to allow her to snuggle against his chest. "Damn, I didn't think he'd . . . it's close enough to walk to . . . I'm sorry, Mandy. I meant to keep what's between us private."

"It is private. We haven't even told each other how we feel. Really feel, I mean."

"Last night I told you I wouldn't chase after you, but I did. That tells you something about the way I feel."

"And I was so glad you did I almost sang alleluias," she recalled. "It was good of Bud to remember us this morning."

"Yeah, Bud has his good points. He gave me something to think about last night when he said I was acting as bad as he does sometimes. That wasn't easy for him to say; he doesn't make a habit of calling me down. He really was worried about you. About me, too, I suppose. Said he hated to see me screw things up for myself over something so stupid."

They lay quietly in each other's arms for a moment, leaving a great deal unsaid. "You said half an hour," Amanda said finally. "How do you suggest we juggle the shower?"

"I suggest," he murmured against her temple, "that we share."

Chapter Nine

The greasy smell of bacon and lard-laden eggs turned Sean's stomach. He drank two cups of coffee, pushed his plate away after toying with the food and offered little conversation. Lacy, too, was unusually quiet, but Bud was in fine form, pleased with the role he had played the previous night. For a change he had shown good insight, and he knew he'd done Sean a service. Probably in deference to that service, Sean suffered Bud's good cheer, wishing all the while that the man would just shut up and eat.

Amanda offered to drive to Mobridge, South Dakota, insisting that Sean was obviously not up to par after the previous night's activities. After a feeble protest he agreed, pointing Amanda in a northeasterly direction before he allowed himself several hours' sleep in the back of the camper.

They had rolled over miles of hills and past countless square-topped buttes when Amanda heard Sean stirring behind her. "I think I've made good time!"

she called over her shoulder. "We're thirteen miles from Omaha."

"You'd better be kidding, lady," he warned, opening the refrigerator. "Otherwise I'll have to pull your pilot's license. How 'bout some pop?"

"Sounds good. You'd certainly have to go a long way to borrow a cup of sugar around here," Amanda commented. She took the can of soda, and smiled at the road ahead when he pulled the hair off the side of her neck and planted a kiss there.

"We believe in a well-stocked pantry and a lot of elbow room between neighbors. I don't suppose that appeals to you." He offered the observation as a matter of fact, dropping into the passenger's seat and stretching his long legs in front of him.

"It would certainly take some getting used to."

"Certainly would," he echoed. "I never did get used to the East. Too crowded. People and trees all over the place. Felt like I was being smothered by trees. You hardly ever see the sky out there."

"Funny. All this unbroken sky seems unnatural to me. I guess it depends on what you're used to."

"I guess it does," Sean agreed absently.

"Are you feeling better? Ready to ride?"

"I feel great." He grinned suddenly. "I'm going to give one hell of a performance tonight."

Mobridge was a small prairie town, hot and dusty on that dry July third afternoon. Perspiration ran freely down Amanda's chest, funneling into the valley between her breasts. She wiped at her forehead often as she cleaned Deke's hooves. Sean had gone to the office at the fairgrounds, and Amanda had busied herself caring for the horses.

"That's Sean Brannigan's horse." Amanda was startled by the small voice, but she smiled when she looked up from her work to see a small Indian boy. He wore the prescribed cowboy attire, and the suspicion in his eyes was apparent beneath the brim of his hat. He held a brown paper bag in one hand, while the other one was jammed into the pocket of his jeans.

"Yes, it is," Amanda confirmed.

"Where's Sean?" the boy asked brusquely.

"He's at the office. He'll be back in a minute." She let the horse put his hoof down, dropped the pick into the tool box and straightened her back. "Do you know Sean?"

"Sure. He's my cousin. He don't like nobody foolin' with his horses, y'know."

"I know he doesn't," Amanda assured him, "but he and I are good friends."

"You Sean's girl?"

"I'm his good friend." She offered an indulgent smile.

"His *girl*friend," the boy insisted.

"Okay, his girl *friend*. My name's Amanda Caron. What's yours?"

"Zack Little Moon. Sean's my cousin."

"So you said. Would you like a soda, Zack? Come on in the camper, and we'll wait for Sean."

"Okay. Sean's teaching me how to rope, y'know."

"Then you have a good teacher."

"When I get good enough I'm gonna go out on the road with him. I hope he don't bring no girls along with us, though." Zack slid into the booth and awaited the drink he had been promised.

"Does Sean have many girlfriends?" Amanda silently chided herself for asking, but she was unable to resist.

"No! Sean says girls are just a pain most of the time."

Amanda choked on a laugh. "How old are you, Zack?"

"Ten. I'm big for my age."

He wasn't, but Amanda nodded agreement, looking very seriously into his small black eyes. "That's pretty tough talk for such a young man."

"You mean about the girls? I got two sisters, and

they're a real pain." Just then Sean pulled the door open and climbed into the camper. Zack's face lit up instantly.

"Hey, Zack!" Sean greeted the boy with a man-to-man handshake. "Good to see you, cowboy. You been practicing?"

"Sure, every day on that calf dummy you gave me. I bet I could work off Medicine Man now."

"I'll bet you could, too. We'll give it a try next time you come down to the ranch."

"Then I can go on the road with you pretty soon, right, Sean?"

"Soon as you can get a permit." Sean flashed a grin at Amanda. "Zack's gonna be a real good hand in a few years." Then he asked the boy, "Did you introduce yourself?"

"Yeah," Zack replied with a note of impatience. "She says she's your girlfriend."

"That's not exactly . . . ," Amanda sputtered.

"Oh, she does, does she?" Eyes twinkling, Sean slid an arm around Amanda's shoulders and gave her a squeeze. "What do you think of her, Zack? Not bad, huh?"

Zack was obviously disgusted by the gesture, but he simply looked down at the table in front of him, tracing the pattern in the Formica with one brown forefinger. "She's okay, but I don't think I'd want her to go on the road with us. Here, Sean, this is for you. Mom made it." Zack handed him the paper bag and offered a toothy grin.

Sean pulled a navy blue Western shirt from the bag, unfolded it and held it up. It was decorated with narrow satin ribbon—strips of red, yellow and white —stitched along the yoke in front and back in several rows. The ends of the ribbons were left to flutter freely. A red and blue star print made up the cuffs and yoke.

"This is great! A ribbon shirt! I'll make a real splash out there tonight—this is really patriotic," Sean de-

clared, and flashed Zack a smile. "And pure Indian."
With a wink Sean confirmed his pride in their shared
heritage, and Zack beamed. "Where's your Mom? Is
she here?"

"She's out at Aunt Arlene's. She just let me off
here a little while ago. We're staying there tonight
. . . unless you're staying over tonight. Then maybe I
could stay with you instead."

"I don't know, Zack; I might."

"It would be fun for you and Zack to camp out and
talk over old times. Then maybe the two of you would
join me for breakfast in the morning." Amanda gave
Sean a pointed look.

"Join you?" She'd lost him somewhere.

"At the motel. You know, where I'm staying."

"Oh." Sean looked at Zack, whose eyes had brightened at this promising turn in the conversation.
"Yeah, I guess we could do that. Meanwhile, how
about warming Medicine Man up a little for me,
Zack? There aren't too many guys I can trust on my
horses, but you're one cowboy who knows how to
handle good stock." Zack beamed again while Sean
ushered him back outside, casting a distressed look at
Amanda as he left.

"I was not going to have you tell that boy he
couldn't stay with you because I would be," Amanda
explained as she turned thick ham steaks in the skillet.
"It means so much to him to stay with you, and it's
only one night."

"Mandy, where do you think you're gonna stay?
This town doesn't have many motels, and I know
every one is booked solid over the Fourth."

Amanda's face registered shock at her mistake. "I
didn't think about that."

"So now what?" Sean leaned back against the
refrigerator, arms folded over his chest, an oblique
smile on his face.

"Well, I can *try* to find a room."

"And then?"

"Don't you know anyone in town who I could . . ."
Sean was shaking his head slowly, still smiling. "You
like watching me squirm, don't you?" Sean's gesture
turned to a nod. "I thought I was being nice."

"You were," he said. "You're a very nice lady. And
if you don't burn supper I'll figure something out."

Sean looked the part of a real country-western
singer in the flashy ribbon shirt, a style adapted from
Indian dance costumes. Though his taste generally
tended to be conservative, he was obviously pleased
to wear this gift from the aunt who had become, in the
way of his mother's people, a mother to him after her
sister's death.

His Aunt Arlene was a stout woman with a ready
smile that seemed to emanate from somewhere behind her sparkling dark eyes. Sean dwarfed her when
he bent down to give her a hug and a peck on the
cheek. She looked Amanda over carefully as Sean
introduced them, and Amanda felt certain that Aunt
Arlene was not convinced that Amanda's intentions
were entirely honorable where her nephew was concerned.

In a discussion of Zack's plans for the night Sean
assured his aunt the boy wouldn't be in the way.
Taking Amanda aside, he told her that he had arranged for Bud to bunk with him, and that she would
stay with Lacy in Bud's gooseneck. He had checked,
and there were no motel vacancies in town. Amanda
flushed with embarrassment over her predicament,
but she had to agree to the arrangement.

Sean's performance that evening was outstanding.
He was introduced as a "South Dakota cowboy," and
the audience loved him. Zack was beside himself
when Sean's times were announced: 9.3 seconds in
calf roping and 4.3 in steer wrestling.

The bull riding scared Amanda, and she was surprised to see Sean's name on the program for that

event. She hadn't seen him ride a bull since Reno. She fought down the urge to go back behind the chutes, to find him and . . . and what? She smiled at her own foolishness.

Sean's bull was a white devil, a monstrous, cross-bred Charolais. The animal fought in the chute, and Sean had to jump back on the railing twice before he could mount the beast. The second time, his foot had been trapped briefly between the bull and the boards, and Sean knew he had twisted his ankle, but he chose to ignore the pain for the moment. He wrapped the braided bull rope around his gloved hand, then nod-ded that he was ready. The gate was flung open, and the bull leaped from the confines of the chute like a canned coil.

This bull refused to perform anything resembling a predictable spin. He reversed his direction with each powerful jump, his body fishtailing in the air like some huge sailfish on a hook. Before the buzzer sounded Sean had lost his balance.

Amanda was unaware that she had come to her feet before anyone else in the stands did. Her instinct told her that something was wrong before Sean landed facedown in the dirt. He lifted himself, dazed, just as the bull's hindquarters swung in his direction, one kicking hoof catching Sean in the chest.

Other people were jumping to their feet, gasping, shouting, but Amanda saw nothing but Sean's still form and the bull turning with the apparent intention of tossing the pesky cowboy over his head. Amanda bounded down the steps and flew along the arena fence, watching as the clown, a skilled bullfighter, successfully drew the bull's attention to himself. Push-ing past all obstacles, Amanda followed the flashing lights of an ambulance. Through the fence she noted that the bull had been distracted and was being chased out of the arena, but Sean had not moved.

A gate was swung open and the ambulance admit-ted into the arena. Amanda followed. Two medics worked quickly to unload a stretcher, and Amanda watched them strap Sean onto it, standing by as helplessly as the dozen or so cowboys around her. Then she saw Sean lift his hand to his face, and she took a few steps toward him, calling his name.

A hand reached from behind her and squeezed her shoulder reassuringly. She glanced back, afraid to take her eyes off Sean for more than a few seconds. "He'll be okay," Bud said, patting her shoulder a couple of times.

She couldn't tell whether Sean's face was injured or just dirty as she watched them load him into the ambulance. "Let me go with him," she said urgently to the driver, who held the door.

"Who are you? Any relation?"

"I'm his wife," she said quickly, feeling that the lie was well worth it if it kept her with him.

"Hop in then."

The medic aboard the ambulance observed that Sean seemed to be coming around as Amanda situated herself at his side. He looked at her through dazed eyes while she took his hand in both of hers, hesitating to touch him for fear of what might be broken. "Mandy?" he said quietly. "Is my shirt torn?"

She glanced down. "No, it's just a little dirty."

"Good. That's good. . . ." He was drifting, his breathing shallow.

"How do you feel, Sean?" Amanda asked anxiously.

"Dizzy . . . a little out of it . . . I'm okay. . . ."

"Do you have any pain? Where does it hurt?"

"Feel kinda numb . . . hard to breathe . . ." Amanda brought his hand to her lips. "Mandy, you look like your puppy just died. I'm okay, really." His free hand clutched at his chest as he talked. Amanda brushed the black shock of hair from his dirt-streaked forehead.

It was a tiny hospital, more like a clinic, but the

doctor seemed to be efficient. Sean winced painfully when the bespectacled man manually tested the left side of his rib cage. "Looks like he hit a rib or two, son. I'm going to ask your wife to wait outside while I get some X rays. I'll have her back in here when the pictures are developed, and we can all admire your skeletal structure together."

When Amanda was readmitted to the emergency room she found Sean sitting on the examining table, looking extremely uncomfortable in a johnny coat. He still had a tight grip on his chest, and he was obviously trying to breathe as little as possible.

"I'm going to keep you overnight anyway, son," the doctor was saying. "You lost consciousness, and you're experiencing some dizziness. I'll want at least twelve hours of observation."

"I don't handle hospitals too well, doc. I'd just as soon be on my way after you tape me up."

A white-uniformed technician glided into the room on crepe soles and handed the X-ray envelope to the doctor, who clipped the film to the viewing screen and flicked the switch. After several moments of study the doctor gave his diagnosis. "I see a fracture here, possibly a hairline fracture here." He pointed to the black-and-white display. Sean touched the matching areas on his chest gingerly as he studied the film himself. "I'll tape you up, but you're staying overnight." The light under the X ray was clicked off.

"Doc . . . I don't . . . we're newlyweds, you see. My wife doesn't know anyone here, and I don't want to leave her alone at the fairgrounds overnight."

"I'll be fine, Sean. You do as the doctor says."

"Your wife can stay here with you. After we get you settled she can take care of the paper work at admitting. You're in for the night, son."

Amanda was advised that several of Sean's friends were waiting in the lobby. The doctor could tape Sean's ribs while she reported on Sean's condition to them. Aunt Arlene and Zack were waiting, along with

Bud and Lacy and several cowboys. Amanda assured them all that Sean wasn't seriously injured, but that he would be remaining overnight for observation. Bud asked her to pass the word that he would look after the horses. Zack begged to see Sean, but Amanda told him that the doctor was bandaging Sean's chest, and tomorrow would be a better time to see him. As she turned to walk back down the hall Amanda caught Lacy's glare.

Sean had given Amanda his wallet to keep for him while he rode, and she took it from her purse to learn the information admitting needed. She found an insurance card, his address, and his birth date, then paused when she saw the pictures of a woman and a young girl, apparently his mother and sister. They were the only pictures he carried.

She thought he was asleep when she approached the hospital bed. Quietly Amanda set a chair close to the bed and sat down. The light that spilled from a wall fixture was restfully dim. The johnny coat was gone, and the white sheet and spread were folded down to Sean's waist. His chest was taped below his armpits for a span of about ten inches. Her eyes traveled to his face and discovered a warm smile and weary eyes. "Hi, Mrs. Brannigan," he greeted her in a soft voice.

"Hi," she said, smiling back. "I had to tell them I was your wife so they'd let me in the ambulance."

"Very resourceful. I like that. If you hadn't been my wife they wouldn't have let you stay, and if you hadn't stayed, I wouldn't have stayed."

"It's a good idea to follow your doctor's orders, no matter how tough you think you are," Amanda commented, rising from the chair.

"Where are you going?" he asked, his eyes following her to the sink.

"Nowhere," she said. She came back to the bed

with a warm, wet washcloth and a towel. "Your face is dirty," she explained, sitting on the edge of the bed.

"I could do this myself," he pointed out.

"I've got nothing to do for the next twelve hours except take care of you, watch out for profound sleepiness . . ."

"You know all the best ways to keep me awake," he said, grinning past the washcloth.

". . . double vision, strange-looking pupils . . ."

"I had a teacher once, said I was a pretty strange-looking . . ."

". . . slurred speech . . ."

"No problem. Speak with straight tongue."

"They didn't mention *absurd* speech. Lift your chin. You look like a little boy with these rings of dirt around your neck." She rinsed the washcloth and returned to sponge his shoulders and the top of his chest. His hand snaked up to flick open a snap on her blouse.

"I won't mind your fussing over me if I can see a little cleavage." Amanda didn't object. "I thought you liberated women had given up bras."

"Not this one. Does it block your view?"

"Sure does. What would it take to bribe you to get rid of it?"

"Ummm . . . just a promise."

"Anything." He grinned.

"That you won't ride bulls anymore."

"Anything but that."

"Okay, I guess I have no business extracting promises from you. But I heard you tell Bud that it was hard on your arm and you ought to give it up. Let me just offer an opinion: I think that was good thinking. You're so good at the other events, Sean. You don't need to risk this kind of thing."

"When I ride the local rodeos, the bulls are mostly for Zack."

"Right now Zack is sick with worry over you."

His hand closed over hers. "What about you?"

She swallowed and looked at their clasped hands. "I was afraid . . . when that animal kicked you . . . and then he started to go after you . . ." She looked into his face, the echo of her fear in her voice. "You were lying so still."

Sean brought her palm to his lips, sending electrical impulses from the point of contact throughout her body. "I'm sorry, Mandy. I didn't plan this, but it's nice to know you care enough to be afraid for me."

"Don't you know by now how much I . . . care for you?" Amanda whispered timidly.

Sean was quiet for a moment. Then he said, "I've heard all the words before, and so have you. I'm not looking for words anymore."

In that case she wouldn't say them. "Are you in much pain now?"

"They gave me some codeine. Breathing isn't too much fun, though, and my ankle is throbbing. Got it caught in the chute."

Amanda pulled the bedding apart at the bottom of the bed to expose his swollen left ankle. She asked a nurse for pillows and a cold pack, which were provided. "I'm sure there'll be no problem, Mrs. Brannigan, but do call us immediately if you are unable to rouse your husband from sleep or if you notice dilation of the pupils. You know, anything unusual," the nurse instructed, and Amanda agreed as the woman bustled out the door.

"Come here, Mrs. Brannigan," Sean teased in a low voice. "Let's see if you can rouse me."

"And if I did, *Mr.* Brannigan, what would you do about it?"

"The pleasure would be worth the pain."

"I'm here to ease your pain, not make it worse."

"Give me your hand, then." She did, and he laid it against the injured side of his chest. "Hold me right there. See if you can keep my ribs from skittering around when I breathe." He winced. "Not too tight. That's good. Now kiss me."

Amanda sat next to him on the bed, brushed his hair back from his forehead and leaned down to touch his mouth with a gentle kiss. "My lips won't break, honey," he whispered, and his hand cupped the back of her head to bring her to him a second time. Their mouths opened against each other this time, their tongues sought one another, and his hand slipped within her bra to cup her breast and taunt her nipple. Beneath her hand Amanda felt Sean struggling to keep the rate of his breathing under control, but a ragged groan finally signaled that the pain had become too much.

"Sean . . . my God . . . just a kiss . . ." Amanda touched her forehead lightly against his collarbone.

"Mmm . . . the pleasure . . . is definitely worth the pain." But the catch in his voice belied his words. "Lie down with me, Mandy."

"Sean, this is a hospital," she protested.

"I want you next to me," he said, taking her hands and drawing her to him. "Don't struggle. You'll make it hurt."

With an indulgent smile she stretched herself out along his side atop the bedspread. "You're certainly using this injury to your advantage."

"A guy's gotta use whatever comes his way."

Something in Amanda's brain nudged her out of sleep. She remembered—she had to be sure Sean wasn't unconscious. Without looking up she shook his shoulder, calling to him. "Sean, can you wake up?"

The response was immediate. "I'm okay, honey. Go back to sleep."

"Shall I ask the nurse for more codeine for you?"

"No."

"But the pain is keeping you awake."

"It's not too bad. I don't want any more of that

stuff. I'll need you to do some driving tomorrow, so try to rest." Offering no further objections, Amanda let herself drift on the cloud of Sean's shoulder, hearing a distant whisper. "Thanks, Mandy."

Despite Amanda's objections Sean insisted on being showered and dressed even before breakfast. He accepted Amanda's help with his clothes, but he referred several times to his aversion to hospitals and his wish to be gone as soon as possible. His entourage of concerned friends arrived in the lobby well before the doctor was there to release him.

Zack asked to go home with Sean, promising to help with the horses, haul bales, clean stalls, anything Sean needed done. Sean was obviously uncomfortable, and Amanda found herself pulling for Zack mentally, but she knew it wasn't her place to say anything. Sean promised Zack a stay at the ranch in the near future. "I'll be out of commission for a few days, Zack; we wouldn't be able to do much together. Tell you what, though. When I see you at Dupree, you show me that you've done some hard practicing and we'll see about mounting you on ol' Medicine Man. How's that sound?" Zack offered a pout and a nod.

Bud had arranged for Gary Reed to pull Sean's trailer, and the horses were already on their way home. "You make this ol' mule take care of himself, Amanda," Bud said. "You oughta lie back and sit a few out now, Sean."

"I'm playing catch-up in the all-around standings as it is," Sean grumbled. "I'll see you in Dupree."

"Are you going to be staying much longer, Amanda?" Lacy asked. It seemed to have become Lacy's favorite question.

"Mandy's agreed to be my guest at the ranch for a few days. Karen and Steve are anxious to meet her," Sean offered, and then the nurse signaled him into the examination room. With Sean's absence, Amanda knew she was in for some awkward moments in the lobby.

Lacy didn't disappoint her. "Bud says you told the ambulance driver you were Johnny's wife."

"It was the first thing that came to my mind. I was afraid he was hurt badly, and I wanted to be with him."

"Yeah, we all did. But you moved pretty damned fast. Doesn't surprise me, though. You've been pretty fast all along—for a *lady,* that is."

Amanda took a deep breath, her blue eyes becoming icy.

"Don't pay no attention to Lacy, Amanda," Bud advised. "She wanted to fuss over Sean herself last night, but they wouldn't let her in. Lacy's a born mother hen. You just pay her no mind and keep that cowboy from getting back in the saddle too soon for his own good."

Sober, Bud definitely had his good points.

Chapter Ten

*B*efore leaving the hospital Amanda was waylaid by a nurse, who pressed two small bottles of pills into her hand. Sean was out of earshot when the nurse explained, "Your husband insists he doesn't need these, but he may change his mind before he gets to Rapid City. By then he'll be looking for a bullet to bite on."

Putting the hospital's fluorescent white lights behind him and stepping into the morning's yellow sun lifted Sean's spirits. "Ah, smell that pure South Dakota air. I swear, hospitals must order their air bottled from some chemical plant."

Amanda invited him to take the trip lying down, but he spent the first thirty miles in the passenger's seat trying to keep her company. His breathing became halting, his discomfort difficult to hide. A second invitation was in order. "Sean, the nurse gave me the prescriptions you refused, one for pain and a sedative. It won't hurt to take something and lie down."

"I don't need any of that stuff," he clipped.

"We don't have to make this trip today if you—"

"I'm okay, Mandy! I'll go lie down for a while. I wanted to keep you company, but not if you're gonna push pills at me."

Amanda drove for another hour, thinking that Sean must have fallen asleep, before she pulled over at a rest area to check on him. She could hear his ragged breathing, but his face startled her. His bronze skin had taken on a sallow tone, and a telling sweat beaded across his angular features. He was clutching the pillow to his chest, one foot on the floor to brace himself against the motion of the vehicle.

"Sean!"

He gave her a wan smile. "I guess I'm . . . not as tough as I thought," he said quietly.

"Oh, darling, what are you trying to do to yourself? You . . ." She soaked a washcloth in cold water, and then she went to him, sitting beside him on the bed. His black hair hung across his forehead in damp tendrils. He had taken off his shirt, and he was bathed in sweat. "You're going to take whatever is in those bottles."

"I don't . . . want to be doped up."

"That's ridiculous. If you could sleep you'd breathe a lot easier, which in itself would lessen the pain. I'm not starting this thing up again until you're sleeping peacefully." Having washed his face with the cool cloth, she fetched the pills and a glass of water. He took them reluctantly.

"There," Amanda said, watching him swallow, "that should get you home." Sitting next to him, she stroked his hair as though he were a sick child. "Why let yourself suffer like that, Sean?"

"When my dad died," he began softly, "well, he'd been in a lot of pain for some time . . . but before he died they had him pumped full of pain-killers. He kept trying to talk to me, but he'd slip in and out of focus. . . . I couldn't understand him. Then he grabbed my arm . . . and it was like he was fighting

for a clear moment . . . and he said . . . he said he
had so many things he wanted to say, but he felt like
he was already dead—couldn't feel anything, couldn't
think, couldn't remember. And then he said, 'Blessed
relief.' . . . It was the drugs, Mandy."

"Did he die right after that?"

"No. He lingered, I don't know, a few hours. That
was the last thing he said to me, though."

"At least he didn't die in agony."

"There were things he needed to say, things I
needed to say . . . but those drugs took the last of his
life away."

"This isn't the same, darling. This will just be
enough to let you rest."

Sean smiled up at her. "I like it when you call me
that."

"And I like it when you call me Mandy," she said,
smiling back. "Do you know that no one else calls me
that?"

"It's *my* name for you. No one else is allowed to use
it." He closed his eyes as she stroked his temples.

"Is it working?" she whispered. "Is the pain going
away?"

He nodded. "It's nice . . . the way you worry over
me."

"I care for you. But then, you've heard all the
words before."

His eyes were still closed, but he managed a smile.
He liked hearing them again. "If we get to Rapid
City . . . in time for the fireworks . . . wake me up
. . . okay?"

Amanda found Rapid City. It was early evening
when she slowed to negotiate an exit, the first demar-
cation of the city. Once she reached the heart of the
small city Amanda noticed that it was pocketed in a
valley, and she decided to head for the high ground
and have a look. A fast-food promise caught her eye,

reminding her that she hadn't eaten since breakfast, and she stopped for a box of chicken.

An imposing brontosaurus beckoned from the top of a hill, and Amanda was lured up the winding road. The nearest approach to the animal seemed to be from the parking lot just below it, where Amanda parked the camper. Now she saw that several prehistoric beasts prowled the hilltop.

"Sean," she called as she smoothed the tousled hair back from his forehead. She was unsure whether to try to wake him from his drugged sleep. His lips were slightly parted, taut with dryness. The powerful, brawny cowboy was vulnerable now, and her woman's heart wanted to gather the whole of him and tuck him safely inside herself, to nurture him with love until he was strong again. Amanda moistened her own lips and then covered his with them, her tongue sweeping all dryness away. His response was the slow, steadily increasing pressure of his mouth against hers. His tongue answered hers, his gentle hand finding the smooth plane of her long back in a familiar caress. Now that he was awake, Amanda plied him with soft kisses and teasing nibbles to his responsive mouth until he groaned, pulling her head down for one more long kiss.

"I'm not dreaming, am I?" Sean asked, his voice gravelly.

"No. Have you been?"

"Yeah. You're a dream come true. Does that sound corny?"

"Um-hmm," she drawled. "Corny, but nice. Could it be that I'm becoming less cynical?"

"I hope so. Where are we?" Amanda leaned back while Sean gingerly eased himself into a sitting position.

"I'm not sure. I've found a lovely spot in a valley that's overrun with dinosaurs."

"Oh. Dinosaur Park. You found Rapid City, then."

"I couldn't resist that brontosaurus, or whatever it is. How do you feel?"

"I'm okay. Hungry."

"That's a good sign. I just got a box of chicken. Where shall we dine?"

"With the dinosaurs."

Sean lay on his back in the grass on the side of the hill, the watchful eyes of the life-sized prehistoric reptilian replicas looming above and behind him in the streaking dusk. He seemed to be enjoying his convalescent role; he had only to open his mouth and chew as Amanda patiently fed him fried chicken and potato salad. "Mmm . . . that bull did me a favor. This is better than Greek Week."

"You don't strike me as the frat type."

"You know, I felt so damned out of place out there when I was a freshman, I actually thought about pledging. When one of the brothers suggested I wear my shorts over my jeans I suggested he go to hell. I wanted friends, but I wasn't that desperate. What about you? I can't see you going in for that stuff, either."

Amanda shook her head. "My college didn't even have sororities."

"So what did you go in for? Mixers? Spring break in Fort Lauderdale?"

"Long hours in the library." Amanda silenced him for a few moments by filling his mouth with food.

"You know, Mandy, you never tell me much about yourself. Have you noticed?" He was trying to talk past a piece of chicken.

"Don't talk with your mouth full."

He ignored that. "I'll tell you a story, and then you'll say something like what you just said, and that's it. I know you have a father and a couple of Morgans, and that you were engaged once."

"And I write about horses."

"And you're one hell of a beautiful woman." He

smiled. "Tell me about the nice family you must come from."

"Mother, father, and Mandy makes three. My father's an investment counselor of some renown—writes a syndicated column. And he's the driving force in our family."

"Sounds ominous. Especially since you say he wouldn't approve of a rodeo cowboy."

"Well, my father has always wanted certain things for me. Frankly, the prospect of a cowboy was never discussed."

"Daddy and I are not going to hit it off, right?"

"Probably not. The only stock that interests him is blue chip."

"What's your mother like?"

"Oh, you'd like my mother, Sean—lovely, shy, compassionate."

"Would she like me?"

"She would *adore* you. You'd get her right away with the country-boy bit."

"Let me talk to her next time you call home."

"I will. I want her to know about you. I want—"

"Am I your declaration of independence, Mandy?"

"What do you mean?"

"Am I your way of telling your parents that from now on Mandy's gonna do as she damn well pleases . . . even with a cowboy?"

He felt the hurt in her silence, and he knew he was wrong.

"What you are to me has nothing to do with anyone else." Amanda spoke evenly, softly. "I'm not playing games with you, Sean. Is that what you think?"

"I guess I just wonder why you avoid talking about yourself and your life back east—unless you want to keep all that separate from this, from me."

"There's very little to tell. My life has been very uneventful until now. My designer facade was the whole show, and without that, there's not much mystique."

"There's one hell of a beautiful woman. But I said that, didn't I?"

"Yes, somewhere back there before you wondered if I was using you to prove my independence."

He watched her put everything back in the chicken box, piece by piece, her movements methodical, as she avoided his eyes, and he felt as though he had slapped her. "I'm sorry," he offered softly. "I guess I'm harboring a little cynic in my pocket. I've been lecturing you about being honest and trusting your feelings, and I'm scared to take my own advice."

"Less than two weeks ago you were anxious to free the woman in me. Now that you've done that, I wonder if you're having second thoughts. Do you want to push me away now? Have I gotten too close for your comfort?"

"No." He took her hand and drew her down beside him, nestling her under his right arm. "No, honey, I don't want to push you away. I want to keep you close to me."

"I'm not a stray dog you found along the road somewhere. You can't just keep me."

"I know that, and I'm trying not to be . . . I'm so damned possessive, Mandy. I'm jealous of your family, just like I was jealous of that preppie reporter."

"That's crazy, Sean. You've filled a place in my life that was empty before. You're trying to create competition for yourself where there isn't any."

"Maybe you have a place for me, Mandy, but my world is—"

The fireworks burst forth over the valley without warning. Showers of red, blue and white light sputtered and popped, filling the starry night with a spectacle of fireflash. Amanda and Sean held each other as they watched, their hearts attuned to the colorful symbol of celebration. After a time they got to their feet, Sean struggling briefly with his nagging pain. Amanda was unsure, when he gathered her shoulders in trembling hands, whether his trembling was from pain or desire.

"I'll show you fireworks," he whispered, and his mouth devoured hers as he pulled her fiercely to him. The hot flow of the emotion that their kiss bore surged between them like a current and left them both breathless and trembling. "Let's go home."

Home was twenty miles from town, two of the twenty made up of gravel road, which caused Sean no small discomfort. Dogs barked when they drove into the yard, and a light came on in the window of the big white house. Then the screened porch was illuminated, and a young woman pushed the door open. Sean and Amanda greeted her at the top of the stairs.

Karen Richter was petite, her strawberry-blond hair cropped short, and she looked like a teenaged tomboy in her tee shirt and blue jeans. She welcomed Amanda, but her concern was for Sean. She chattered as they moved into the kitchen, telling Sean that she had prepared the guest room right after he had called that morning, that Bud Eliot had called earlier to see whether he was back yet, that Gary Reed had dropped the horses off, and that he was lucky he hadn't ended up with more than a cracked rib from what she'd heard.

Karen's husband, Steve, met them in the living room. A midsized man, Steve reached up to put a square, callused hand on Sean's shoulder as he asked if Sean could use a beer. Steve had apparently been in bed when they arrived; he was squinting in the light. Karen asked her husband to bring Amanda's luggage from the camper and deliver it to the guest room upstairs.

Easing himself into a chair in the living room, then sitting stiffly upright, Sean asked for straight whiskey rather than beer. "That's a switch for you, Sean," Karen shouted from the kitchen. "You must be hurt-

ing." There was a pause as she rummaged in the
cupboard, and then she said, "We don't have any hard
stuff except some red-eye left over from Steve's
cousin's wedding."

"That oughta do it," Sean answered. Then, lowering his voice, he said to Amanda, "It's gotta be better
than pills. Couple o' belts of that stuff and I'll sleep
like a baby. Want something?" Amanda shook her
head.

Karen brought Sean's drink and the bottle, which
she set on the table next to him. "Don't overdo it,
now; that stuff can make you howl at the moon." She
turned to Amanda. "Can I get you anything,
Amanda?" Again Amanda declined, noticing the
sound of Steve trudging up the steps, presumably with
her luggage. Karen turned to Sean. "Well, the horses
are all fine, fences are fine, hay's coming along, and
we thought we'd go to Custer for a few days. How
long do you think you'll be home?"

"Few days. I want to get to Dupree."

"You're crazy," Karen sighed, "but we'll be back
by then."

Steve bounded down the steps and joined them in
the living room. His grinning face was slashed by deep
creases at the corners of his mouth. It was an expression that his face fell into easily. "Cracked rib hurts
like hell, don't it?" he said, sitting in a chair near
Sean. "Think I'll join you. Could you get me a glass,
Karen? I cracked one once, too. Feels like you're
breathing fire, huh?" Sean nodded, sipping the liquor
in his glass with a grimace. "That stuff'll kill the pain,
though. Thanks, Karen," Steve said as he took the
glass that was handed him and poured himself a shot.

"What is that stuff?" Amanda asked.

"Something the Germans around here brew up
whenever they drain the oil from their tractors," Sean
explained with a grin. "They can't have a wedding
dance without it."

"What's in it?"

"High-proof grain alcohol. Taste it." She did, and then gagged as it burned its way down her throat.

"My God, Sean!" she gasped. "How can you . . . ?"

"We might as well plan on carrying these two up to bed tonight, Amanda. Come on, let me show you the house," Karen suggested.

It was a fine old farmhouse, one that reminded Amanda of somebody's—anybody's—grandmother's house. Upstairs were four bedrooms, including Sean's room and the room that had been prepared for Amanda. Sean's room looked like Sean, with artifacts, pictures of horses, trophies and books filling the shelves on the walls. There was a large four-poster bed covered with what must have been an heirloom white crocheted bedspread, and hand-braided rugs adorned the polished hardwood floor. The small brick fireplace shared a chimney with the large one downstairs in the living room. Two dormer windows with window seats flanked the huge bed.

After the tour of the rest of the house Karen insisted on making tea, and the two women sat in the big kitchen and listened to the talk in the living room become louder and fraught with increasing laughter. Karen and Amanda, meanwhile, exchanged backgrounds, and Amanda explained how she had met Sean. She wove a convincing story about the article she was writing and what a tremendous help Sean had been, but when she finally detected the knowing look in Karen's eyes, Amanda stopped midsentence. "I guess I'm pretty transparent. The article was the reason I gave myself for going with him, but it's hardly foremost in my mind right now."

Karen smiled sympathetically. "When Sean told me on the phone that he was bringing a lady home with him, I nearly jumped for joy. I could tell you were special by the way he talked. I'm going to tell you something, Amanda, but don't ever tell him I said this. Sean's so good-looking, he's got women falling all over themselves trying to get in bed with him. And he's such a nice guy, well, Sean's everybody's friend. But he won't let anybody get too close, not the women, not the friends—nobody. He's lonely, and I was afraid he was going to let that be a permanent condition."

"I may not be able to change that, Karen. It's too soon to know whether I'm the cure for his loneliness."

"I hope you are. I was beginning to think he might marry Lacy Cook just for convenience."

"Lacy is . . . very important to Sean," Amanda admitted.

"Lacy helped Sean through a rough time, and he'll never forget that. But she's not the woman for him."

"She's in love with him."

"Are you?"

Amanda glanced down at the table. "I'm not sure."

"Yes, you are. Tell him. He needs to know that. Really."

"Mandy! Karen! Bring your sweet selves in here!" It was Sean's voice, his drawl more pronounced than usual. "Mandy! Come on, honey, I'll sing to you," Sean coaxed. He grinned when she walked into the living room. Amanda was wary of his glazed eyes, but she smiled back and put her hand in his as he held it out to her. She sat on the arm of his chair, slipping an arm around his shoulders.

"Well, how's the anesthetic working, cowboy?" Amanda asked.

"I can't feel a thing, hon. I'm ready to give that ol' Charolais another crack at me."

"Poor choice of words, dear. I'm afraid that's exactly what he'd do to you."

"I like 'darling' better. 'Dear' sounds too stuffy, like some stockbroker's ol' lady. I like it when you call me darlin'."

"And I like your house, Sean. It's very—"

"It's very old, very country. I'm just a country boy,

Mandy. I don't even own a three-piece suit or a single share in GM or . . ."

"Are you going to do that country-boy number on me again? We'd better call it a night while we can still walk, *darlin'.*"

Sean grinned up at her. "I might have some trouble walkin', but you're gonna prance up those stairs just as pretty as always." He lifted his glass in salute.

"Please, no more, Sean. I'm afraid you'll get sick. You can't afford to start retching with that fractured rib."

"Yeah, you're right. That'd be pretty stupid. But don't worry, honey, I won't get sick." He turned to Steve. "Mandy's always worryin' over me. Is that what it's like to have a wife? Is Karen always worryin' over you, Steve?"

"Hell, yes, always worryin'. Just like a mother hen. Always worryin'. Women have to worry."

"You oughta give Karen a baby. She needs a baby to worry over," Sean judged with overblown seriousness.

"Already did that, Sean. That's our big news. Karen's pregnant," Steve announced.

"Great!" Sean beamed. "That's great news! Did you hear that, honey? They're gonna have a baby."

"And you're going to be a godfather, Sean," Karen promised.

"Hey, now that's something to celebrate," Sean declared, lifting his glass again. "And my godchild's gonna have the best roping horse in South Dakota. Birthday present from an all-around champion godfather."

"You're gonna do it, too, Sean. Travis Steele's gonna be eatin' your dust." Steve punctuated his prediction by slamming a meaty fist on the arm of his chair.

"I can't afford to be laid up now, though. Steele's hitting two or three rodeos a weekend, buzzing around in that Piper Cub. Wins pretty consistently in saddle bronc and bareback. Picks up some cash in calf roping once in a while."

"How do you get a horse in a Piper Cub?" Amanda wondered.

"You don't, hon. You use somebody else's horse."

"So why don't you do that?" she asked.

"Win or lose, I ride my own stock. That's part of the game for me. I raise 'em, train 'em, ride 'em myself."

"And can you win enough that way to beat Travis Steele?"

"Course I can," Sean assured her with a squeeze of her waist.

"Damn right he can," Steve echoed.

"But I can't sit out very long with this." Sean spread a hand over his chest.

"Then you'd better get some rest now that you've got a little pain-killer under your trophy buckle," Amanda suggested.

"Right," Sean agreed, rising carefully from the chair and finding a precarious balance on feet that didn't quite feel like his own. "G'night, you guys. Congratulations on the baby."

Sean made it up the stairs without mishap, but he knew he'd overdone it, and he never liked the hazy feeling that gave him. "Sorry, Mandy," he mumbled. "I'm sorry. I didn't mean to get drunk."

"It's a relief to know you're not hurting," she said, turning a lamp on in his room.

"You've been so good to me. So damn good to me," he mumbled. "Mandy, would you ever . . . be willing . . . to have my baby?"

"Certainly," she said quietly, unsnapping his shirt and thinking that he'd never remember this in the morning. "If we were married I would."

"Well, of course. I meant if we were married." She sat him in a chair and began working on his boots. He grinned. "Are you gonna undress me *completely*, Mandy?"

"Not quite."

"Mandy . . . what if I asked you to marry me? I mean, I'm not askin', not right now . . . but if I were to ask you, what would you say?"

"That's not fair, Sean," Amanda protested, laughing. "You're asking me for the answer to a question you're not asking."

"Yeah, but what if I did ask you? What would you say?"

"I guess you'll just have to ask to find out."

"Come on, Mandy, give me a hint."

"I've given you a lot more than a hint, Sean Brannigan. Now stand up so I can take your jeans off."

"There's that direct approach again. I'm an invalid, honey; you'll have to help me up." He enjoyed letting her strip him down to his shorts, luxuriated in being waited on as she turned down the bed for him. He favored his left side when he pushed himself out of the chair and lowered himself into the big bed. "I don't suppose you'd want to stay with me tonight."

"I suppose I'd want to, but I also suppose I'd better not. I hope you sleep well, Sean. You need to rest."

"Sean darlin'?"

"Yes . . . Sean darling. Sleep well."

"You, too, Mandy. Have pleasant dreams . . . about me . . . and you . . . and no more damn . . . bulls. . . ."

Chapter Eleven

$\mathscr{F}$or two nights and most of two days Sean did little but sleep. Karen and Steve left for their trip, leaving Amanda free to work. She finished typing the wild-horse series, which it seemed she had started a lifetime ago. Then she toyed with some of the notes she'd taken on rodeo, shaping the scenes and character sketches that stood out in her mind.

"How's it coming?" Amanda turned from the type-writer, startled, as Sean's voice ruffled the stillness in the room.

"Fine." She smiled, pushing her chair back. "You look as though you're feeling much better."

"I don't know which was worse, the cracked rib or the red-eye headache. Either way, I guess I asked for it."

"Supper should be ready pretty soon." She went to him, spreading her hands over his chest. "And after we eat, let's go for a walk. Do you feel up to that?"

"Definitely. The patient is definitely ambulatory."

It was a long, leisurely walk, Sean holding her hand

as he often did when they were alone. They followed the fenceline of the broodmare pasture. Sean pointed out the most promising colts, talking about bloodlines and performance records, and Amanda listened with interest, asking astute questions.

"Well, what do you think of the place?" he asked finally, as though he were almost afraid of her answer.

"I think I like these Quarter Horses of yours. Of course, I'm not familiar with their bloodlines, but you've obviously developed a successful breeding program. I'd like to get my hands on that big blood-sorrel mare you've got in the corral. She'd make a wonderful hunter."

"You can ride her if you like. She's just a four-year-old, but she's saddle broke. I thought about training her for cutting, but that's not right for her. She's a pleasure horse." They walked quietly for a few minutes before Sean said, "You still haven't told me what you think of the place."

"I like it," she said, as though she were trying to convince herself. "It smells so good here, with the pine trees and the clean air. And it's nice and quiet—peaceful."

"So's a graveyard."

"I haven't always lived in Boston, Sean. I appreciate quiet beauty like this."

"But you feel a little isolated."

"I don't feel that at all. It's not that far to Rapid City, which seems to be a very nice town. With the hectic pace you set for yourself, this must be a nice place to come home to."

"Yeah, I really like this place. One of these days I'll settle down and run it myself."

"This must've been a fun place to grow up in—a barefoot boy's paradise," Amanda said, imagining a young Sean, looking much like Zack, playing on a stack of bales by the barn.

"It was fun—and work. Chores every morning before school and every evening after school. My

grandparents lived with us until . . . my grandfather
died when I was twelve, Grandma a year later. They
belonged together, those two, and she didn't stay
around long after he was gone. They're buried over
there, along with my parents and Shelley, my sister
. . . and my father's brother, who was killed in World
War II." Amanda's eyes followed his gesture to a
grove of pines, where several stone markers were
visible.

"Let's go back to the house and sit in that wonderful porch swing," Amanda suggested. "We'll pretend
you're courting me, and we'll be sixteen and sip
lemonade and listen to the crickets." The mood could
stand a lift, she thought.

"Hell, I'd *never* go back to being sixteen again. I
was too awkward, always trying to figure out how to
get my hands inside some girl's blouse." He chuckled,
remembering.

"I'm sure you had plenty of opportunities."

"Long on opportunity, short on dexterity. Must've
been a woman who invented those crazy little hooks."

With each lazy motion, the porch swing creaked its
accompaniment to the crickets. Amanda was snuggled
under Sean's arm, and neither had spoken for some
moments as they rocked the old porch swing and watched
the darkening sky through the porch screen.

"I wasn't a cheerleader, you know. I'll bet you only
went out with cheerleaders," Amanda commented, as
though what she said were connected with something.

"Cheerleaders, barrel racers and carhops were my
favorites. What did you do in school?"

"I was a debater."

"Ah, a brain. The proverbial good girl, right? 'A
good girl goes out on a date, goes home and goes to
bed. A *nice* girl . . . ,'" he recited.

"Right. You'd never have asked me for a date."

"On the contrary, I'd have taken you to the prom. I
always took a girl like you to the prom."

"Why?"

"Nobody wanted to go to the *prom* with some chick who'd been hashed over a hundred times in the locker room. Didn't your mother always take pictures of you and your date in front of the fireplace before you went to the prom?"

"Of course. Actually, my father did."

"There, you see? Who'd want to get all dressed up and have his picture taken with some girl who'd been scored on more times than home plate? On the other hand, beautiful, smart, hardly touchable Amanda Caron would be worthy of the eight-dollar orchid, and a guy wouldn't mind having his picture pasted in her mother's scrapbook."

"My, my. I had no idea there was such meticulous thought given to the jock's double standard," Amanda observed dryly.

"You'd have gone to the prom with me, no question."

"Yes," she agreed. "I'd have told my girlfriends you were probably only after *one thing* but I knew I could handle you."

"And you would have, too. Especially if you had tricky hooks." They laughed, enjoying the mental image of their former adolescent selves steaming Sean's car windows.

"What do you think of the house?" he asked later.

"I think it has a lot of character."

"I've never done anything to it. The furniture has been the same, sitting in the same places since my mother died. A lot of it was my grandmother's. It's a haunted house, I guess. I should do something with it . . . remodel."

"You could do a lot with a house like this, but don't change too much and spoil its charm."

"Charm. That's an interesting choice. This is what's left of the Brannigans—this old house and me."

"Both charming. Must be the Irish." Amanda ran a lazy finger along the open vee of his shirt.

"Irish charm gets 'em every time." He smiled slyly as he shifted away from her slightly, lifting her chin with a hand that was bound for the back of her neck. "But it's the Sioux that keeps 'em coming back." He cut off her groan of disbelief with a demanding kiss, his tongue plunging past her lips to find hers waiting to caress it. Their heartbeats began racing instantaneously, their mouths moving with each other, their bodies moving closer. Amanda moaned softly when she felt his tongue flickering just below her earlobe. She felt the release of two snaps on her blouse, knew that her clothing was being pushed off one shoulder, but then she began to lose touch with reality and knew only the sensual touch of his wet mouth trailing a path of hungry kisses to the quivering breast he had uncovered.

His groan penetrated the mist of total sensation, and she managed to ask him whether his chest hurt him. "Not as much as I ache where you're touching me," he answered, and she realized where her hand had fallen. "Let's go upstairs, honey," he whispered. He slipped her blouse over her shoulder, and they stood, Amanda leaning heavily against him. He wished he could sweep her into his arms and carry her up the stairs. Instead he held her against his healthier side and led her to his room.

Evening light poured through the tall windows, bathing the room in a soft glow. They made an unspoken agreement to undress, and each watched the other peel away clothes. Naked, she went to him and slid her arms around him, fingering the bandage around his chest. "Oh, Sean, how can we do this now? Heavy breathing isn't good for a man in your delicate condition."

"It's all right, Mandy . . . I can hardly . . . I want you so bad I can't stop now." He rained kisses over her face between phrases, pulling her against the full length of him. He whispered his desire for her, seating himself on the edge of the bed and drawing her to stand between his legs. His mouth teased her breasts, drawing her nipples to an excruciating tautness, while his hand stroked her long back and her soft, round bottom. She became weak, leaning heavily on his shoulders for support, her fingers clutching at his hair. He lay her back on the bed and persisted in his teasing, stroking the plane of her abdomen, nibbling at her breasts until she felt a hot rush of molten need swirl in the pit of her stomach.

"Please, Sean," she whispered urgently.

"I am pleasing, honey. I can tell . . ." His voice was hoarse with his own desire, and he stifled her pleasured moan with a kiss before he whispered, "You'll have to make love to me this time. Will you do that for me, Mandy?"

"Yes, darling . . . just show me . . . what to . . ."

"No, you show me." He chuckled wickedly, lying on his back beside her. He moved her over him, guiding her where he wanted her. "Most ladies ride astride nowadays," he whispered. "Now show me, sweetheart. We'll judge our own performance." He slipped himself inside her, and his presence there electrified her. He told her how to move with him, but she needed no coaxing. They soared together with a quickening rhythm.

Drained utterly, they lay in each other's arms, Amanda feeling too languid to move and too awed by the beauty of his face to close her eyes. They watched one another, recognizing the joy reflected in each other's faces. Sean smiled as he stroked her hair. "Tell me how you feel, pretty lady," he whispered.

"I feel like a woman . . . who's very much in love with you." His hand froze for a second, and neither of them breathed. Then he traced her cheekbone with his thumb. "Do you believe me?" she asked shyly. His thumb followed the smooth curve of her jawline. "I know you've heard the words before, but that had nothing to do with us. I want to tell you how I feel, and it feels good saying the words. I love you, Sean."

He moved slowly, as though she were fragile and precious, carefully pulling her against him. His lips brushed her forehead, and then he spoke softly, slowly, as if he were working things out in his mind. "I don't know whether you belong with me, Mandy, but right now we sure as hell belong to each other."

It wasn't what she wanted to hear. "All that exertion didn't make your chest worse, did it?"

"No." He chuckled. "You were the one exerting yourself. I'd give you a blue ribbon if I knew where to pin it."

"And you have definitely earned . . . Reserve Champion."

"Reserve!"

"I'll let you try for a Grand—later. Where's your guitar?"

"There's one in the closet. You want a music lesson?"

"You promised to sing to me the other night."

"I was drunk the other night."

"But you do remember telling me you'd sing for me. I want to be serenaded. Wouldn't that be romantic?"

"You want romantic? I'll show you romantic. Shall I stand under the window? Maybe we could do a balcony scene."

"I wouldn't want you to fall and crack another rib."

He was pulling on his jeans. "I don't know what happened to that sophisticated lady I met in Reno. She would never have gone for this."

"She was a drag until she fell in love," Amanda said quietly as he left the room.

The reflection of the flames flickered in Amanda's blue eyes as she tucked her legs under the big bathrobe in which Sean had wrapped her before he built the fire in the bedroom fireplace. Perched at the foot of the huge old bed, she watched Sean uncork a bottle of shimmering rosé that he had bought to celebrate the Fourth.

"This is what I call romantic," Amanda observed, accepting the glass of wine he'd poured for her. "A fire in July. Does it usually get this cool here at night?"

Sean set his glass down after sipping at it briefly and cradled the guitar in his lap. "Um-hmm. Before you tell me what you want me to sing, just remember: If you want to call the tunes, you're gonna have to pay the piper." Her stomach tumbled around a bit when he winked at her.

"Sing my song." She watched Sean's long fingers pluck skillfully at the strings. When she turned her attention to his face she saw his eyes brighten at the sight of the firelight in hers. He sang of love for his lady, and his eyes told her that he sang from the heart. Without pausing in between he sang several love songs as he watched the red-gold firelight glow in Amanda's chestnut hair.

"You have a wonderful voice," Amanda said, watching Sean carry the wine glass to his lips. "In my wildest fantasy I see myself singing onstage. Unfortunately, I can't sing a note."

"You should've heard my dad sing. He had me singing with him all the time when I was a kid. Dad dreamed a lot, too, of being a singer, a musician, a football player, bronc rider—you name it. Dad was a dreamer."

"I pictured your father as a very practical man. You said he wanted you to be a veterinarian."

"He wanted me to be *educated*. He said a man had to have an education to be somebody. Dad was a rancher by default. The ranch was given to him. He dreamed life; he didn't live it. My grandfather built the place up, and when Dad took over, it was Mom who ran it. She was a hell of a rancher, too. She knew the birth and weaning weights of every calf any cow on the place ever raised."

"Didn't that make your father feel rather useless?"

"Mom was very skillful at making Dad look good. 'Kevin has decided to crossbreed this year. Kevin thinks we should feed the heifers out.' And he wasn't a total washout. He had some interest in it. He was good with horses, got us started with Quarter Horses. But after Mom died he lost interest even in that."

"And now you're left with the ranch. Is it what you want?"

"Yeah, but I'm not gonna sit around here dreaming about all the other things I could've done."

"Like being world champion all-around cowboy?"

"I've got Dad's horse fever and his thirst for glory, too, I guess. But the excitement's in the doing, not the dreaming. The ranch is here when I'm ready for it."

"You're lucky to have Steve and Karen here."

"They're making a good living. They'll be looking for a place of their own one of these days, what with the baby coming now."

"Do you envy them?" Amanda asked, holding her glass out for more wine.

"Sure. I want what they have . . . someday. What about you? You envy them?"

"Yes. As you say, someday." She glanced away from his eyes.

They watched the fire and sipped wine, talking of things past and present, dreaming of the future, but each time they came to a point at which discussion of a possible future together seemed imminent, they backed away quietly. When Sean picked up his guitar and played, Amanda took the lyric promise to heart. In the soft glow of the dying firelight they made slow love, taking time for touches and whispers, building a need in one another that both hoped would endure beyond the night's satisfaction.

"I'm not sure when I'll be home. Mother, I've met someone."

"Your father seems to think you've taken up with a

cowboy. He's beside himself with worry," Amanda's mother said.

"Is he there?"

"No. You should have called him at the office this time of morning."

"I wanted to talk with you. I want to tell you about Sean. I'm in love with him, and I've never felt so good about anything in my whole life."

"You haven't known him very long, Amanda. Aren't you being a bit hasty?"

"Mother," Amanda sighed, "please forget about what Daddy will say and just be happy for me."

"What's this cowboy's name, Amanda?"

"Sean Brannigan. Oh, Mama, you'd like him, I know you would. He's a kind and gentle man, and he makes me feel . . . like a woman. That sounds corny, doesn't it?"

"You haven't called me that for a long time, Amanda: Mama." The voice at the other end of the line sounded wistful. "You do sound happy . . . for a change."

"I am," Amanda laughed. "I am happy, and I have changed."

"Why don't you bring him home to meet us?"

"I don't think he's ready for that. And I'm sure Daddy's not ready for it. I'm certainly not ready for them to clash." Amanda heard the back door and knew that Sean was back from the barn. She was using the kitchen phone, and she mouthed, "My mother," when he crossed the linoleum floor in her direction.

"Hi, Mother!" he shouted, grinning.

"That was Sean," Amanda offered with a laugh. "I'll let him introduce himself properly." Handing him the receiver, she said, "Here, wise guy."

Amanda listened anxiously to Sean's end of the conversation. "Hello, Mrs. Caron, I'm Sean Brannigan. . . . Your daughter and I have become very good friends, and she's agreed to be my guest here at the ranch for a few days . . . *my* ranch.

. . . Yes, near Rapid City. . . . Well, she's told me a lot about you, too, and I'm sure I'd enjoy meeting you. . . . Don't you worry about her, now. I'll take very good care of her. . . . Nice talking to you, too." Sean grinned as he returned the receiver to its cradle. "I have a way with mothers."

"I told her all about you."

"So she said."

"She's happy for me," Amanda said with a smile.

He looked surprised. "You mean you told her . . . everything?"

"Not the intimate details, silly. I told her I'm in love with you."

"How soon do you think Daddy can get here with the shotgun?"

"We're both consenting adults, right?"

"Yeah, right. And your mom sounds like a real nice lady. But I suspect that when she tells your dad about your cowboy, he'll be very anxious to blow my head off."

"Oh, Sean, he's not *that* bad. We've been close, probably too close, and he assumes I want what he wants."

"Why don't you set him straight?"

"My father is the epitome of straight, and he's also set."

"I guess you'll have to handle that situation in your own way, sweetheart."

They were both startled by the rude sound of a blasting horn. "I didn't hear anyone drive up," Sean said as he headed for the back door. "Probably that idiot Eliot," he said to Amanda, and then, to whoever was disturbing the peace, "You can quit laying on the horn. I hear you."

Amanda followed Sean out the back door. The horn blew steadily, insistently, but there was no visitor. Sean lifted the hood of the camper, and Amanda stood back while he perused the engine for some way to shut off the irritating noise. After a few minutes the sound stopped as unexpectedly as it had begun.

"How did you fix it?" Amanda asked, stepping closer as he threw the hood down impatiently.

"I didn't. I don't know a thing about mechanics. It just stopped."

"That's weird." Amanda stared at the camper. "Must be haunted," she added with a shrug.

Sean turned his eyes on her almost reproachfully. "What makes you say that?" he clipped.

"I was just kidding." His tone caught her by surprise, but he didn't comment further as he looked thoughtfully back at the camper. "What is it, Sean?"

"It's nothing," he said, relaxing a bit. "I guess it's my superstitious nature or something. I had a strange dream last night, and it's kinda been nagging at me ever since I got up this morning."

"What kind of a dream?"

"It was about Zack. He was running in a field, and all of a sudden he fell off the edge, rolled down a rocky embankment. It was one of those dreams . . . you see everything happening, but you can't do anything. So . . . real."

Amanda put her hand on Sean's arm. "It was only a dream."

"Yeah. As I said, I have a superstitious nature. Indians put a lot of stock in dreams, and I . . . have a lot of dreams."

"Sometimes it's hard to get them off your mind the next day when they're realistic like that."

"Let's forget about it, then," he said, dismissing the matter. "This thing's been on the road too long. Time to put it in the shop for a physical." He reached for her hand and flashed a smile, offering an instantaneous mood change. "Follow me, lady. I've got a birthday present for you."

"It isn't my birthday." She fell into step beside him.

"That makes it the best kind of birthday present."

The blood-sorrel mare stood saddled and tied to the

corral. "Take her out and see how you like her," Sean
said, gesturing toward the horse.

"The mare?" Amanda didn't see a present anywhere.

"Her name is Lexie. She's a daughter of Great
Alex, a champion cutting horse, out of one of my best
mares. If you like her, she's yours."

"Sean, you can't just give me a horse!"

"I can give you anything I damn well please. It's my
horse."

"But I can't take it. How could I?"

"You can ship her back east. She's well worth the
effort. Or I can keep her for you . . . if you decide to
stay around awhile. In any case I want you to have
her . . . if you like her."

"Like her!" Amanda approached the big mare,
incredulous. "Sean, she's magnificent! And you're
generous to a fault, my darling. I just can't—"

"Ride her, woman!" Sean roared with a grin.

Sean leaned on the gate he had just closed after
letting Amanda and the mare into the yellow-green
pasture. Watching her put the horse through its
paces—walk, trot, canter, hand gallop—made him
feel warm inside. He loved her; he knew that, and he
wanted to shout it to the world, but he couldn't bring
himself to say it quietly to her. She knew how he felt.
She *must* know. He'd shown her over and over again.
He wanted to keep her with him, but the gift wasn't
just a ploy. His horses were part of him, something of
himself that he could give her without risking . . .
whatever he was afraid to risk. The horse would show
well, and maybe he could persuade her to go to the
big stock shows . . . if she'd stay. And weren't they a
pair, the woman and the blood-red horse? The effect
of Amanda's chestnut hair glinting like fire in the
sunlight was repeated in the mare's flowing tail, which
Sean had carefully combed an hour beforehand.

Amanda's body moved sensually with the rhythms

of the horse's gaits, and Sean remembered the pleasure of having her body move that way with his the night before. He thought of her now as his woman, and he watched her ride with a possessive pride in her smooth proficiency.

"She changes leads as smooth as butter, and her gaits are easy and fluid," Amanda assessed. "I've won some pleasure classes, Sean, but never have I ridden a more graceful animal." She dismounted and walked beside him, the mare following like an old friend.

"I knew you'd like her. Like you, she was born for pleasure." His ever-endearing wink brought a girlish blush to her cheeks.

"You can't mean to give her to me, though."

"For God's sake, Mandy, can't you accept gracefully? I want you to have a real horse so you won't have to fool around with those prissy Morgans."

"Oh, Sean, you know a Morgan is a good horse," she objected, clipping him on the shoulder with a dainty fist. "But I've never had a horse of my own. The Morgans are Daddy's."

"Ha-ha, Daddy! I'm one up on you. I gave Mandy her first horse," Sean crowed, squeezing Amanda's shoulders with genuine glee.

They were making spaghetti when the phone rang. Sean answered it, predicting that it would be Amanda's father threatening to have his head on a platter. His back was to her when he answered, and then he stretched the cord into the dining room. She tried not to listen, although his end of the conversation was quiet and monosyllabic. Diligently she rinsed the pasta, stirred the sauce and told herself that the call was obviously private.

Sean hung up and disappeared into the living room before Amanda had a chance to look up from her chores. With an ominous feeling that she shouldn't disturb him, Amanda waited. Long moments of si-

lence passed before Sean appeared again in the doorway. His face was drawn, his lips chalky, as though he
were in terrible pain again.

"It's Zack," he said almost inaudibly. "He's dead."

"Oh, my God," Amanda whispered.

Sean walked briskly through the kitchen, avoiding
her eyes, but he paused at the back door. "I'll be back
in a little while, Mandy," he said without turning
around. Then he was gone.

Amanda laid a fire in the living room fireplace,
wanting to drive away every possibility of chill. It was
dark when she heard the back door open and close
again. She went to the kitchen, but when she saw him,
she couldn't speak. Her unshakable cowboy was
heartbroken. She went to him and put her arms
around him without a word.

They sat together on the couch watching the fire, his
arm around her shoulders, and she held his hand in
both of hers. She told herself not to ask, to let him tell
her when he was ready. After a long silence he spoke
quietly, but with little emotion. "I told him to do
some hard practicing. He did. He got on a green-
broke horse and tried to swing a rope on him. The
horse bolted. I don't know why he was wearing tennis
shoes. He got hung up in the stirrup, and they don't
know how far the horse dragged him. He was dead
when they found him." Amanda watched the whole
story in her mind's eye. When he finished she turned
her face to Sean's chest and wept. "I knew something
was wrong," Sean mumbled.

Sean said little that night. He made several phone
calls, arranged for someone to feed the stock and got
things in order. Then, without a word, he went to bed.
Amanda followed after seeing to the fireplace and
cleaning up the kitchen. She got ready for bed,
wondering whether Sean meant to shut her out and
bottle up his pain. Standing in the doorway of his
room, she asked quietly, "Do you want to be by
yourself tonight, Sean?"

"No."

She undressed and slipped under the covers, offering him her warmth. She reached out to him, but there was no response as he lay on his back, studying the ceiling. So she lay beside him, tracing the pattern of muscle on his chest with a delicate hand. He finally turned to her, laying his face against her breast, whispering her name.

"I'm here, Sean," she answered. "I know how much you hurt. Don't bottle it up inside."

"Just hold on to me, Mandy. I don't want to be alone. Just hold me."

Sean suggested that Amanda stay at the ranch and wait for him, but she insisted on attending the funeral. He accepted her decision wordlessly as they prepared the camper for the trip. She wondered about taking the cumbersome vehicle, but she asked no questions as she cut the tape from his chest and wrapped him tightly with an elasticized bandage.

Amanda offered to drive, but Sean shook his head and took the seat behind the wheel. He persisted in his silence as they traveled eastward, and Amanda watched as he smoked several cigarettes. She had seen him smoke only once before, when he had been angry with her.

The house could have been any tract house in any suburb, but here on this South Dakota reservation it sat by itself, about a mile off the paved road, in the middle of nowhere. There was another small, run-down house sitting along the rutted dirt road leading to the bigger house, and Sean told her that his aunt's family had lived in the little three-room house before a government project provided the newer home. A log rail corral stood in the back, a wire chicken coop on one side. A squaw cooler, a structure of poles topped with leafy willow branches, shaded several people who lounged on folding chairs beneath the dry, rustling leaves.

There was no real lawn surrounding the house. The yard blended into the wild prairie grass that stretched across the rolling plains. Several mongrel dogs greeted the camper as Sean parked it among the dozen vehicles that were already there. As he shut off the engine he drew a deep breath, then released it slowly, his eyes fixed on the house. Almost convulsively he reached for the cigarettes on the dash, shook one out, popped it into his mouth and struck a match. As he drew deeply on the smoke Amanda reached over and put her hand on his thigh, needing to find a way to comfort him.

Sean covered her hand with his, but his eyes were on the house as he exhaled quickly and brought the cigarette to his lips again. Smoke drifted from his mouth as he said, "This will go on through the night. When you've had enough I want you to feel free to come out here and rest, Mandy."

"I'll be fine. Don't worry about me."

The house was packed with people. Sean held Amanda's hand, releasing her only to embrace his aunt, who cried when he took her in his arms. Amanda stood aside and watched him, hoping that now he could let go. His eyes glistened, but he held back the relief that could come from tears, muttering over his aunt's head, "I should have taken him to the ranch with me. He wanted to come, and I put him off. I told him to practice. . . . I told him to . . . oh, my God . . . I'm so sorry." His voice trembled only slightly as he spoke.

Arlene grasped Sean's shoulders and shook him once. "I was afraid you'd feel this way, and you must not. You will not blame yourself for this." Sean stared at her, not responding, and she shook his shoulders again. "Do you hear me, son? This is not your fault," she whispered.

He nodded slowly, rasping, "I hear you."

"I have said I should have been watching more closely. Sam blames himself for letting him use the horse. Sam told him to stay in the corral. It is just something that happened, son. We have to find a way to accept it."

Sean closed his eyes and nodded again. "He called for help," Sean said. "I had a dream the other night . . . a warning, and I ignored it. But yesterday he called out to me for help. I knew something was wrong, but I didn't know what. . . ." He sighed, and the woman nodded her understanding. Amanda wondered at this exchange, this tacit acknowledgment of a premonition, which she still found hard to recognize as more than a strange coincidence.

"I see you brought your pretty girlfriend with you," Arlene said, dabbing at her eyes with a wad of tissue and turning to Amanda.

Sean reached for Amanda's hand. "Amanda wanted to come," he said, drawing her to his side.

"Zack and I became friends in a short time, and I feel very sad about his death. I think he and I understood each other because . . . because we both loved the same man."

"Thank you for coming." Arlene smiled sadly and reached for Amanda, who embraced the small woman. "Since his mother died, Sean is my boy, too. And he has needed someone like you for a long time. I worried about what this would do to him." Arlene pulled back and looked steadily into Amanda's face. "Don't let him be alone too much."

The small coffin stood open in the living room, which was packed with folding chairs and people. "Do you want to see him?" Arlene asked Sean. Amanda glanced up, waiting for his response, and realized that his eyes were pointedly avoiding the little box. "Come," Arlene was saying, "we'll go together."

Amanda's hand was suddenly crushed under the pressure of Sean's. "No," he said hoarsely. "No, I . . . not yet."

Arlene patted Sean's arm, nodding her understanding of the fear lurking in his eyes. "Go speak to your grandmother," she suggested, gesturing toward the dining area.

Sean introduced Amanda to a small, square-shaped Indian woman, whose proffered handshake seemed to Amanda to be less than hearty. He told the older woman where Amanda was from, what she did, and finally that she was his "girl." The woman peered up at Amanda through heavily lidded eyes, nodding solemnly at each bit of information. Amanda felt as though she were being sized up for something, but she was unsure what it was.

With the intention of gaining a friendlier look from this, the family matriarch, Amanda asked if she might be of some help in the kitchen. Her face softening, Sean's grandmother nodded and led Amanda past the counter separating the dining area from the kitchen. Women and girls stood hip to hip there, and Amanda was set to work washing dishes as the hips gladly shifted to make room for her.

Conversation was subdued, but Amanda became acquainted with Sean's nieces, cousins and aunts as she washed an endless succession of kettles and cups. It had been at least an hour since she had seen Sean, when he appeared at the other side of the counter and motioned her to him. "We're going to the graveyard now to get started on the grave."

"Get started?"

"Digging the grave. We bury our dead ourselves. I'll be gone a few hours. Do you mind?"

"Of course not. I'm fine."

He squeezed her upper arm. "I like the way you pitched right in." She had his attention for a moment, and then the faraway look crept over his face again. He dropped his hand and detached his mind at the same moment, moving mechanically toward the door.

Several hours and many pounds of potato salad later, the men returned from their chore at the cemetery. They ate, smoked, and talked in hushed voices. The air in the house was thick with smoke and the slightly rancid odor of hot lard, in which square pieces of raised dough were deep-fat fried to produce frybread. Amanda felt as though she were watching a movie, but she busied herself, trying to deemphasize her constant awareness of the small corpse that lay so close by.

During the evening prayer service Sean disappeared, but later, when several guitars were produced, he returned and was invited to sing hymns with four others. Then someone asked Sean for a solo of "Amazing Grace," which he did in a clear, steady voice, the edge of which betrayed raw sadness.

This time Amanda followed Sean when he left the house, hurrying to catch up to him as he wended his way among the parked cars. He turned when he heard the sound of her footsteps and took her under his arm when she came to him. Beneath the bower of the squaw cooler Sean lit another cigarette, drew deeply and ejected a stream of smoke into the night. The strains of another hymn carried an even lonelier feeling out there in the darkness. "I'm sorry I brought you here, Mandy."

"Why?"

"Because it's unfair to subject you to this."

"Are you holding back because of me, Sean? Are you trying not to let me see how heartbroken you feel?" He brought the cigarette to his lips in a cupped hand, dragging the life out of it. "I'm here for you, Sean. Let me help you. Talk to me."

"He's dead. There's nothing else to say."

"You've been very careful not to look at Zack," she said gently.

"That's not Zack," he protested. "Zack's gone."

"Why can't you look at him?"

"I know what death looks like. I've seen a lot of it."

"There's no shame in grief. You need to face it so you can deal with your loss."

"The senseless loss of a ten-year-old boy's life? Don't tell me about grief, Mandy. I don't need any advice on dealing with death. I'll deal with it my way." He had dropped a curtain around himself.

She touched his jawline delicately. "How is your chest?"

Sean dropped the cigarette and ground it out beneath his boot. Then he reached for her, gathering her into his arms. "I'm fine, sweetheart, but you're tired, and I'm tucking you in."

"And yourself with me?" She snuggled against his chest.

"Maybe later."

Zack was buried atop a windswept hill in a desolate prairie graveyard. There was no clipped lawn, and the only shrubbery was scrub pine. The scattered white crosses and small stones were all but hidden by the same tall grass that blanketed the surrounding prairie.

Amanda stood beside Sean at the graveside, only half listening to the words of the funeral service. In her mind she saw the image of the man who stood beside her as he had been an hour before, his broad shoulders sagging, standing beside the dead child's casket. She hadn't seen Sean's face, but she had watched his hands clench and unclench as he stood there, and then the fingers of both hands had stretched steadily toward the dead boy's smooth cheeks. A low, ragged groan tore at Amanda's heart. Sean's warm hands had met the cold shock of reality. But when he had turned from the casket there had been no tears in his eyes, nothing to reflect the anguish of the moment that had passed.

Amanda's reverie was interrupted by another anguished sound, and, startled, she glanced about to find the source of the plaintive, high-pitched keening. It was the universal wail of a mother's grief—timeless, bottomless, inconsolable. Arlene's mournful tremolo carried the jagged edge of shattered glass, and it split the high-plains wind with ancient maternal sorrow.

Chapter Twelve

$\mathcal{I}$f the camper had had wings Sean would have flown it back to the ranch.

Once they got back Sean's brooding silence pervaded the atmosphere through supper, and afterward it accompanied them to the porch, where they sat together and watched the night fall. They made token conversation about leaving for Dupree in another day, about going for a ride the next morning, and about the fact that Sean's injury wasn't bothering him much, but each exchange was brief, broken by intervals of loaded silence.

Unexpectedly Sean suggested, "Let's go into town for a while. Have a drink, listen to some music, see some people." He was already pulling her to her feet.

"It'll take me a few minutes to change."

"No, you're fine. We're not going anyplace fancy."

Within minutes he had loaded her into the pickup and they were barreling down the road, leaving a trail of flying dust and gravel. Sean gripped the steering wheel with the intensity of a man with a purpose.

Amanda had the feeling that she would need to remember the way back to the ranch later on.

Sean was no stranger to the clientele at the Silver Dollar, a cowboy joint with a blue jeans dress code. He seemed to come alive with the attention he got there from friends who recounted his career with video-taped accuracy. He made a concentrated effort to draw Amanda into the conversation. He refused the occasional requests that he dance with other women, and when a friendly cowboy approached Amanda for a dance Sean led her to the floor himself, quipping that he'd asked her first.

Pulling her into his arms, Sean smiled, sliding a hand just below her waist and pressing her against him. "How am I doing tonight in the attentive department, Mandy? Are you having a good time?"

"Um-hmm. I could dance with you all night," Amanda said, tightening her arm around his neck.

"Or at least until closing time. And then . . . I intend to take you home and make love to you," he whispered.

It was a thought that became sweet torture as he held her body tightly against his, moving slowly, swaying slightly to the music. "Have you gotten what you were looking for here?" she asked.

"What do you mean?" he responded.

"The sudden need to come to town. Did you find what you were looking for?"

"Yeah, I guess I wanted some bright-light distraction. Now I'm feeling mellow and lusty, and closing time is too far off. Let's go home."

They hadn't quite reached the door when a familiar voice drew Sean back to the bar. Bud Eliot had ordered drinks for them both before Amanda had time to refuse. She wasn't about to perch herself on a barstool, and Sean suggested a booth. After another beer Sean became boisterous, and after two he was melancholy.

"What's going on with Sean?" Bud asked after

Sean had disappeared into the men's room. "He's not one to go out and get loaded. Looks like I might have to drive *him* home for a change."

"His little cousin, Zack, was killed in a riding accident. We just came from the funeral," Amanda explained.

"Oh, no. That kid was like a brother to him. Why didn't he tell me?"

"You've known Sean for a long time, Bud. Why *didn't* he tell you?"

"He never talks about these things. I remember after the accident when his mom and . . . hell, you don't know what to say to a guy. . . . Try to tell him you're sorry, he'll just stare right through you or shrug it off."

"He's bottling this up inside himself, too. Worse, I think he blames himself somehow."

"It's a wonder he hasn't gone crazy, everybody dyin' on him like that. Lacy says you're gonna leave him, too."

"Oh, she does, does she?" Amanda said with disgust. "She'd like that, wouldn't she?"

"Anybody's got eyes can see you care for Sean. Lacy's jealous as hell because she knows he's head over teakettle in love with you. Anybody can see *that*, too. Lacy's worried about losing something she never had." Bud glanced up as Sean returned and grinned. "Hey, cowboy, we were just talkin' about you."

Sean slid into the booth next to Amanda. "Don't you ruin things for me, Bud. Mandy thinks I'm not half-bad."

"But you are half-shot," Bud pointed out. "I was just sayin' how you always have to drive me home, but tonight it's my turn."

"I am perfectly capable—"

"Correction," Amanda interrupted, *"I* am perfectly capable of driving."

Sean grinned sheepishly as he leaned back to allow his hand access to the front pocket of his snug-fitting

jeans. "This lady is a hell of a driver, Bud. I'd trust
her with the keys to my pickup anytime. Here,
honey," he said, handing her the keys. "I'm capable,
but not perfectly."

Once in the pickup, Sean slid down in the seat,
pulled his hat over his eyes and slept. Getting him out
of the pickup was a difficult matter since he'd made
himself comfortable where he was, but Amanda reminded him of the comfort of his own bed. Sean went
quietly to his room, leaving Amanda to decide that
she would prefer the guest room that night.

As she undressed she pondered her limited wardrobe and made a mental note of the fact that this was
quickly becoming a summer away from home, which
she had not intended when she packed. When she
thought about it she felt a little foolish about what she
was doing. Love him or not, she could not go on
staying there indefinitely. She wasn't sure what Sean
expected, nor was she sure of her own expectations.
They were living in the present.

"What are you doing in here?" She turned from the
mirror above the bureau to find Sean leaning in the
doorway wearing a black robe and a sly smile.

"I thought you were asleep."

"And I thought our plans for tonight were firm," he
said, still smiling. His demeanor was awkward, and
the glazed gleam in his eyes bothered Amanda.

"Frankly, I think you've incapacitated yourself with
drink, my darling." Amanda laughed, her voice too
flip, too challenging under the circumstances.

"You underestimate the extent of my capacity,"
Sean advised, pushing himself away from the door-
frame. "I'm in the mood for a woman."

"That doesn't sound very romantic," she said,
unconsciously taking a backward step when he
reached for her. "Why don't we wait until you're
more yourself?"

"More *myself?*" Sean chuckled, catching her upper
arms in his powerful hands. "I'm *never* more mysel

than when I'm looking for a woman. Haven't you heard, lady? I am one fantastic stud." His lips bore down on hers, the pressure of his mouth so hard that she couldn't respond. Crushing her to him, Sean locked his mouth over Amanda's soft lips, and his hands kneaded her shoulders, back and buttocks.

When he tore his mouth away, his breathing hard, his mouth dropping to her neck, Amanda was able to gasp, "Sean, this isn't . . . like you. Stop this . . . please."

The straps of her nightgown were dropped over her shoulders, and when the gown wouldn't give he pulled at it with impatient hands until it ripped and fell open. "Sean, this isn't necessary," Amanda said as she struggled.

His face came up from under her jaw, where he had been nibbling at her tender skin. His countenance was dark, his eyes glowing hotly. "It's necessary," he growled, pushing his hips against hers. "Damn necessary. You're not leaving me, Mandy."

She started to protest, but he devoured her mouth again, and she felt a strange churning in the depths of her stomach, strange since there was real fear in the forefront of her mind. She was backed toward the bed, lifted and settled across the chenille bedspread. Despite her quiet protest Sean dropped his robe on the floor and lowered himself to the bed, covering her. "I won't hurt you, Mandy. But I won't let you go. . . ." The hands were not unkind, but they were not Sean's. The plundering mouth was not Sean's. This wasn't his way.

"No, Sean, not like this . . ."

"Yes, Mandy," he hissed. "Any damn way I please. You're my woman." The hard driving of his body against the soft vulnerability of hers underscored his insistent, *"My woman!"*

Amanda still lay trembling even after Sean had fallen asleep, one of his arms flung across her hips.

She hadn't thought him capable of this, and she didn't think drunkenness was the cause of his behavior. But she throbbed with his brutality, and she resented what he had done. After carefully extricating herself from Sean's arms, Amanda left him sprawled on the bed. She put her torn nightgown back on and found solace in the empty bed in his room. It was a long time before she was able to let herself sleep.

Then the mattress creaked beneath the weight of another person—another person who slipped into bed beside her. She became aware of the stale smell of alcohol and a warm physical presence. The fog cleared in her mind, and she started to move in the opposite direction, but he caught her in his arms.

"Don't go, Mandy, please," Sean whispered hoarsely. "I'll be good, I promise. Please stay with me tonight. I need you . . . I can't stand being alone . . . right now." He felt her settle back warily, holding herself away from him. "There are ghosts . . . ghosts that haunt my dreams, Mandy."

"Go to sleep, Sean," she whispered. "We'll talk about it in the morning."

Sean prepared to leave the house at first light, while Amanda still slept. In the soft morning light he looked down at her lovely sleeping face and grimaced at the puffiness of her lips. He'd done that, and he didn't know why. He remembered every moment. He had watched himself behave like a madman, but he had been powerless to stop himself. He had felt a deep, inexplicable pain, loneliness clutching at his gut, anger of the most insidious, unreasonable nature. He had been driven to possess her, driven to push her, to punish her for her future leave-taking and for all those who had left him in the past. Oh, God! Had he lost his mind?

He saddled the bay and rode him hard in the gray light of morning. Listening to the pounding hooves against the hard-packed prairie path and bathing his face in the morning-cool wind helped Sean drive the nighthaunts from his mind. It had always been this way. He was angry, driven to lash out, but his tormentor had no face, and so he put himself in motion, hurling himself like a battering ram against the unseen antagonist. He topped a rise and drew the horse to a prancing halt. They stood there, the horse blowing, his sides heaving under Sean's legs, while Sean faced east and opened himself up to the warmth, the light, the promise of life that his soul craved. He drew deeply of the sustenance of sunrise.

Amanda woke to find Sean, fully dressed, seated in a chair some distance from the bed. "What time is it?" she asked, yawning and pushing herself up on her elbows.

"It's early," he said quietly.

"How long have you been up? I thought surely you'd sleep in this morning."

"A man doesn't sleep well when his conscience is bothering him."

Amanda eyed him suspiciously as she swung her feet to the floor. Then she noticed the gaping bodice of her nightgown, and she pulled the front together. His boots sounded heavily on the hardwood floor as he approached the bed and sat wearily beside her, dropping his elbows on his knees and casting his gaze to the floor.

"I don't know what happened to me last night, Mandy. There's no excuse for what I did."

"You scared me, Sean. And you hurt me." She spoke softly, but she leveled her gaze at him.

"I know. God help me, I wanted to hurt you, Mandy. I don't know why, but I did."

"Why don't you be honest with me, Sean? What ghosts were haunting you last night?" He looked at her without understanding. "When you came in here you talked about ghosts haunting you."

"Did I say that? I must've been half-asleep. Nothing I said or did made any kind of sense. I wasn't even that drunk. I was just so damn . . . I don't know . . . mad, I guess, or crazy, or both."

"Well, I was scared, Sean. Scared and angry and humiliated."

"I'm sorry, honey," he mumbled. "I feel like the lowest . . ."

"Sean, why? Why did you want to hurt *me?* Why take whatever it is out on *me?*"

"I don't know. . . ."

"That's not good enough! I want an answer, Sean. I want to know what I did to deserve—"

"I don't know!" he growled, stiffening, but then, with an effort, he relaxed again. "The people I care about just seem to slip away from me. One day I'm with them, the next day they're gone." He took her hand, but avoided her eyes until he said, "Look, Mandy, I was mad at the world, and I wanted to hurt somebody because . . . because I was mad."

"Because you were mad?" she asked quietly, looking into his dark, inscrutable eyes. "Or was it because you're hurting?" She waited for his affirmation, but it didn't come. "I know you hurt, Sean. You've lost someone you love, and it hurts. Be honest about what you feel—your advice, remember?"

"Yeah, I remember. You're right, of course, but I'll get over it. I always have."

"Over what? The anger, or the pain? You vent the anger and hang on to the pain, Sean. Last night was no answer."

"I know. I should be horsewhipped for treating you the way I did last night. Can you . . . forgive me, Mandy?"

He was refusing to hear her, but she heard him, and she heard his sincerity. "Yes . . . as long as you understand that I'm not willing to let you take your frustrations out on me like that again. I'm not Lacy."

He stared at her for a moment, remembering Lacy's sacrifices for him, knowing this woman would not offer that, and knowing it would disgust him if she did. He lowered his eyes as he answered. "I know you're not. I'm not looking for another Lacy. You're . . ." His eyes met hers again. "It won't happen again—my promise."

Sean rode a bull in Dupree. He told Amanda about the bull riding only moments before getting his gear together and heading for the chutes. Amanda refused to follow, but at the last moment she scrambled onto the fence nearby and watched. Her glimpses of Sean were brief, but when the bucking animal whirled in her direction she saw the furor in Sean's face. His chaps flapped wildly as he dug the rowels of his spurs into the bull's shoulders, the fire in his eyes matching that in the bull's. Amanda empathized with the bull. Sean was still angry, still driven to punish. The pain was there, too, but he had succeeded in making it something physical that he could deal with.

Sean made an effort to relax his posture when he heard the camper door open, and Amanda caught his attempt to appear at ease. He was sitting on the couch, his face drawn, and Amanda made a mental note not to feel sorry for him. She busied herself in the galley, doing nothing in particular, until she could stand it no longer. "Why did you enter the bull riding, Sean? You're in no condition to—"

"I need the money."

"Right. Try again."

"Rodeo is a very pragmatic sport. The more money you win, the higher you climb in the standings. That's how you get to the finals." He closed his eyes and let his head fall back.

"You could've put yourself out of the running with that stunt today. You risked compounding the damage you've already done."

"Risky business, isn't it?" he tossed back.

"All you're really risking is your neck, which seems

to be of little value to you. *Real* risk scares you, though, doesn't it—the risk you'd have to take on all those words you've heard before."

His head snapped up. "What does all this have to do with the price of bologna? If I want a shot at the all-around, I have to ride. I'm always up against the chance of getting hurt. I live with that."

"We all do, Sean." Amanda approached him with slow, steady steps. "You told me you rode bulls mostly for Zack. You wanted to kill that bull, Sean. Was that for Zack?"

"Let it go, Mandy," he sighed. "Zack doesn't care anymore. I wish you'd stop trying to analyze me."

"*You've* got to let it go. Let go of whatever's festering inside you." She sat beside him, but she didn't touch him except with the words, "Let Zack go, Sean. Let them all go. You can't beat death by riding a bull."

"Damn it, Mandy, I'm not ready for the psych ward! Zack's dead, and that's that. I rode a bull today because I'm in the rodeo business."

"You're also suffering from a cracked rib," she said quietly.

"Yeah, well, that wasn't really bothering me before I"—he glanced at her, giving her a crooked smile— "rode the bull."

"After all the worrying I've done over you, I should crack your skull," Amanda grumbled sullenly.

Taking her by the hands, he pulled her toward him. "I like it when you worry over me. That's when you put your arms around me, like this, and you cuddle me up and make me feel better all over."

"You're wasting your time, cowboy," she groaned as she laid her head against his chest and ran her fingers gently along his rib cage. "I don't feel the least bit sorry for you."

"But do you still love me?"

"Yes."

"I need to hear you say it."

"I love you, Sean."

His arms tightened around her, and he buried his face in her hair, memorizing the smell and the texture and the taste of it. "I treasure that, Mandy, believe me. I treasure your love."

"Then trust me. Talk with me. You're carrying a burden of grief that's eating away at your insides because you won't let it out. Share that with me, Sean. If you believe I love you, then you know I won't think less of you if you let yourself—"

He put her away from himself, confused. "What do you want me to do, Mandy? Cry? Wail at the heavens? I don't need that. What I need is for you to let me forget it."

"All right, Sean, you handle it your way," she sighed.

"Mandy," he groaned, holding her close again, stroking her back, "of course I'm grieved by Zack's . . . death. But I can't . . . there's not a damn thing I can do. I just have to get busy and . . ." There was always that wrestling. It would leave him alone for a while, and then there it was again, and he'd have to . . . "Let's get out of here, honey. We'll find someplace where we can be alone and make mad, passionate love."

"Not mad love, Sean," she warned. "I don't want any more mad love."

"Gentle love, then." He offered a smile. "Tender, gentle love. I'll drive you crazy with gentleness."

"Give me a sample," she whispered, lifting her chin. His full lips made slow, teasing contact with hers, his flickering tongue taunting her. Slipping her hands behind his neck, Amanda responded as her fluttering heart demanded, her lips caressing his while her tongue darted into his mouth.

He smiled against her kiss. "Easy, girl."

"How far away is this private place?"

"Just down the road a piece," he assured her with a sly wink.

Having driven down the piece of road, Sean was stretched out on the couch a short while later, his feet propped up on the back of the driver's seat. He was wearing only a pair of jeans. He'd been fed and had enjoyed a shower, and now he lifted his head and shoulders while Amanda tucked herself under him, letting her lap be his pillow.

What an ingratiating female she'd become, she mused, and in such a short time. But she smiled, lacing her fingers into the thick shock of black hair, still damp from his shower.

"You're getting pretty used to having me around, aren't you, cowboy?"

"I'm enjoying your company, lady. Have I forgotten to tell you that lately?"

"I've enjoyed yours, too."

"Past tense? Is this leading up to an announcement?"

"I can't follow you around indefinitely. I'm not getting much work done, and I'm not in a position to take a sabbatical."

"Why not move to Rapid City? Get an apartment."

It wasn't the suggestion she'd expected. "Move? Why?"

"I go to a lot of the big stock shows in the winter. We could go together. Wouldn't that fit in with your career?"

"This is a different circuit out here."

"A better circuit, and you can be part of it. Show the mare, Mandy. Earn me a reputation for raising good pleasure horses."

"Who says it's a better circuit?"

"I do." He grinned. "You meet a better class of people."

"*Moving* is such a big . . . I don't know anyone."

"You know me. You'll make new friends."

"But my family is—"

"Mandy, you've got your own life to live. You're not going to depend on Daddy forever, are you?"

"I don't depend on him. I have my own—"

"This is the first time in your life that Daddy hasn't been around to call the shots. Am I right?"

"It's not like that. He *offers* his advice, but . . ."

"Wait 'til the advice comes down on me, honey. You can bet it won't be in my favor."

". . . but I don't always follow it."

"What I'm offering is a suggestion. Will you think about it?" She glanced away, obviously troubled by the idea that she pull up stakes and move with some vague notion of following the Western show circuit. "Answer me, Mandy. Will you consider it?"

"Yes, I'll think about it, but you know it's a crazy idea."

"It's an excellent idea. My first idea was a good one, right? For you to come along with me?"

"Was that your *first* idea?" Amanda teased. "Kind of fun to come up with, aren't they? And now a *second* idea follows hard on the heels of the first! Be careful, cowboy; you start using that brain too much and all your brawn might turn to flab."

Sean's eyes brightened steadily, and the corners of his mouth twitched with delight as she teased him. "We wouldn't want that to happen, would we?" he said, rolling easily to his feet. "You like my body pretty well the way it is, don't you, pretty lady?" Before Amanda had time to react he had pulled her to her feet, put his shoulder to her midriff and whisked her into the air over his shoulder like a sack of feed. He laughed when she squealed, demanding to be set down.

"Enough talk, woman!" Sean growled, turning off the light. "Brain weary. Body frustrated."

"They say push-ups help," she bellowed, swatting at his bottom, a target somewhere below her dangling head.

"Exactly what I had in mind—after a fashion."

"Sean Brannigan, you can be so crude! Put me down!"

With a chuckle and an affectionate smack on her bottom he unloaded her on the bed in the back of the camper. "Crude is part of the package," he reminded her. In the shadowy moonlight Amanda watched his fluid motion as he shed his jeans. His contours were smooth and sleek, like a jungle cat's, but it was Amanda who purred, "Mmm, yes . . . I like your body *very* well the way it is."

"How about unveiling yours for me?"

With one hand she pressed him back against the pile of pillows, and then she uncovered her body with deliberate slowness, feeling hotly seductive. "You're so gorgeous," he mumbled.

Amanda knelt over him and began touching him, caressing him all over with soft, cool fingertips. She felt him shiver just before he reached for her. "Oh, Amanda," he groaned. "Come here, temptress. Let's make love."

"Sean," she whispered, stretching herself along the length of him, electrified by such total contact with his warm skin, "I want to make you want me, just me. I want to drive every other woman from your mind."

"There's no other woman in this world, Mandy," he whispered close to her ear as he lifted himself over her. "I've never wanted anyone this way, never felt this . . ."

His lips were warm and wet and tantalizing. Amanda's body quivered with delight. Loving hands caressed her tingling flesh, her breasts, her belly, making their way lower. She shifted to allow access to those adept fingers, and the gentle acquaintance they made with her caused a delicious shivering deep inside her.

"You're driving me wild, my darling," Amanda moaned.

"I told you I would." His voice was gravelly.

"Don't ever stop . . . oh, Sean . . . so good . . ."

"I'll make it even better," he murmured, his tongue

tracing wet circles below her navel. He loved the cool smoothness of her, the sweet taste of her. The sound of her soft, urgent moaning drove him, despite her feeble protest, to seek the source of her need, to taste the honey of her desire, and to help her reach the crest of the wave of sensation she'd been riding. Then he moved quickly to gather her in his arms and hold her fluttering heart against his. "You're the most exciting woman," he whispered, nuzzling her neck, "because you're *my* woman, because you've given yourself to me completely, and I've made you mine. I need you, Mandy. I need you."

As if to verify the truth of his words Amanda reached for him. The need within her grew as she stroked him and coaxed him to fill her with his own essence. Her body welcomed him, reached for him, cradled him, arched itself to receive all he had to give her. Their names became a litany as they reached out to one another and were pitched as one beyond the limits of reason.

In the afterglow of lovemaking they held each other, kissing and touching and whispering hints of their pleasure. "Forgive my possessiveness, Mandy," Sean said quietly. 'Calling you 'my woman' . . . but I hate the thought of anyone else touching you. I want you to be mine alone."

"No one else has touched me the way you do. I don't come with a bill of sale, Sean, but you do have my love."

"I know that." He hugged her against his chest. "I know that."

"You know, but you don't trust. Why don't you trust me?"

"One day," he sighed, "you're going to go back east, and you'll settle back into your city life, and you'll wonder how anyone could be content to live in this empty prairie."

"Why do I get the feeling you see Alisha when you look at me?"

"Alisha? I don't even remember what she looked like."

"But you remember how yóu felt. You loved her, and she hurt you, and you can't let go of that."

"You were hurt once, too, weren't you? You learn to be a little more cautious, a little less foolish."

"Our past romances are hardly comparable," Amanda said quickly.

"We were each the third corner of a triangle, sweetheart. Your fiancé's other girl couldn't have been more beautiful than you are. Was it money or sex?"

"Oh, for heaven's sake, Sean, let's not talk about that."

"Why not? Does it hurt even now? Can't you let go, unburden yourself, let bygones be bygones?"

"I never think of it anymore. There's no reason to."

"It still bothers you when you think about it." And the idea that it might bother her bothered *him* very much.

"It was a disgusting situation, and I was disgustingly naive." She sighed, the whole scene creeping back into her mind, the memory she'd carefully bricked up in the cellar of her subconscious. "I caught him with someone else, that's all."

His jealousy retracted its claws. "Tell me what happened, Mandy."

She knew then that it was time to take it out and see whether she could handle it sensibly. "I went to his apartment one day—his birthday, in fact. I had this ridiculous little cake to surprise him with, and I thought he had a class. He did. He was holding his own private little anatomy class with a very adept little blonde. I walked in on the lab session."

"What did you do?"

"I think I actually said 'excuse me.' Really!" She giggled. "I excused myself and backed out the door. Then I cried myself sick. *Then* I thought I'd do the *reasonable* thing and let him apologize, talk the whole thing out. . . . You know what he said to me?"

"That he had temporary amnesia?"

"That I was like a mermaid. He was still *willing* to marry me because all he expected of me was to sit across from him at the dinner table and look pretty." Her giggling became infectious. "He said a mermaid wasn't expected to perform anything that was physically impossible for her."

Sean touched her warm, smooth thigh. "The man failed anatomy and became a dentist, and the moral of the story is: Don't send a doctor to do a veterinarian's work."

When their laughter died down Amanda was able to confess, "It was so humiliating, and it's stayed with me all this time—the disgust. Mostly with myself."

"Did you believe him?"

"I guess I thought it might be true—that I was sort of cold. But I decided I wouldn't be flattered or cajoled or betrayed again. I waited for someone I could love . . . and it was worth the wait."

"And worth the trip?"

"Worth every mile. Lacy was right; once you've known a cowboy, other men seem very ordinary."

"They are ordinary. Lack imagination. Paul, for instance—the boy had no imagination." Sean propped himself up on an elbow and traced a finger along Amanda's breastbone. "Now a cowboy—he's got an imagination as big as Texas. Come on and let me show you, little mermaid."

Amanda awoke during the night and realized first that it was raining. As she came fully to her senses she realized that it was storming, and that it would be wise to close some windows. After slipping quietly from the bed, she put on her robe, groped her way forward and discovered rain pelting through the window and soaking the couch.

She had found a towel and was blotting water from the cushions when a bolt of lightning illuminated the dark room, a crash of thunder rending the night's peace after a second's delay. The thunder was startling, but the echoing cry joining it from the back of the camper momentarily paralyzed Amanda with icy terror. Then she realized that it was Sean, and she stumbled to her feet and made her way through the dark to get to him.

Sean sat bolt upright in the bed, both hands clutching the sheet beside his hips, and when the lightning flashed again Amanda saw the horror in his dazed eyes. Another raspy cry from the pit of his tormented subconscious chilled Amanda to the marrow. Bracing one knee on the edge of the bed, she reached for him, shaking his shoulders. "Sean, you're dreaming," she said, willing her voice to remain calm. "Wake up, darling. It's a dream."

A long, drawn-out, hollow groan began somewhere in Sean's body. His arms coiled around Amanda's waist, and he buried his face in her belly. She held him there, smoothed his hair back and felt the terrible shudders that wracked his body. "Oh, my God!" he gasped again and again. "Oh, my God!"

She held him that way for what seemed like a long time, and when her hand brushed across his face and came away wet he turned his face squarely into her stomach so she couldn't touch his tears again. Then suddenly he drew away and started out of the bed. "Sean, where are you . . . ?"

"I don't know what's the matter with me," he rasped. "I need a cigarette."

"I'll find them. Let me turn the light—"

"No! Leave it off."

"But I can't—"

"They're . . . never mind." He sighed raggedly, settling back on the bed. "I . . . don't want you to see me like this. This is crazy. I must be crazy."

She sat beside him and put a cool hand on his arm.

"Tell me what's haunting you, Sean. It's something to do with Zack, isn't it?"

At the mention of the boy's name Sean pushed her hand away and sat up abruptly. "I'm not a kid anymore, Mandy. Don't baby me. I don't need anybody to wipe my nose or tie my shoes for me." He rolled to his feet and left the room, returning moments later with a glowing cigarette in his mouth. Sitting heavily on the side of the bed, he sucked in a lungful of acrid smoke and then heaved it from his chest with an awful sigh. "I'm sorry, Mandy. But I guess 'I'm sorry' is getting a little old, isn't it?"

"Why won't you let me get close to you, Sean?"

"I hardly let you out of my sight, Mandy; what are you talking about?"

"You've shared everything with me but this, and I've watched it eat at you for days now. Darling, you don't have to carry this grief in stoic silence. Crying because someone you love is dead doesn't make you less of a man."

Amanda watched the cigarette tremble slightly as he brought it to his mouth and drew on it again. "I'm a hell of a big man during the day, but at night I'm afraid of ghosts. Look at me. I'm shaking all over."

"It was a nightmare," she said, emphasizing the obvious.

"Nightmare," he echoed. "My ghosts haunt me at night."

"Does this happen to you often?"

"It's been a long time, but I've had them before. I've never acted like this before, though, never actually . . ."

"Cried?" she finished gently.

"Damn it, Mandy, I wasn't really . . ."

"Yes, Sean. Yes, you were. Did you cry when your mother and sister died?"

"No."

"When your father died?"

"Hell, no!"

"You needed to. You've held it all inside you. And now Zack. Tell me about the dream." He finished the cigarette in silence. "Smoking doesn't help much, does it?" she asked quietly.

"No, not much."

"Neither does a wild bull, or a night on the town, or . . ."

"Or forcing myself on you," he finished for her.

"So talk to me, Sean. See if it'll help to tell me what haunts you." Her hand rested on his thigh, and he covered it with his.

"Yeah, it was Zack," he sighed. "I saw him die. I heard a horn blowing, kind of off in the distance at first, but it got louder and louder. I saw the horse galloping full blast across the prairie, dragging that little boy, his body bouncing over the rocks and through the brush and getting all torn up, just like . . ." He turned his head aside.

"Just like what, Sean?"

"The accident that took Mom and Shelley was caused by a drunk driver . . . my father. He was thrown from the car right away—before it rolled down an embankment. Mom was thrown into the windshield. Her face was . . . battered. Shelley's body was mangled. I couldn't believe it, couldn't accept it until I saw them, and now that's the last memory I have of them . . . the way they looked . . . God! How I hated him for that! I hated him almost as much as he hated himself. I kept the place up and watched him drink himself to death . . . hating every minute he breathed after they were gone. He'd get drunk and cry over them, and it made me sick."

Amanda sat quietly, listening to the rain and the distant rumbling of thunder, and she waited. He was nearly crushing her hand in his, and she knew that he was struggling with the last of his terrible memories. "Maybe I could've helped him," Sean said at last, his voice hollow. "I thought I wanted to see him die. Hell, he had nothing to live for anyway—a ranch he couldn't run, a son who hated the sight of him. He was nothing but a drunken dreamer. He *deserved* to die."

"You loved your father, didn't you, Sean?" Amanda asked in a quiet, understanding voice. "You loved him, but you couldn't bring yourself to admit it."

"That's right," Sean whispered. "I loved him, and I let him go to his grave thinking he'd lost his son."

Amanda reached to touch his cheek and found it wet with tears. There had been no tears in his voice, and she was surprised to find them on his skin. "Let them all go, Sean. Grieve for them, and then let them go. They haunt you because you hang on to this regret and remorse."

"I didn't want to let them go. They died too soon."

"I know. That's why you're angry. It's easy to get angry, but being heartbroken isn't easy for a man like Sean Brannigan."

"I've been alone too long, Mandy."

"I know that, too. But I love you, Sean. And I'm here, and I'm going to hold you through the night, just to remind you that you're not alone, not now."

"Are you going to rock me to sleep, too?" he asked with a sardonic chuckle.

Amanda untied her robe and let it slip to the floor. "I'm going to cradle your head between my breasts and your hips between my thighs. If you need to be rocked," she whispered, moving fully onto the bed and reaching out to him, "I'll do that, too."

Thunder rumbled intermittently throughout the night, but Sean Brannigan was troubled no further.

Chapter Thirteen

Amanda climbed onto the fence near the roping box when she heard Sean's name called. Her heart hammered for him, sharing his anticipation. He was apparently unaware of her presence, or, for that matter, of any of the crowd of cowboys who stood along the fence. The piggin string was in his mouth, he built his loop, and his focus was on the edge of the chute, from which the calf would emerge like a shot when the gate flew open. Sean's nod triggered the flow of motion whose flawless continuity still amazed Amanda. Horse and rider sprang from the box as the rope was quickly whirled, thrown and jerked. There was no hesitation in the procedure: dismount on the right, throw the calf on its side, tie three legs—all in nine seconds.

"That's what I call smokin'!"

Amanda turned toward the voice and returned Bud Eliot's smile. "Bud! Good to see you," she said, lowering herself to the ground. "Where have you been lately?"

"I haven't been doin' too good, thought I'd slack off, get some work done at home. Glad to see you two are still together."

"I'm pleased with the story we're putting together. Sean's been a great help." It was a transparent grab for justification, an old habit.

"You look great, Amanda. You look happy. And Sean's doin' real good from what I hear."

"Is Lacy with you?" Amanda tried not to dread the answer.

"Not this time. Lacy found herself a new driver. Sean's gonna be madder 'n a dog with a snoot full o' quills when he finds out she's runnin' around with Travis Steele."

"Travis Steele? If she hasn't learned her lesson I doubt Sean will waste his time worrying about her at this point."

"Listen, Amanda," Bud warned her seriously, "if he does, don't let it bother you. Sean's got a soft spot in his heart for Lacy, but it's like she's his sister or something. She's just doing this to get his attention, and even if it works, well, it's nothing for you to worry about."

The topic of conversation shifted when Sean joined them, his hand settling naturally at Amanda's waist. "Hey, Bud, you trying to steal my girl?"

Bud reached for Sean's handshake. "If I thought I had a chance I'd sure try, ol' buddy. Hey, you heal fast. That was a hell of a run on that calf."

"Thanks, Bud; you did a good job tonight, too. Where's Lacy?" If it wasn't the first question Sean asked Bud, it was inevitably the second, and Amanda flinched when it came.

"She's around," was Bud's reply.

"She with you?" Sean asked. Bud shook his head.

"Bud was just telling me that Lacy is with Travis Steele," Amanda said, trying to help Bud out.

"Steele? What happened? You two get into it?"

"I've been home for the last week. Guess she was afraid she'd miss something."

"She's gotta be out of her mind," Sean sighed.

"She's a big girl, Sean. She'll do what she wants." A trace of regret had crept into Bud's voice.

"Yeah, well, she knows what she's getting into this time. I hope she can handle it. I could use a hazer, Bud."

"Tonight? You gonna bulldog with that rib?"

"I've got enough elastic wrapped around me to bandage a gorilla. You with me?"

"All the way!"

Molding herself along the length of Sean's back, Amanda snaked her arms around his chest and beneath the shirt before he could finish snapping it. The bandage seemed tight. "I couldn't help noticing the pain in your face when you pulled that steer over, cowboy," she said.

"No real harm done, though. I did get second."

"Watching you perform has a strange effect on me."

He turned into her embrace and added his. "Really? What sort of strange effect, pretty lady?"

"I get a fluttering, churning sensation deep in my stomach."

"So do I. I've been in, I don't know, hundreds of rodeos it seems like, but I still get . . ."

"Mine isn't nerves, Sean. It's pure lust. I like the way you move with the horse, the way you make it look so easy to do everything at once, the disciplined strength in your body. It makes me want to ravage you," Amanda growled, ducking under his chin to nip at his neck.

"Well, I'll be damned! I don't know as I've ever been *ravaged*, ma'am, but I don't think I'd put up much of a struggle."

"You know you'd love it. You know what else I like?"

"I'm afraid to guess," Sean laughed.

"The way you mount a horse—that little hop into the stirrup and the way you swing up into the saddle."

"If I'd 'a known that, I could have . . ."

Her hands slid slowly along the muscled ridges of his back toward his belt. "You have this long, powerful back that tapers so perfectly to this small, tight bottom, and your jeans ride your hips kind of low."

"You like that, huh?"

"Even the most scrupulous lady secretly admires the rear view of a well-proportioned male."

"Hell, I wondered why I was always getting jumped from behind."

The rodeo at Aberdeen was part of the Brown County Fair, and the town had prepared itself for cowboys. The favored night spot had once been a lumberyard, but the transformation had left no sign of the establishment's lowly beginnings. A country-western band rocked and twanged atop the huge stage, which was surrounded by a spacious dance floor. Patrons could choose from a number of bars, each with its own share of tables, some overlooking the dance floor from a loft.

Amanda wore a softly flowing, ivory-colored knit dress that flattered her shapliness even more than her usual tight blue jeans. By the look in his eyes she knew that Sean approved, even though many of the women wore jeans. They had dinner and drinks, greeting and meeting a procession of Sean's acquaintances. By the time they got to the dance floor the crowd was beer-boisterous and rodeo-rowdy. Amanda found the atmosphere intoxicating, and she abandoned her normal reserve, clapping and stomping and twirling happily.

When the tempo of the music slowed she snuggled against Sean's chest, draping both of her arms around his shoulders. Sean held her tightly against his body. He could feel every curve under the soft, clinging fabric of her dress. "You feel as good as you look, Mandy. Dancing close to you is always such sweet torment."

"And you, sir, feel—" The couple behind Sean caught her eye, and when the woman turned to face her Amanda cut herself off, recognizing Lacy.

"I know. It's Lacy and Steele," Sean muttered. "I saw them."

"I hope this doesn't mean it's showdown time."

"Always save that for high noon. Lacy's not putting up a struggle over there, and I only rescue ladies in distress."

"Well, the picture of distress is sitting over there at the bar by himself. What do you say we keep Bud company for a while?" Amanda suggested.

When they joined Bud, he revealed that he had come to a realization that seemed to surprise him. "I miss her, Sean. I really miss her. I didn't treat her so good, walkin' out on her that time in Reno, always yellin' at her and callin' her down. Now she's got herself mixed up with that toad, Steele."

Amanda searched for words of consolation. "She doesn't like Travis Steele. She told me that. She just wants to stir up a little jealousy."

"Tell you what, Bud," Sean added, taking a drink from the bottle in his hand before he continued, "she's trying to make us both mad, but this is one game I'm not playing. The limits of my friendship won't stretch that far, not even for Lacy. Just let her play her game out, my friend. She'll be back."

At the words "my friend" Bud glanced at Sean, pleased by the declaration. But then gloom overcame him again. "I won't want her back after she's been with that scum. Won't take her back, not after she's been with him."

"That's up to you, Bud. Lacy's making a big mistake trying to prove God-knows-what. Let's hope it doesn't backfire on her."

Bud's eyes hardened. "If he does anything . . . if he hurts her . . . damn, I'll kill him, Sean."

Sean gave Bud a wry smile. "Lacy'll love that, especially if you spill a little blood in her honor."

Lacy flaunted her ploy in Sean's face before the evening was over. She and Travis sauntered over to the table, Lacy starting the conversation with a breathy compliment for Sean's performance at the rodeo. "I was worried about your broken rib, Johnny, but it looks like you're really on the mend."

"I'm fine, thanks, kid."

"Well, Amanda," Lacy said, turning a smile in her direction, "have you decided to spend the summer on the road like the rest of us bunnies?"

Amanda felt Sean's hand close over hers under the table, but her reply was quicker than his. "Actually, Lacy, my plans are quite flexible. I've decided to make this a working vacation, and thanks to Sean, I'm enjoying every minute of it."

"That's real nice. You'll like the Deadwood rodeo. It's not a big town or anything, but they have the big motorcycle races in Sturgis at the same time as the rodeo. We'll be there; right, Travis?" Lacy glanced back at her companion, who appeared to be totally bored.

"You still riding, Steele?" Sean asked. "Haven't heard your name mentioned lately."

"Then you haven't checked the standings in the *News* lately. I didn't hang around South Dakota over the Fourth. Gotta go where the money is." Steele's eyes shifted in Bud's direction. "No score on your bronc tonight, huh, Bud? Competition with the big boys got you rattled?"

"I'll match you ride for ride, Steele," Bud ventured.

Travis hooked an arm around Lacy's neck. "What do you think, Lacy? Think ol' Bud can match me ride for ride?" Lacy stiffened, her eyes on the floor. "I've

made some good rides lately, haven't I?" Travis
sneered, tightening his hold on her in a travesty of a
hug.

Bud made an attempt to rise to his feet, but Sean
gripped his arm in a face-saving gesture. "I oughta kill
you, Steele," Bud mumbled, falling back into the
chair. Travis laughed.

"Take it easy," Sean said quietly, but his eyes slid
coldly past Travis and he shot a dark look at Lacy.
"Listen, kid, nobody here cares for the company
you're keeping. I think you're making a mistake, but
you do what you want. Just don't bring your friend
around me and try to make small talk."

"What's the matter, Johnny?" Lacy retorted with a
cat-eyed glare. "Got no time for your common friends
now that you're shackin' up with a fancy *lady?*"
Travis's laughter was the only sound that filled the
next seconds as Sean and Lacy glared across the cold
distance between them. Sean pushed his chair back
from the table and stood slowly, the look of disgust
visibly retreating from his face until there was only
pity and a hint of regret in his eyes.

"Be careful this time, kid," Sean advised as he
reached for Amanda's chair. "If you get yourself in
trouble you might be short on friends to help you
out." As he dropped a hand on Bud's shoulder Sean's
parting remark was, "Just take it easy, Bud. We'll see
you later."

Amanda assumed that they were headed for the
door, but as they passed the dance floor Sean took her
purse from her hand and set it on a table. Pulling her
into his arms, he guided her smoothly against him
without missing a beat of the music. "I admire your
self-control," he said.

"And I admire yours. I'm glad she didn't get the
scene she wanted from you."

"The scene she was hoping for was with you. Most
women would have gone for her throat after that

remark. She was looking for an excuse to tear your hair out."

"You're kidding." There was disbelief in Amanda's half-smile.

"Nothing more entertaining on a Saturday night than a barroom cat fight. Lacy's pretty handy with her claws."

"Amazing. I've never seen women fight. I don't think I'd know what to do," Amanda laughed. "I suppose you guys stand around and make bets on the outcome."

"All my money's on you, honey." Sean leaned back to give her a wink. "Everyone knows the pen is mightier than the claw."

Later that night Sean drove the camper several miles from town to a small lake, where he parked in tree-sheltered isolation. At his suggestion they headed for the water for a midnight swim. The water was warmer than Amanda had expected, and they swam in earnest for a while before finding a chest-deep spot close to shore where they lingered, talking quietly, floating lazily, teasing each other with little splashes. Their proximity to one another, the water, the quiet and the starry night were delicious, and Sean enjoyed this prelude as he anticipated what would naturally follow.

He began by kissing her, warming them both with the tender promise of parted lips exploring, tongues darting to excite one another. Amanda shivered, and he lifted his mouth from hers. "Cold?" he asked.

"Mmm, no. I'm . . . the way I always am when you kiss me . . . trembling . . . all over."

"All over?" He slipped the straps of her swimsuit off her shoulders. "I need to check this out, Mandy— see if you're quivering all over just because I kissed you." He pushed the suit down to her waist and admired the alabaster breasts afloat in the water. Then he lifted her, his hands at her waist, until his tongue could tease and his hungry mouth could devour first one sensitive nipple and then the other. Amanda gasped with pleasure, her fingers laced through his thick, wet hair.

He stripped the suit from her easily, letting her body float back down as he took his own trunks off and tossed both suits to the shore. Beneath the water their hands slid along wet skin as their bodies drifted against one another.

"Is it possible . . . in the water?" Amanda groaned.

"I think it's possible anywhere." His hand moved between her legs, and he lapped the lakewater from her shoulder. "I could make love to you in midair. Free fall. Wanna try it?"

"Right now I'd try anything."

"Touch me, then, Mandy . . . yes . . . there." They watched each other's faces as the delightful tension increased quickly. Suddenly able to stand it no longer, Amanda wrapped her legs around his waist, and Sean found passage. Amanda lost touch with reality, lost herself in the water, drifted in pleasure. There was security in the knowledge that the water could not carry her from Sean, her mooring. He would let her enjoy the freedom of the water, and he would not let her drift away from him.

Her head dropped to his shoulder. Lifting her in his arms, Sean carried her from the water and wrapped her in a blanket he'd left on shore. He carried his bundle to the camper, dried her and himself, and then snuggled with her beneath warm blankets, vowing to himself that tomorrow he'd hire a plane.

They spent the days before the Deadwood rodeo at the ranch. Sean watched Amanda begin to school the mare for show. She told herself that she was only doing it for fun; there was no way she could go home with a horse. Still, the mare was an excellent show prospect.

More interesting than show schooling was watching Sean train a sleek young gelding destined to be a calf horse. The horse, Sean said, had natural cow sense, and Amanda marveled at the way he tracked calves like a bloodhound. With great patience Sean worked at perfecting the spunky roan's ability to stop on a dime. In the interest of her research he explained his methods, which involved making use of calmness and gentleness to bring about control. He decried those who used harsh methods and cruel pressure devices, and he explained to Amanda that he'd seen many a good horse ruined by an impatient trainer.

With Karen and Steve in the house, Amanda couldn't bring herself to share Sean's bed. Sean felt that Lacy's remarks had caused Amanda renewed embarrassment, and he respected her wishes despite the nightly loneliness. He would miss her when she left him, but he tried not to think about that too much. They would spend time together in the hills when they went to the Deadwood rodeo, and she would love it there, and maybe she would see . . . what the hell. He would take each day as it came.

One evening they walked together, hand in hand, needing the time alone. "What did you and Karen do in town today?"

Amanda shrugged. "Oh, we shopped. I bought a few things for myself and a gift for her. She was planning her nursery. It was fun."

"What do you think of Rapid City? Have you thought about . . . staying?"

"I've been thinking about it." Her voice seemed very small.

"And . . . ?"

"I haven't come to a decision; I've just thought . . . just tried to imagine myself . . . Sean, I'm not sure where I fit into your life, or where you fit into mine."

He was quiet for a time, and then he decided to tell her. "I talked to your father today."

Amanda was surprised. "He called?"

"Yes, while you were gone. Since you weren't there he settled for me. Wanted to know why you'd been here so long. I told him you'd been doing some writing, but he wouldn't buy that. He asked me whether we're sleeping together."

"What did you say?"

"Told him it was none of his business. Then he went on a tirade, said I'd brainwashed you, that his daughter wasn't going to waste herself on some worthless cowboy. I'd have hung up on him, but I kept telling myself, he's Mandy's dad."

"I appreciate that, Sean. He's overly protective, even now."

"You're not his little girl anymore, Mandy. You're my . . . you're a woman. Your father resents the idea of losing you to another man."

Amanda sighed. "My father has introduced me to more insufferable bores than—"

"Mandy, your father has an idea that all you see in me is that I'm not his choice for you. He thinks you were looking for somebody who isn't his kind of people, and I'd sure fit the bill."

Amanda digested this theory slowly. "No three-piece suits, no *Wall Street Journal.*"

"He assured me that your intelligence and good breeding would triumph, and that after you'd had your adventure you'd—"

"My adventure! My declaration of independence! My God, doesn't anybody think I have any capacity for love?"

"The men in your life have all managed to underestimate you, Mandy. You're the gift wrapped in a dozen boxes—hard to get at, but the center box holds a diamond."

She smiled up at him. "And you are becoming quite the poet. It's poetry I crave, not adventure."

"I think you'll have a tough time convincing your father of that."

"Will we be able to stand up to him?" Her grin was a challenge.

Sean chuckled, slipping his arm around Amanda's shoulders. "He said if you didn't call him back, he was coming out here."

"And?"

"And I told him I didn't know whether you planned to call, but that I had an extra guest room, and he was welcome."

"I'll call him tonight and tell him . . . something."

"Just tell him Mandy's a big girl now, and Sean's a hell of a nice guy."

Calling her father didn't help Amanda make any decisions. When her father asked whether Sean had offered any suggestion of marriage, Amanda had to admit that he hadn't.

"Not that I would tolerate a marriage between you and a cowboy, Amanda, but the man obviously has no scruples, and what you're doing is indecent by any standards."

"You have no idea what—"

"Of course I have an idea. Do you think I was born yesterday, for Pete's sake?"

He demanded that she return home, and she ended the conversation with a calm declaration that she would be there when she was ready. Later, when the house was quiet, Amanda found herself unable to sleep. She crept into Sean's room, closing the door quietly behind her, and slipped into bed beside him. She was gathered into his arms immediately, and his hands played over her smooth curves as she snuggled close to him. "I thought I knew your nightgowns. This a new one?" he whispered.

"I bought it today. Like it?"

"Mmm, nice. Let's get rid of it." He tugged at it while Amanda shrugged out of it. "I nearly went crazy lying here with you in the next room."

"I know the feeling. It's just that Karen and Steve are nice people, and I don't want them to think of me the way Lacy does, even though I'm sure—"

"Hey, we're nice people, too, Mandy. Are we doing something wrong?"

"I don't know. I know I love you, and you . . . I think you really . . . care for me." She held her breath a moment.

Sean stroked her back, trailing his fingers down the long, sleek curve to her buttocks and then back up again. "You came from another world," he whispered. "The sky opened and dropped you in my lap. I'm afraid I'll wake up one day and you'll be all packed and ready to go back where you came from."

Amanda sighed, impatient with him for not seeing the depth of her feeling. "Sean, do you have any idea of the risks I've taken in loving you? I have never, ever let a man be as close to me as you are. Leaving Reno with you was insanity for me, but it was exciting; you're exciting, and it's been worth the risk. Why can't you take that risk for me? I need to know how you feel about me."

"I've told you how I feel . . . in a hundred ways."

"I need the words, Sean."

"Okay . . . I've been in love with you since I first saw you in Reno, standing there like a goddess in that white satin outfit, looking surprised, a little scared. But I was the one who was taken by surprise." He chuckled, remembering. "Blew my cool all to hell when my heart leaped into my throat at the sight of you, and I couldn't talk sense."

"I thought you were pretty cool," she said, picturing the scene. "I thought you were fantastic."

"And I thought I was wearing my heart on my sleeve all this time. Haven't you known all along how I feel about you?"

"I've needed to hear the words."

"I love you, Mandy. Don't go back to Boston. Stay here. Stay with me."

"Stay here and do what, Sean? I can't just stay with you and be your . . . your lover or whatever."

"Be my lover, my friend, my partner, my woman . . . be my wife, Mandy."

"Sean, I—"

"No, don't say anything yet. Stay a while longer and see if you . . . could live in this 'godforsaken desert.' See if I can take the girl out of the city and keep her happy in the country. I'm part of a package deal, honey, all wrapped up with this ranch and rodeo and South Dakota, and that's a lot of change for you. But, God, I don't want you to go back to Boston."

"I know your life is here, Sean. There's nothing I want in Boston. Nothing I can do there that I couldn't do here, too."

"I'd . . . like to have children," he ventured, realizing that he wasn't sure how she felt about a lot of things. "Would you?"

"You asked me once if I'd be willing to have your baby."

"If we were married. And I was a little . . ."

"A little drunk, I know. But I wasn't, and I answered you honestly. Shopping with Karen today, I imagined what it would be like to be carrying your baby. And I've imagined a dark-eyed little kid following you around outside. . . ."

Sean chuckled, planting kisses on her eyes. "I've imagined blue eyes . . . ," he said, kissing her hair, "and chestnut hair glinting with red highlights in the sun . . . and perfectly shaped, finely cut lips." His thumb traced the soft curve of her lower lip. "Sometimes I sit back and watch your lips move when you talk, and I have a terrible time controlling the temptation to"—his lips brushed hers—"kiss them."

He kissed her slowly, and then again, still slowly, but Amanda had waited long enough, and she responded with more urgency. She touched him, caressed him, coaxed him to become one with her, reveling in the assurance that he did truly fill her with himself, that he gave her his love.

Chapter Fourteen

$\mathcal{D}$eadwood was a small community tucked in a crack between steep hills. Wild Bill Hickock and Calamity Jane had put the town on the map by living and dying there, providing the elusive fantasy of the past, to which time, simply in passing, had added a considerable touch of romance. Amanda was gratified to see that the town's many saloons had batwing doors, but much disappointed that Boot Hill was not a collection of lonely wooden markers on a dusty hill.

The lively spirits of Calamity Jane and Wild Bill would have approved of Deadwood's night life. Cowboys dressed in colorful Western shirts and Stetson hats bellied up to the bar next to motorcyclists in leather jackets and faded blue jeans. The carnival atmosphere seemed to promote an unexpected congeniality between the two groups.

Sean and Amanda attended the first performance of the rodeo as spectators. They ate popcorn and cotton candy, and when he wasn't cheering for his favorite

contestants, Sean evaluated the riders and horses for
Amanda's benefit. During the rough-stock events he
noted form, style, and "try," and scrutinized each
roper carefully; if a horse made a mistake, Sean
identified the cause. Sean knew horses as well as any
horseman Amanda had known.

Travis Steele's ride was allowed to pass without
comment, but Sean was surprised when Lacy appeared in the ladies' barrel racing. "What got into
her?" Sean wondered. "Hell, she hasn't run barrels in
two years or more."

"Was that a good time?" Amanda asked.

"She won't place, but it isn't bad. She used to be
one of the best. I've been telling her to get herself
back in the saddle, but she . . . That looks like her
sister's horse."

"Well, she took your advice. No doubt she'll be
anxious for your critique of her performance."
Amanda feigned interest in the clown's shenanigans
near the fence.

"Which I'll be glad to give her." He caught her
daggers with a grin. "You sit a horse better than she
does, Mandy. Think I should tell her that? Would that
even things up this round?"

"I hardly think we could ever be *even*."

"She's jealous—you're jealous. That much is even.
Your barbs might be a little classier than hers, but
that's to be expected, isn't it?" He squeezed her hand
and offered a smile. "That frown doesn't become you,
either. Forget about Lacy, okay?"

They stayed at an old lodge in Spearfish Canyon,
whose steep walls were covered with green conifers.
Sean liked the rustic accommodations there—the old
tub without a shower, the absence of a telephone and
television in the cabin. He had used the lodge before
to indulge himself in solitude. Now he walked with
Amanda, and it was good—*damn* good—just to feel
her shoulder brush against his arm. Needles and cones
crackled under their boots as Sean unhooked his hand

from his pocket and took hers, ostensibly to help her balance herself on the steep grade.

When the message came that Amanda's mother had called Sean was in the bathtub. The boy from the lodge office suggested she ride back with him and call home immediately. From behind the bathroom door Sean told her to wait for him, but she told him to meet her at the office.

Amanda climbed into the pickup beside the boy, thinking that her mother must have gotten the phone number from Karen, and that something must be wrong for her to call like this.

The pickup stopped well short of the lodge driveway. Amanda's preoccupation delayed her reaction when both doors flew open. Surprise gave way to the chill of terror when a meaty, callused hand silenced her gasp and immobilized her head. She glimpsed a grisly face and greasy brown hair to her right. Both doors slammed shut, and the tires squealed, accelerating Amanda's pulse rate. The man's second arm pinned her left arm to her side and crushed her right shoulder to his chest.

"There's a six-inch blade in your belly, lady. You plannin' to make any noise?" His hand tasted of oil and dirt, and she couldn't breathe. Amanda moved her head slightly from side to side. "That's real nice," he drawled, moving his hand away from her mouth. She glanced down at the fist at her waist and saw the knife handle, but no blade. "It's push-button," the man explained, clamping both arms around her. "You behave yourself and I won't need to flip out the steel."

"What do you want with me?" Amanda managed a steady voice as she looked to her left at the driver. The sandy-haired boy was gone. "Travis! What are you doing?" Recognition of the cowboy at the wheel brought some measure of relief. "Is this some kind of joke?"

"We're just havin' a little fun, Boston. What d'ya think? Think ol' Brannigan's gonna bust a gut laughin'

after he combs the woods lookin' for you?" The grin
on Travis Steele's face was frightening, but his glassy
eyes were even more disturbing. Both men reeked of
beer, but the man who held her against his black
leather jacket smelled filthy. Looking past his face,
which was inches from her own, Amanda saw that
Lacy Cook sat quietly on the other side of him.

"Lacy?" There was no response from the other
woman, and Amanda abandoned any thought of
asking Sean's "best friend" to intercede in her behalf.
Summoning her composure, she turned her head, the
only part she could move, in Travis's direction.
"Where are you taking me?"

"We're havin' a party. Celebratin' Miss Lacy
Cook's return to the circuit. Thought you'd wanna be
there." Travis grinned.

"Where is this party?" Amanda's voice gained
strength as she willed herself to stay calm.

"Where nooobody ain't gonna bother us, sweetheart," the grizzled stranger offered.

"Is this man a friend of yours, Travis?"

"Yeah, we're real *compadres*. Both got a talent for
straddlin' something mean and wild and raisin' lots o'
hell."

"You ain't gonna be disappointed." The man's
breath was nauseating. "You Boston 'ladies' start out
cold, but you learn real quick."

"You realize this is kidnapping," Amanda said.

"Kidnapping!" Travis laughed. "You're Lacy's
friend, aren't you? Been together since Reno. We're
just givin' you a ride to the party." The pickup
groaned when Travis ground the gears as he turned
onto a dirt road.

"Sean rides tonight. You want him to miss the
rodeo. Is that it?"

"Brannigan doesn't worry me. He's too lazy to
come after me in the standings."

"Then why are you doing this?"

Travis's boot found the brake pedal, and the pickup lurched in protest at the sudden stop at the edge of a sloping ravine. "I wanna try out Brannigan's finest stock." Travis grinned again.

There had been no phone call, and no boy had been sent to their cabin with a message. It didn't take Sean long to ascertain those facts. The police suggested that Sean look around again; she might have gone for a walk, and after all, she hadn't been gone very long. He should call them back, they said, after he made sure she was really gone. Sean wondered if he should've said, "My wife has been kidnapped," rather than, "My girlfriend disappeared about half an hour ago." He needed help, so he called the ticket office in Deadwood and left a message for Bud. Then he searched again.

What did you do when someone disappeared? Where would she have gone? If the boy had kidnapped her, who would he contact? And how? And when? And for God's sake why? By the time Bud showed up Sean was frantic. The manager at the lodge had been of little help, obviously suspecting a lovers' quarrel. Cowboys and their women were a dramatic lot when it came to quarreling.

"She's okay, Sean," Bud said quickly, clapping a stubby-fingered hand on his friend's back. "Let's go get her. I've got someone out in the pickup who knows where she is."

"Who?" Sean asked, striding toward the door.

"Miss Lacy Cook," was the answer, underscored with disgust.

"Lacy? What the hell's going on?"

"I picked her up on the way over here. She was walking, coming to get you."

As soon as he reached the pickup Sean jerked the door open, and Lacy immediately scooted to the middle of the seat. "Where's Mandy?" Sean barked, climbing inside. Bud was behind the wheel in a flash, and the tires squealed at the sudden takeoff.

"I thought they were just joking around, Johnny, just to scare her a little, so you'd miss the rodeo tonight . . . just kind of a trick. I didn't know they'd do anything to hurt her!"

Sean's hands gripped her shoulders, and his voice shook with rage. "Shut up and tell me who's got her!"

"Travis . . . and some guys on motorcycles. We got in with these guys at the bar last night, and Travis . . . well, I don't know whose idea it really was. I just wanted to see her squirm a little."

"Where did they take her?"

"They're out a ways on a dirt road. . . . I didn't see any houses around or anything. They said we'd just have a little party, but then they started talking like they were gonna . . . rape her or something." Sean's hands crushed Lacy's small shoulders as he shook her until her head whipped back and forth like a rag doll's. "I . . . I didn't think. . . ."

"You didn't think!" Sean roared. "You didn't think! Damn you!"

"Take it easy, Sean," Bud said quietly. "Lacy slipped away and ran to the highway. Lucky I came along, saved a lot of time. We'll find her."

Willing himself to calm down, Sean opened his hands slowly and let Lacy fall back against the seat. "How far?"

"Not far, Johnny," Lacy whispered. "Honest to God, I never meant for her to get hurt. I got scared when they started talking like that."

"I'll kill him," Sean croaked. "If he lays a hand on her . . . if any of them touches her . . . my God . . . Mandy." His eyes were fixed on the road ahead.

Travis's pickup was parked on the high ground, but they could see nothing else. The sound of motorcycles became louder as they approached, but they saw no cyclists.

"There's a draw over there, on the other side of the pickup." Lacy pointed in the direction she meant. Bud downshifted, barely hesitating at the edge of the ravine before barreling down the hill.

Amanda stood in the middle of the draw, her arms hugging her body, her eyes shut tight. No fewer than a dozen cyclists raced from hill to hill, up and down the draw, in a demented game testing how closely each could pass to the terrified woman without running her over. They were good at it. They whizzed by her from all sides in quick succession, skillfully bypassing one another in the process. As Sean watched one cyclist's knee sideswiped her, and she tottered. The next one knocked her over, but she scrambled to her feet. Sean felt a sickening urge to lash out at Lacy as the pickup drew close enough for him to see the trembling that wracked Amanda's body. His right hand gripped the door handle, his left the padded dashboard. "I'll kill that bastard," he muttered from between clenched teeth.

One by one the cyclists became aware of the approaching vehicle. They peeled away from their formation, scattering over the hillsides like a swarm of flies after the swatter hit the table. Sean hopped out of the pickup before it even stopped. Amanda was frozen to the spot. Her eyes flew open in terror, and she seemed not to know him when he took her in his arms. Her sobs were silent at first—deep, shuddering, soundless sobs. Then she was able to give voice to her anguish, to wail mindlessly as the tears finally came. Scooping her up and cradling her in his arms, Sean took her to the pickup. She curled herself into a ball and huddled against his chest.

Travis Steele leaned against the hood of his pickup, apparently in no hurry to follow his retreating friends. Bud drove to the top of the hill, not sure whether he should stop near Steele and let Sean settle the matter, or drive on. Steele pushed himself away from the pickup and closed the distance between them with a few steps. He grinned, pulling a piece of grass from his mouth. "These guys can get pretty wild. They were just havin' a little fun, Brannigan. She ain't hurt . . . much."

At the sound of that voice Amanda's grip on Sean's shoulder became viselike, and she turned her face into his chest as if she could hide there.

He realized that he couldn't leave her for even a few minutes, not then. "I hope the cops don't catch up to you right away, Steele. Not before I break your face."

"Cops!" Travis chortled. "What cops? I gave Boston a ride, that's all. She got in with a rough crowd. Hell, Brannigan, you ain't gonna bring the law in on this. Little Miss Lacy might be in serious trouble, and you wouldn't want that, would you?" With that Steele turned and headed for his pickup, tossing back, "See ya 'round, cowboy."

Bud took them directly to the cabin. Amanda trembled all over and said nothing, clutching Sean's shirt in both hands. "Bud, would you bring us some brandy or something? And something to eat," Sean said, lifting Amanda as he slid off the pickup seat.

"Sure thing, Sean. She gonna be okay?"

Sean didn't look back as he headed for the cabin. Ignoring the question, he shouted over his shoulder, "When you come back, Bud, don't bring *her*."

Bud returned quickly with brandy and a paper sack, which Sean set aside while he poured the brandy into motel water glasses. "Thanks, Bud," Sean said, turning from the bureau, glasses in hand. Bud stood awkwardly by the door and cast a sympathetic look at Amanda.

"I'll be around for a while if you need me," Bud said, then added hesitantly, "Lacy feels real bad, Sean. I think she was telling the truth about not expecting them to—"

"I don't want to hear about Lacy right now, Bud. You really came through for me, though, and I appreciate it."

"Is she . . . hurt?" Bud asked quietly. Sean gave Bud a look that asked him not to say any more. "Let me know if there's anything . . , well, see you later." Bud backed out the door.

Sean hadn't asked her anything yet, had talked very little, in fact, and he dreaded the answers to the questions he had to ask now. She sat quietly, looking down at the hands folded in her lap. Her blouse was torn and dirty, her face streaked with dirt and mascara, and her hair was a mass of disheveled curls.

"I want you to drink this, honey," Sean said, squatting in front of her and bracing one knee on the floor. She stared expressionlessly at the glass he held out to her. "It's just brandy. It'll help you relax." She took the glass, considered it for a moment and then took a sip. "Good girl," Sean whispered. She sipped twice more, and then sighed long and hard. "Can you tell me what happened, Mandy?"

Amanda swallowed more brandy. "I'd like to take a bath," she said quietly.

Oh, God, Sean groaned inwardly, *if they raped her, she mustn't take a bath.* He drained the brandy from his glass. *If they raped her, she'll have to see a doctor. If they raped her . . . If they raped her . . .* "Mandy," he said, trying to maintain the calmest possible tone, "honey, did they hurt you?" She nodded, tears welling in her eyes again. "How? How did they hurt you?"

She thrust the glass toward him. "I'd like some more of this."

He took the glass, refilled it and knelt in front of her again. "Mandy," he said, "you need to tell me what they did. Please trust me, now. You need to let go of it."

"I just need a bath." Her shallow breath fluttered. He brought her hand to his lips and kissed her fingertips. "If they . . . Honey, I have to get you to a doctor right away," he rasped.

Her hand was cool against the heat of his cheek. "They didn't . . . rape me. They talked about it, threatened to, but they didn't."

"What did they do?" he asked again.

"You saw what they did. I was terrified that I wouldn't be able to . . . They kept knocking me down. . . . If I hadn't been able to get out of the way . . . They told me to . . ." She was crying, trying to gain control. "Sean, I need a bath."

"I'll get it ready. Just relax and drink your brandy. I'll take care of everything else."

He undressed her carefully and helped her into the hot water. He ground his teeth at the sight of the bruises on her hips and thighs. Lovingly, tenderly, he washed her body and hair. Then he sat by the tub and listened to the outpouring of her ordeal.

"Sean," she said finally, "I don't want you to miss that rodeo. That's just what he wanted, I know it."

"If you're feeling all right tomorrow I can ride in the slack. I'll call and trade with somebody. You just take it easy now. The rodeo is the last thing we need to worry about."

"I'm okay now," she protested.

"Well, I'm not sure I am. I still feel like killing somebody. Here, let's get you dried off. Are you hungry?" He helped her out of the tub and blotted her skin gently with a towel.

"I'm not hungry. I'm just very tired." She leaned against him, and he took the cue to lift her into his arms and carry her to the bed.

Before undressing himself he poured more brandy for both of them. Amanda settled back on the pillows, which were propped against the headboard, and sipped her drink. Sean slid into bed beside her and tucked her under his arm. "I want to hold you, Mandy," he said, brushing her damp hair back from her temple.

She snuggled against his shoulder. "I was so scared."

"So was I, honey. I've never been so scared."

"I'm going to the police tomorrow."

Sean raised the glass to his lips, offering no comment.

The room was quiet while they dressed, and when there was nothing more to do they sat down almost simultaneously—Sean in the chair, Amanda on the bed—and looked at each other. "Do you want breakfast first?" Sean asked quietly.

"I'm not hungry. I'd just as soon get it over with."

"It won't be over with. It'll just be the beginning."

"I know." She watched her hand smooth the corded bedspread.

"If you're sure it's what you want to do, we might as well—"

"What I *want* to do!" Amanda retorted, exasperated. "This isn't *my* doing, Sean. I ache all over from their little joke, and they're not getting away with it."

"I know," he said, looking down at the floor. "I know how you feel, and you're right."

"You don't know how I feel! You have no idea what it was like!" She had been terrified and hurt, and now it was time for anger.

"I know what it was like for me. I was so scared, I couldn't think. I didn't know what to do, where to look."

"But you don't want me to go to the police."

Sean stood quickly and walked toward the bureau, as though he needed space to think. "I want to go after Steele myself. And Lacy . . . I don't know . . . I can't forgive her for what she . . ."

"*You* won't be able to forgive! *I'm* the one."

He moved to the bed and sat next to her, obviously at odds with himself more than with her. He touched her hand, but she drew away. "She's been in trouble before. She could go to jail."

"You're still protecting her, aren't you?" Amanda asked, truly surprised. "You don't care what she's done."

"If she walked in the door right now I don't know if I could keep from hitting her. I could never trust her again, but damn it, I don't want to see her go to prison, Mandy. Do you?"

"What would they have done to me out there if you hadn't gotten there when you did?" Amanda shot back.

"I don't know. But if Lacy hadn't come after me, I guess we would've found out."

Amanda felt no need to counter the point. "This isn't something you can take care of yourself, Sean. It's a police matter." She stood quickly and walked to the door. When she opened it Bud Eliot was standing on the other side.

"I just came to tell Sean that I got Jimmy Stephens to take his calf last night." Amanda moved aside, and Bud stepped just inside the door. "Can you make the slack at two?" he asked Sean.

"I don't know," Sean replied, reaching for his hat.

"Steele roped last night. He's leading."

"We've got some business to do in town. I don't know how long it will take."

Bud turned to Amanda. "You going to the police?" he asked gently. Amanda nodded. "Look," Bud said with a resigned sigh, "I don't blame you. You're probably doing the right thing. I trailered Lacy's horse home for her last night, and I stayed with her for a while. She feels real bad. Guess I never really thought much about her feelings before. She was just good-time Lacy. But now I . . . well, I'd hate to see her maybe . . . end up in jail."

"Poor Lacy," Amanda sighed. "Poor, misunder-stood, mistreated Lacy. I won't even try to compete with her for sympathy."

"I'm not feeling sorry for her, Amanda. She did wrong. I'm just saying she's not all bad . . . and I'm telling you, out loud and sober . . . that I care about her."

Amanda looked from Bud to Sean and then walked to the bed, seating herself wearily. She only heard half the brief conversation between the men. After Bud left Sean sat next to her on the bed. "You've got every right to do what you think best, honey. I'll be there with you, and I'll back you up."

"I've decided not to go to the police," she said, her voice flat.

"You sure?"

"Not for Lacy, or even for you, but for Bud," she explained, and Sean nodded his understanding. "I wish him luck with her," Amanda concluded. "He'll need it."

Sean took fierce pleasure in beating Travis Steele that afternoon, first with his rope, and then with his fists. That they would have it out was a foregone conclusion. No one wanted to stop it—or to miss it. As though by arrangement the two men drifted together in a far corner of the grounds, where the contestants parked their trailers and campers. There were no preliminaries, no words; suddenly they confronted each other, and the rest inevitably followed.

Amanda was drawn to watch the fight. She felt no urge to protest, but she offered no encouragement, either. The few punches Steele landed caused Amanda to flinch, but when Sean cornered Steele against a trailer Amanda had no desire to see it end yet. There was too much satisfaction in watching Steele's face bleed, in hearing the dull thud of his head hitting the side of the trailer, in listening to the grunts of pain when Sean buried his fists in Steele's midsection. It was only when Steele offered no more resistance and could no longer support himself on wobbly legs that Sean backed a few steps away and surveyed the results.

"Are you all right?" Amanda asked.

Sean wiped his mouth with the back of his hand as they walked to his pickup. There was just a trickle of blood from the corner of his mouth. "Never better!" he declared with enthusiasm. "How 'bout you?"

"Revenge is sweeter than I imagined," she said with a wicked smile. "I do hope Mr. Steele knows a good plastic surgeon."

Chapter Fifteen

As Sean backed the trailer up to the corral gate Amanda planned the call she would make to ask her mother to send some things out to her. She'd decided to look for a short-term lease in Rapid City. The way Sean traveled she probably wouldn't need much of an apartment, especially if she was going on the show circuit, but she felt the need for someplace of her own. In Denver and Amarillo there would be new editors to meet, proposals to offer. She had to remember to have her mother send her portfolio. . . .

"Amanda, your mother called this morning." Amanda had been too preoccupied to notice Karen run out of the house, but now she looked out the open window of the pickup into Karen's concerned face. "She wants you to call home right away. Your father has been taken ill. He's in the hospital."

It had been a heart attack, and Amanda's father was in intensive care. As she waited for her plane at the tiny Rapid City airport she felt that Sean had put a distance between them already. His mind seemed to be elsewhere, although he glanced at his watch and at the sky frequently, as though he were anxious to have this leave-taking over quickly.

They watched the plane arrive, watched passengers file into the terminal and said nothing. Finally Amanda leaned down to pick up her bag. Sean's hand flashed out of his pocket almost convulsively, fastening itself to her upper arm. She let the bag fall back to the floor and straightened, looking at the changed expression in his face. The detachment had vanished, and for a moment he allowed himself to be vulnerable. "Are you coming back to me, Mandy?"

She reached out to him, and she knew a sublime ache in her chest as he pulled her into his arms. "Do you want me to?" she whispered, laying her cheek against his shoulder.

"Of course I want you to. God, I miss you already."

"I was afraid you were angry with me."

"I know you have to go. I'm being selfish," he confessed.

"I have more work to do on this story. It has real potential. Saga potential, in fact."

"Saga." He gave her a thoughtful look. "Won't that run into children and grandchildren?"

She smiled. "And great-grandchildren. I know what I want, Sean. I'll be back as soon as my father is out of the hospital."

She still felt his lips long after she had boarded the plane. They had branded her with a statement of possession, a demand that she remember how she felt at that moment and let nothing deter her from fulfilling her commitment.

Donald Caron's recovery was an inordinately slow process. Seeing him in the hospital shook Amanda's sense of security to the very core. Here was a man who had always taken care of everything and was now being tended by nurses for every simple need. Amanda spent several days with him before mention of her "escapade out west" was even made. She thought it best to minimize anything that might worry him; his face had become gaunt, the flesh under his eyes forming deep, puffy pockets. She told him that she was home now, and that he was not to concern himself about anything. He seemed to take comfort in that statement, no doubt choosing to believe that what had happened between Amanda and "that cowboy" was over.

During the first two weeks Sean was concerned about her father's progress, and Amanda wanted to hear every detail of Sean's day each time he called. She visualized each story he told and longed to be with him. When her father came home, she told herself, she would explain her plans.

She tried once. He had been home for two days, and she broached the subject by telling her father about the mare Sean had given her.

"That was a pretty grandiose gesture, don't you think?" her father responded. "He knew it would be too much trouble to bring a horse this far. A Quarter Horse wouldn't be worth the effort," Donald judged with an impatient snort.

"Daddy, I wasn't planning to bring the mare here. I'm planning to . . ." She caught a frantic glance from her mother.

"Planning to what, Amanda? Surely you're finished with that little fling," Donald clipped.

"I wish you could meet Sean, Daddy. He isn't at all what you think. He may talk and dress a little differently from the men you've . . . but he's a wonderful man. He's . . ."

"That's it, isn't it? He's a real he-man. You didn't want anyone who might possibly fit my requirements for a son-in-law, so you threw yourself at some honky-tonk hero. For Pete's sake, Amanda, where's your sense of . . ." His face reddened as he spoke, and Amanda rushed to his side, begging him to be calm. In the end the doctor was called, and Donald Caron had to be taken back to the hospital for another two days.

"And you feel guilty as hell," Sean summarized for her. She had related the incident to him, explaining that she couldn't even move back to her own apartment until her father's health improved.

"What can I do, Sean? The doctor warned me not to upset him, to give him time to recover his strength. He's still very weak, very susceptible to . . . Any shock could . . ."

"I understand, honey. I don't want to cause him any trouble, but I miss you—you know that?"

"Yes," she said quietly. "I miss you, too."

"Nights are the worst. Morning is a long time coming."

"I know."

"It's almost September. I'll be on the road a lot. You won't be able to get hold of me most of the time, but I'll call you."

"There is such a thing as writing, you know."

"I'm no good at that, and your letters would be too long in catching up to me. Besides, I want to hear your voice. I can see you in my mind, those perfect lips moving as you talk. . . . It's lonely around here without you."

"Don't, Sean," she whispered. "It won't be much longer."

But it was. Sean's calls were frequent at first, but as October drew into November, he began to lose patience. They often argued, and Amanda accused him of being insensitive where her father was concerned.

"Insensitive? People here are telling me that I'm overly sensitive lately. A powder keg, Bud said the other day."

"You might be a little more sensitive to my situa-

tion, Sean. Even though he and I don't always agree, I
do love my father, and I don't intend to cause—"

"What's that supposed to mean?" Sean's voice was
cold steel. "Is that supposed to be something I
wouldn't understand?"

"I don't know. You don't seem to."

"You *do* know. You know I've been through . . .
oh, the hell with it. Look, take your time. The more
you listen to him, the less attractive I'll seem; and the
longer you take to make up your mind about growing
up, the less likely it'll be to happen."

"You're being unreasonable."

"I'm not talking reason, Mandy, I'm talking love.
You want me to talk reason? Here it is: I can't afford
to mess up my mind worrying over what you're going
to do. So I'll let you worry about it, and I'll attend to
my business. See ya 'round, Mandy."

Fifteen hundred miles apart, they stood glowering
at their phones.

After that he didn't call. Amanda immersed herself
in writing, but everything she wrote was connected
with Sean somehow. She took long walks in the brisk
fall afternoons, swished her feet through piles of
brittle brown leaves and told herself to be patient. Be
patient with her mother, who continued to ask her to
wait a little longer, maybe until after the holidays.
Amanda didn't bother to ask which holidays. Be
patient with her father, who seemed his old self one
day and debilitated the next. And be patient with
Sean, who could not be patient himself.

Mild weather lulled Amanda into December. She
moved back into her own apartment, and she envi-
sioned herself becoming a hermit. Her happiest times
were spent riding the Morgans, and she hoped the
weather would hold in deference to that one small
pleasure. She knew she'd lost weight, because her
mother bemoaned the fact each time they were together. She began to tell herself she'd probably delayed too long; there was a clear message in Sean's

silence. It would never have worked anyway, she told herself; they were just too different, too far apart. But she thought about him constantly, listened to his music and waited for the phone to ring.

"Amanda, this is Bud Eliot."

"Bud! Is something wrong? Is Sean . . . ?"

"Sean hasn't called you lately, has he?"

"N–no, he . . . It's been a month since . . . Is he all right?"

"That's what I thought. Listen, Amanda, he's too damn proud for his own good. He said it was all over between you, that you didn't wanna move out here."

"That's not true, Bud. I've never said I wouldn't."

"Well, he finally admitted you never *said* that, but he thinks that's the way it is. He's been ridin' himself into the ground, and just lately here, he's been partyin' to beat hell between rodeos."

"Is there . . . another woman?" Amanda hated herself for asking.

"Yeah, lots of 'em, but only for show. He goes to bed alone. He misses you."

"I miss him, too, Bud. It's just that my father . . ."

"He knows that's how it started out, your father being sick and all. But it's been a long time, and now he thinks you've changed your mind. It's tearing him up inside."

"Why doesn't he call me?" Amanda asked, tears slipping down her cheeks.

"I told you, he's too stubborn, and proud as they come. He'd kill me if he knew I was calling you now."

"Where is he?"

"We're in Oklahoma City for the national finals. If he has a good finals he'll take the all-around. Nobody can touch him in calf roping."

"Oh, Bud, if I could just talk to him. I've been sitting by the phone all this time. When we last talked he got angry, and I was afraid . . ."

"How's your dad now?" Bud asked.

"He's doing pretty well. The doctor says he can go to the office a couple of days a week."

"Sounds like he doesn't really need you anymore."

"Probably not. We have to avoid . . . *he* has to . . ."

"Amanda, Sean *does* need you. He loves you, and he needs to see you. I thought maybe if you knew how it was with him, you'd wanna come out for the finals. It'd make the victory a whole lot sweeter for him if you were here."

"I . . . yes! Yes, of course I'll be there, just as soon as I . . . Don't tell him, though. Pick me up at the airport?"

"You betcha! Call you back in half an hour for the time and flight number."

There were plane changes in New York, Chicago, Kansas City—the flight seemed interminable. Bud's smiling face was a welcome sight. He seemed a little embarrassed when Amanda flung her arms around his neck, but he returned her hug.

"Why, Bud Eliot, you're blushing!" she teased.

He reached for her bag. "Sean'd kill me if he saw that. I'm sure glad you're here. He's touchier'n hell lately. Long flight?"

"Awful! I left at ten-thirty last night—five hours in Chicago—I don't even know my own name. What's Sean doing?"

"He's at the hotel. He doesn't ride 'til tonight—this goes on for a week, you know. I imagine he's getting dressed about now. We were up pretty late last night."

"Partying again?"

"Mostly just seeing old friends. It isn't that he drinks real hard—in fact, last night he took it real easy. He just seems to want people around him, and even then he seems pretty . . . I had a heck of a time keeping from spillin' the beans last night." Bud beamed with the anticipation of his surprise.

"Is Lacy here?"

"No. I been seein' her once in a while, but I haven't taken her on the road since last summer." The look on Amanda's face told him that she had one more question. "Far as I know, Sean hasn't seen her at all. Don't think she dares try anymore."

"Let's not wait for the luggage. We'll just have it sent over to the hotel. Good Lord, it's almost noon. Do I look all right? I can't sleep sitting up. I must look awful," Amanda chattered as Bud held the terminal door for her.

"You look great, Amanda. Everything's in just the right place."

Amanda stood to the side as Bud knocked on the door to Sean's room. She had planned this scene for hours, and now she was too nervous to remember the lines she'd chosen.

"Sean?" Bud called. "You decent?"

The doorknob turned, but the door was left for Bud to open himself. "Decent enough for you," was the answer.

"I've got a girl here with me. She wants to see you."

"You bring her in now, she's gonna see a lot of me. Who is it?"

"She says you went out with her a few times. She thought you'd remember her if you saw her again."

"Uh . . . if she'll just wait in the lobby, I'll be—"

"She says she's waited long enough, ol' buddy." Bud swung the door open for Amanda, who took two steps inside and stopped, seeing Sean's face in the mirror seconds before he saw hers. He was combing his hair, his shirt hanging open in front and his feet bare. He turned slowly to face her, disbelief registering in his dark eyes. Bud closed the door, leaving them alone.

"How . . . ?" Sean muttered. "Where did you come from?"

"Out of the sky and into your lap."

"But I mean . . . Bud?"

She nodded, moving toward him. "Bud is a good friend. Don't you dare be angry with him."

"I didn't think you'd . . ."

"You crazy cowboy. Why haven't you called?"

"I couldn't think of anything to say, short of begging you to come back. I quit calling before I resorted to that."

They reached for each other, and the embrace was a moment of desperate relief for them both. "I thought your father had you where he wanted you. I thought he'd changed your mind," Sean groaned.

"Oh, Sean, when will you believe I love you?"

"You damn well better love me, lady," he swore, his hands stroking her back, pressing her tightly to him. "You're not getting away from me again."

"That's not what I came all this way to hear, Sean Brannigan."

"I love you, Mandy. I wanted to call you a thousand times, but I thought . . . Hell, I couldn't have stood it much longer. I'd have gone after you sooner or later."

"I got tired of waiting."

"What about your dad?"

"I didn't tell him. I asked my mother to handle it. He's a lot stronger now. He'll be all right. The greatest stress in his life is his business, and he's going back to that."

"He'll find out I'm not so bad. After the finals I might even be a celebrity. Think he'd like that?"

"I don't know," she said, kissing his neck, her hands finding the thrilling expanse of his bare back. "I don't care. All I know is what I like. . . ."

"I'm glad you'll be here for the finals, honey. I kept wishing . . ."

"I'm not sharing you with any buckle bunnies, darling." She was unsnapping his cuffs. "You weren't going anywhere, were you?"

Sean grinned as she slipped his shirt off his shoulders. "I never worry about changing my plans. We've got plenty of time for . . . whatever you have in mind."

"A little loving won't spoil your performance, will it?" she asked, unbuckling his belt.

"A *little* loving? Lady, it's been four long months! I need a *lot* of loving. How 'bout you?"

"I don't know whether you've noticed, but I'm about to . . . remove your pants, and I'm still fully clothed."

"That's because you're using that direct approach of yours. Here, allow me. . . ." Sean stepped out of his jeans and unzipped Amanda's dress. "What've you been doing, Mandy? You're skin and bones!"

"I've been waiting for my father to be well enough so I could tell him that I was leaving. I've been waiting for you to call. And I've been waiting to feel the warmth of your skin against mine. . . ."

Sean swept her beautiful skin and bones into his arms. "The waiting's over, love," he whispered. "I've been starving for you for four months, and I'm about to feast on what's left of you." He laid her on the bed and drove her wild with kisses and love words. His tongue made sweet buds of her nipples, and every inch of her skin became sensitized to the delicate touch of his hands. She began to shudder with ecstasy before he entered her, holding himself at bay while she strained to receive him. He wanted to hear the words, needed to hear her say that she needed him, and he plied his magic until she gasped, "Oh, Sean, please make love to me!"

"I am, sweetheart. This is love . . . love . . . love. . . ."

Amanda stood in front of the mirror in her turquoise Western shirt, white Western-cut pants and heart-shaped belt buckle. She looked good like this. She smiled at that thought and then at the other reflection as Sean slid his arms around her waist and fitted her against him. Lowering his mouth, he bit the top of her shoulder. "How soon can we get married?" he asked.

"Not 'will you' but 'how soon'?"

He grinned and winked at her in the mirror. "How soon?"

"Anxious to make an honest woman of me?"

"Anxious to make an honest man of me." He kissed her temple and the hair she'd just fixed. "Let's find a courthouse tomorrow and make it a finals wedding."

"Sounds ominous. Sort of like the last roundup. You sure you can handle all this right now?"

"I'm very good at tying knots," he reminded her, and stifled her groan with a kiss.

At the National Finals Rodeo cowboys walked tall and rode hard because a finalist's boots were a challenge to fill. Sean had been right: Cowboys were a diverse breed, exhibiting a whole range of characteristics. They all had a competitive spirit in common, though—what they termed "plenty of try."

For Sean the competition within himself had always been the toughest. It was Brannigan against the senselessness, Brannigan against the numbness, Brannigan against the dark void. No more. Now it was Brannigan against Travis Steele, and compared with his former adversaries, Steele was an easy mark.

As Bud had predicted, Sean was unbeatable in calf roping, so edging Steele out of the all-around depended on this week's work in steer wrestling. Steele had had a good finals week, but Sean's had been far better. Sean and Amanda had discovered that a lot of loving tended, if anything, to enhance Sean's rodeo performance. He claimed that getting to bed early was going to become part of his training program.

By the last go-round Sean had closed in on Steele's formerly formidable lead. Already mounted for his last steer, Sean made his way to the box, passing Travis Steele, who was watching the arena from the fence. Sucking on a cheek full of tobacco, Steele spat a stream of brown slime into the dirt as Sean passed, but Sean simply ignored him.

Sean Brannigan was quite capable of wrestling steers. At just the right second he slid neatly into the slot behind the animal's horns, and a quick jerk brought the steer down to cinch the go-round and the title. The crowd knew it before it was announced, and approval thundered over the arena. When the money was tallied Sean Brannigan was world's champion calf roper and all-around cowboy. Head held high, he rode out of the arena.

"Sean, you did it!" He swung down from his horse and reached to catch Amanda in his arms. "You were wonderful—the best you've ever been!"

"I just get better and better," he laughed, then whispered in her ear, "as you'll see when we get back to the room."

"Mmm, do I get credit for being your inspiration?"

"Sure do. Tell that guy over there with the microphone. He's about to ask me how it feels to be a winner, or some stupid question like that."

"And how does it feel?"

"I swear, you journalists are all alike."

"Congratulations, Sean!" The man in the pinstriped Western suit had cornered them. "We have your winning run on videotape. Will you come over to the monitor and give us a short interview?"

Amanda reached for Deke's reins, but Sean tossed them to another cowboy and hooked an arm around her shoulders. "You're coming with me, lady. You know all about this stuff."

Protests were useless. She stood quietly, listening to the commentator and Sean discuss the slow-motion tape on national television. In humble cowboy tradition Sean gave the horse credit for doing all the work.

"Well, Sean Brannigan, you've had quite a week,"

the announcer drawled. "You've just become world's champion calf roper and all-around cowboy, and you placed third overall in steer wrestling with tonight's win. How do you feel?"

"Pretty damn good, Bob."

The announcer reacted with a TV laugh. "You've got a mighty tight hold on this pretty lady's hand. What's your name?"

The microphone was thrust at Amanda, and her face suddenly felt hot. "Amanda Brannigan."

"We didn't know you were married, Sean."

Sean grinned proudly. "Have been since yesterday."

"This *has* been quite a week for you! And how does it feel to be Mrs. Sean Brannigan?" the man asked, turning to Amanda.

She smiled demurely. "Pretty damn good, Bob."

Silhouette Desire ®

CHILDREN OF DESTINY

A trilogy by Ann Major

Three power-packed tales of irresistible passion and undeniable fate created by Ann Major to wrap your heart in a legacy of love.

PASSION'S CHILD — September

Years ago, Nick Browning nearly destroyed Amy's life, but now that the child of his passion—the child of her heart—was in danger, Nick was the only one she could trust....

DESTINY'S CHILD — October

Cattle baron Jeb Jackson thought he owned everything and everyone on his ranch, but fiery Megan MacKay's destiny was to prove him wrong!

NIGHT CHILD — November

When little Julia Jackson was kidnapped, young Kirk MacKay blamed himself. Twenty years later, he found her...and discovered that love could shine through even the darkest of nights.

Silhouette Classics ™

COMING IN DECEMBER

#27 MORNING STAR by Kristin James

Nashville star C. J. Casey was the man Cathleen blamed for her father's downfall, yet he alone could call forth the music in her soul. Could she ever forget the past and surrender to his love?

#28 GOLDEN ILLUSION by Ginna Gray

Claire Andrews was determined not to be a figurehead senator. She fought to show Matt Drummond that she was cool and capable, but soon she couldn't hide the explosive passion only he aroused.

COMING IN JANUARY

#29 BLACK DIAMONDS by Nancy Martin

Someone in Bree's coal company was trying to sabotage her land-reclamation efforts. Ryan's job was to find out who. He desperately hoped it wasn't Bree herself—the woman who had already infiltrated his heart.

#30 WHEN MORNING COMES by Laurey Bright

Scott Carver's name spelled temptation in Claire Wyndham's convent-school world. The playboy and reckless traveler was a despoiler of hearts—and the man to whom she had given hers.

AVAILABLE THIS MONTH:

#25 MOMENTS HARSH, MOMENTS GENTLE
Joan Hohl

#26 SOMEDAY SOON
Kathleen Eagle